**Christine could hear her heart thudding. She felt more scared than ever.**

She tried to keep her voice steady. "Mam," she said quietly, "I think that man is the getaway driver."

"You can't see his ponytail," Emily said accusingly.

"The cap he was wearing covers that," said Christine tightly. She gripped the arms of the chair, watched her mother and wondered how she could stay so calm.

"Best get on to the police, then."

Christine felt a surge of panic. "I don't know, not after last night. They'll think I'm nuts. I mean, I don't know his name or anything."

"So what are you going to do?"

What should she do? Christine felt the fear grow inside her. She'd have to try something....

**EILEEN ROBERTSON**

lives in Gosport. *We'll Be Watching You* is her third novel. Her previous novels are *Miss McGuire is Missing* and *Blackmail for Beginners*.

# EILEEN
# ROBERTSON

# WE'LL BE
# WATCHING
# YOU

TORONTO • NEW YORK • LONDON
AMSTERDAM • PARIS • SYDNEY • HAMBURG
STOCKHOLM • ATHENS • TOKYO • MILAN
MADRID • WARSAW • BUDAPEST • AUCKLAND

Recycling programs
for this product may
not exist in your area.

ISBN-13: 978-0-373-06297-3

WE'LL BE WATCHING YOU

Copyright © 2013 by Eileen Robertson

A Worldwide Library Suspense/March 2014

First published by Robert Hale Limited

www.Harlequin.com

**Printed in U.S.A.**

## Acknowledgments

My sincere thanks to my much-loved nephews,
Nick and Zischi, for their
constant encouragement and support.
Also in fond memory of their mother, Hedy,
who is greatly missed.

# ONE

EMILY BRETT SCRUBBED at her binoculars, eased herself onto a chair at the dining table and peered out of the window. 'You and your Neighbourhood Watch, Christine. More trouble than it's worth, I say. Spying on folk! Makes me feel as if I've joined MI6.'

'Whatever you say, Mam, only you keep an eye on things while I get on with the veg.'

Emily waited until Christine went into the kitchen, then she dipped her hand in her cardigan pocket, brought out a miniature bottle of vodka, tipped its contents into her orange juice and swirled it around.

'I saw that, Mother!' Christine's outraged voice came from the doorway.

'It was only a drop. It is medicinal. It improves the circulation, see.'

Christine strode towards her and sat down. 'Don't you think it's a bit early to start tippling? You've had a stroke. Your body needs time to recover.'

Emily took a defiant gulp. 'That was six months since. It's you that's not recovered. You should get out and have some fun instead of prowling around watching me and everyone else. Get a life, love, and let me have one, too.' She lifted the glass in salute. 'This at least eases the monotony.'

Christine got up and marched back to the kitchen. 'I'm not going to argue. If that's how you feel, on your head be it.'

'Don't go wishing a hangover on me,' Emily called, but

there was no response. Emily sighed. At times like these she felt like a prisoner. The lass meant well, of course, but she could manage all right. The physios up at the hospital made sure of that. They'd not let you go home unless you could fend for yourself. She leaned her elbows on the dining table and looked around the living room. True, her furniture was a bit worn and weathered, like her, she supposed, but it was home, and there, in the corner, was her flat-screen TV, a much-treasured gift from Christine last Christmas, so she shouldn't really complain about her. She shot a glance in the direction of the kitchen. She didn't want to upset her daughter. The girl had been through enough; what with a lousy divorce, followed by the loss of her job as a bookkeeper, it was no wonder Christine felt frustrated, stuck in here, bored out of her skull.

Emily leaned forward, tweaked the net curtain and looked down the road. After a while she called, 'Christine!'

'Now what?' Christine peered round the kitchen door.

'A police car has just pulled up at Harry Myers's house.'

Christine's face reddened and she disappeared back into the kitchen.

'Oy! Don't dash off. I thought you'd be interested, seeing as it's Harry.' Emily looked again through the window. 'They're knocking on his door. Now he's standing in the doorway talking to them. He doesn't look very pleased. Oh, the bobbies are grinning; they're getting back in their car and driving off. Yep, that's them gone but Harry's still standing there with a face like thunder.' She looked towards the kitchen with suspicion. 'I wonder what's happened?'

She waited for a response. None came. 'You know something, don't you?' She peered again through the window and said, 'Christine, it's not that I want to worry you, but it looks like our Mr Myers is heading this way.'

Christine hurried into the room. 'He's coming here?'

Emily nodded. 'Sure is.' She looked at her daughter's face. 'So? Now what have you gone and done?'

Christine joined her mother at the window. 'It's not me that's done anything, it's him.' They watched as Harry stormed across the road and winced as he kicked open their gate until it swung off its hinges and onto the flower-bed, neatly decapitating several innocent dahlias. The doorbell buzzed incessantly.

Emily said sharply, 'Let him in, for crying out loud.'

Christine hurried to the door; Emily grabbed her walking stick, and limped after her.

Harry Myers stood, red-faced and fuming on the door-step.

'Come on in,' Emily called.

He wiped his feet vigorously and snapped, 'This isn't a social visit. There's something that has to be said.'

'You could at least say "hello" to my mother,' protested Christine.

Harry nodded briefly at Emily. 'Good day, Mrs Brett.'

Emily beamed at him and said, 'Nice day again, isn't it?' Harry scowled at her, stone-faced. Emily returned to the living room. 'Well, it was,' she muttered. 'Don't let him stand there, girl. Make him come in here and sit down.'

'I'd rather have a word in private,' said Harry tersely.

Christine ushered him into the living room. 'You can speak freely, Harry. Mother and I don't have secrets.'

'Neither does anyone else,' said Emily. 'Least, not if she can help it….'

Harry scowled at the two women. 'I have just suffered the embarrassment of being questioned by our local constabulary. It would seem that, for some reason, my car is suspected of being the getaway vehicle in a robbery that occurred recently.'

'Was it?' Emily leaned forward in her chair. 'Well, I never—'

'The police say it's a routine inquiry, but my guess is that someone,' Harry paused and stared hard at Christine, 'who lives not a million miles from here, has reported me to them.'

Emily sighed. 'She's at it again....'

'All I can say, Harry, is that I'm sorry about it being your car,' Christine said, 'but as a member of the Neighbourhood Watch team, I've got to do my duty.'

'What made you think it was me? What proof do you have that it was my car?'

'It's the same make and colour as the one in the newspaper photograph,' Christine replied.

Harry's eyes widened. 'The car shown in the photo is a Vauxhall Corsa.'

'So's yours.'

Emily snorted and hastily downed the rest of her orange juice.

Harry spoke slowly as if to a child. 'Do you have any idea how many motorists own a Vauxhall Corsa?'

'No, but then I don't have the luxury of owning a car any more.'

'Woman, there are thousands!'

'But they're not all silver.'

Harry groaned. 'I could understand it if the number plates had been similar.'

'The photo didn't show the number plate, I just thought—'

'You did not think! You hadn't a single fact to go on, yet off you rush again down to the cop shop, reporting your neighbours and causing mischief. I don't know why you always pick on me.'

'Don't flatter yourself!' Christine bristled. 'I report

anyone who breaks the law. That woman over the road got a right telling-off when I complained about her parties. It was after eleven and I've got Mother to consider.'

'Oy!' said Emily. 'I never said nothing. I likes a good rave-up, I do. Just wish I'd been invited.'

Harry gaped at Christine. 'Let me get this straight. You reported that young widow for having a party? Doesn't poor Kay deserve some enjoyment?'

'Poor Kay nothing,' Christine said angrily. 'She's more like the merry widow; you should see the number of young men that beat a track to her door.'

'I wish one would beat a track to your door,' Emily muttered. 'Then you might get a life.'

'Christine, can't you mind your own business instead of spying on Kay and keeping count of her admirers?' Harry said.

'Is that what you call them? I could think of a better word.'

Harry shook his head and strode towards the door. 'I feel sorry for you. You've upset me and everyone else around here. Carry on the way you're going and you'll end up a neurotic old witch.' The door slammed behind him.

'That's telling you,' Emily said. 'You shouldn't have got him riled like that. You're not daft. There are other ways of getting a man's attention....'

'I don't know what you mean,' snapped Christine.

'Of course you don't,' said Emily, 'and I just saw a pig fly past our front window.' She sighed then said gently, 'You have to be sure of your facts if you're shopping folk. Harry's always been very fond of you.'

Christine tossed her head. 'He's even fonder of Kay.'

'Ah, I thought so. Is that's what this is all about, then?'

'Of course not. I was being absolutely fair.'

'Try being absolutely certain.'

'That's it. I've had enough!' Christine brushed away a tear and marched into the kitchen. 'No one's on my side,' she sobbed. 'Now everybody hates me.'

Emily limped into the kitchen and touched her arm. 'They don't like you reporting them when they've not done anything wrong. It's not as if we live in Leeds city centre. Rossforth is a quiet suburb, where hardly anything happens…until you started interfering.' She peered up at her daughter. 'Can't you understand?' she asked gently. 'Would you like to be spied upon?'

'If something's wrong, I report it. There's nothing worse than indifference.'

'There was no need to report that fella at number 22 for being a litter lout; all that happened was his dustbin blew over…and you did go on at them lads for riding their bikes.'

'They were on the pavement, Mam, that's illegal.'

'There wasn't a soul about, yet out you dashed—'

'I was trying to protect you, Mam.'

'I wasn't even on the street; I was sitting at the window minding my own business like you should have—'

'I was doing what's right,' Christine shouted. She scrubbed vigorously at a potato and tossed it into the pan. 'I don't care if the whole neighbourhood hates me. Tomorrow I'm going to boycott the lot of them. I'll go into Leeds and do our shopping at that big hypermarket in Seacroft. Do you agree, Mother?'

'Wouldn't matter if I didn't, you'd take no notice.' Emily watched as Christine picked up an onion, tore at its skin and then put it down.

'Neurotic old witch indeed.' Christine dried her hands and ran into the hall.

Emily stared after her. 'Now where are you off to?'

'Got to live up to my reputation, haven't I? She pulled

on her coat. 'I'm going to the police station to report him again.'

'What for?'

'For breaking our gate and murdering the dahlias.' She swept out of the door.

# TWO

---

THE NEXT DAY CHRISTINE, loaded down with carrier bags, eased her way through the doors of the hypermarket; she'd not shopped there since her divorce and now with her 'mission accomplished', felt an overwhelming sense of relief. She took a few steps, put down the bags and checked her watch. It would be another twenty-five minutes until her bus was due. She looked across the main road to where a line of taxis beckoned, but she remained resolute; taxis cost money, and besides, she'd bought a return ticket.

She wondered if Harry had noticed that she'd not visited the local shops today. By now he'd be wondering if everything was all right. Maybe he was sorry for what he'd said yesterday. Mother was right; Harry had been kind to her when she'd first moved back in, but it was hard to trust any man after Charles....

Christine looked down at the groceries she'd bought. She'd been impressed by the cleanliness of the hypermarket, and she'd forgotten just how much choice there was there. Even better, she could see what other people had bought without anybody noticing. Not that she really was 'nosy', whatever Harry said. She was just interested in people. He didn't understand. She was glad that she'd not gone and reported him about the dahlias. She didn't like the idea of Harry hating her.

Earlier, she'd stood at the checkout and watched a young man pay for a bunch of roses, a bottle of champagne and some chocolates. No prizes for guessing that he was heading for a romantic night out. She thought again about Charles, her ex-husband, and her bitterness returned. She was well rid of him. Folk were right when they said, 'The cure for love is marriage.'

ALUN INCHED THE car through the heavy traffic and cursed. They were late! His eyes shifted to the two passengers in the rear and his lip curled. It was not his fault. His gaze returned to the road ahead in the hope of seeing a gap in the traffic, but there was nothing, just car after car. He sighed. He'd had to keep his cool; there was no point in starting a row just now. He scowled at the reflection of Pete and Rick in the rear-view mirror. Both of them looked pale and hungover, and this in spite of the many warnings they'd been given in the past.

How many times had he told them they'd to behave like athletes on the night before going on a 'job'? No pot, no sex, no booze. Those were the rules. Why couldn't they keep them? He looked once more from the road to the two men and fought to control his anger. Even a one-eyed man could see that they'd been on the piss last night. If he confronted them now, though, they'd deny everything and then they'd go in and do the job in an aggressive mood. That was when mistakes were made.

A car horn blared and Alun braked sharply and stared at the tail light of a truck that was inches away from his bonnet. 'Focus,' he told himself. The last thing he needed was to have a bump. He saw a gap in the traffic, nursed the car through it and let out a sigh of relief as he found the road clear. Glancing at his watch, he rammed his foot down on the accelerator.

CHRISTINE SHIVERED, BENT down and rearranged her groceries so that she had the right amount of ballast. She had plenty of time to spare. She looked around; now where was the bus stop? There used to be a shortcut round by the rear of the hypermarket. It might still be there; she would find out. She picked up her bags and strolled towards the rear of the building.

She thought about yesterday's row with Harry and felt her indignation grow again. What was it about him that made her so angry? And why did she still feel so hurt by his remarks? Well, she'd show him, and the rest of them. From now on she'd shop here. The carrier bag handles cut into her fingers and she winced—she would have to invest in a shopping trolley. She would also have to take into account the cost of the bus fares in her budget.

As she crossed the delivery yard a tin can rattled loudly underfoot, making her jump. Christine stopped and clicked her tongue at such untidiness. She put her bags down, picked up the can and looked around for a dustbin. On the far side of the yard she saw a door marked 'staff entrance'. Opposite the door was a large industrial dustbin; she walked over and tossed the can into it.

THE GREEN CONVERTIBLE roared into the backyard of the hypermarket and Alun cursed out loud as he applied the brakes. Too late he realized his anger had made him careless and that he'd given way to his nerves. He should have allowed the car to glide smoothly into the yard without noise or fuss.

Quickly and without speaking, Rick and Pete pulled their balaclavas down over their faces, leapt out of the car and raced towards the staff entrance.

Alun watched them anxiously then turned the car round, cursing as he manoeuvred past a pile of carrier bags that some idiot had dumped in the yard. He drew a deep breath and tried to relax. He knew that it was his own kind of stage fright that was making him feel hot. Taking off his sunglasses and opening his shirt he allowed the breeze to cool his skin; it couldn't do any harm, just for a minute.

Time passed and Alun sat with his eyes riveted on the staff door. Without thinking, he revved the engine impatiently. The lads seemed to be taking longer than usual, or was he still jumpy? He tried to reassure himself. They'd done these jobs so many times before; he'd been stupid to allow things like lateness and a traffic jam to make him panicky. He knew that as a driver he was the best there was—of that much he was sure.

The staff door burst open and Rick and Pete came bounding towards him. In an instant they were in the car and he was turning the wheel.

It was then that he saw the woman.

CHRISTINE HAD JUST located the old footpath and was about to return to collect her shopping bags when the screech of brakes and the arrival of a green, open-top sports car stopped her in her tracks. She watched as the car pulled up near the staff entrance and two large men with balaclavas over their faces jumped out and raced through the doors. The third man, the driver, turned the car then remained at the wheel with the engine running.

Some primal instinct made her press against the bin without moving. She felt the hairs at the back of her neck rise and a coldness slither down her spine. Without knowing why, she wanted to run; to hide, to be any place except here, yet some sixth sense forced her to remain rooted. She watched the driver who, as the seconds ticked by, became more and more restless.

He was dressed in black, his face was long and pale,

his eyebrows thick and dark. She couldn't see his hair; it was covered by a kind of black cap. She pressed against the dustbin and watched as the driver became impatient and revved the engine loudly. She risked a glance across the tarmac to where her four carrier bags were marooned. She shivered. What if the driver should notice them in his mirror? Even worse, what if he should reverse over them? There were free-range eggs in those bags, needed for the omelette for mother's tea. Christine hesitated and eased herself loose from the dustbin. Maybe there was nothing wrong. Perhaps this was all a figment of her imagination. Everyone was always telling her that she made mountains out of molehills. Perhaps she should just stroll across the yard in a carefully casual manner?

At that precise moment the staff door burst open and the two men charged out clutching canvas money sacks. They leapt into the rear of the car, which was already moving off.

Christine's eyes focused on the driver. There was some-thing…she had seen him somewhere before. But too late; as the car raced off the driver glanced in her direction. She saw his startled expression as he stared at her. Then he hunched over the wheel and the car roared out onto the main road.

Christine felt her heart begin to thud. Had she really seen what she thought she'd seen? Her legs felt as if they'd turned to water and once more she leaned against the grubby rubbish bin for support. After a few seconds she straightened up and forced herself to walk slowly across the yard to her shopping. She'd just reached it when an alarm sounded. The staff door burst open and a pale-look-ing man in a dark suit stumbled out. He was immediately followed by several members of staff.

Then all hell broke loose. Christine stood rooted whilst police cars with sirens and flashing lights zoomed into the yard. Both the manager and the police converged on her, yelling questions.

She felt elated. All eyes were upon her and notes were taken of every word she uttered as she relayed the events that she had witnessed. To her delight she found herself being escorted to the manager's office. But, as minutes ticked by into hours, and time and again she was asked to recall every detail, she grew uneasy. By now Mother would be worried, yet if she telephoned her to explain it might make things worse. She sipped her third cup of tea and tried not to lose patience at the policeman's persistent questions. This was what she'd always wanted—to be the key witness in some important crime—but already the whole thing was becoming frightening. She'd told them all she knew. Except for that one thing…she knew the driver's face.

The officer spoke again in a kindly manner. 'I think we've questioned you enough, Miss Brett. Now, if you could accompany one of my drivers to the station we can take a statement from you and then run you home. Shouldn't take too long. If you would like to call your mother? As you said earlier, she'll be getting worried.'

'May as well wait until I get home now…as long as I am going to get home soon?

'Of course,' the officer replied. He escorted her to the waiting car and opened the door. 'Meanwhile, if you should remember anything further?'

Christine nodded. 'I'd be in touch.'

In the car she leaned back against the upholstery and thought about the events of that afternoon. Today had given her all the excitement she needed, and although money had been stolen, she'd been the one to give useful information that might lead to the capture of the thieves. She felt fulfilled and righteous. She, as a citizen, had contributed to the maintenance of law and order.

A green car pulled up alongside them at the traffic lights. Christine started and thought about the driver of that other green car and the way he had stared at her. A shiver ran through her and she pulled her coat collar tight around her neck. Would she then have a price to pay for being in the wrong place at the right time?

# THREE

---

*Tuesday*

IN A MULTI-STOREY car park, some seventeen miles east of Leeds, a green convertible made its way to the level three and backed into a parking space.

Alun switched off the engine and, for a moment, he, Rick and Pete sat in silence.

Alun looked at them. 'Any bother, there, at the hypermarket?'

'Nope, well…nothing to worry about….'

'Rick had to smack someone,' Pete blurted.

Alun straightened, eyes alert. 'You stupid sod! What someone?'

'Were just a tap,' muttered Rick, 'manager got a bit close.'

'Weren't no damage done, not even a scratch,' Pete added.

'You're an idiot. The boss'll have to be told,' Alun shouted.

'You reckon?' Rick stared coldly at him and reached for the door.

Alun hesitated. He saw the challenge in Rick's eyes, and he thought about the gaff that he'd made by taking off his sunglasses outside the hypermarket. What if Rick should shop him and mention that to the boss? He rested an arm on the steering wheel and forced a smile. 'Half a mo'.' He grinned, but his eyes were hard as stones. 'Why were you two late?'

Pete shifted uneasily. 'It were only a few minutes.'

'Try holding your breath that long,' Alun snapped.

Rick muttered softly.

'What did you say?'

Rick glared at Alun defiantly. 'I said, you can talk, I mean last thing we need is a driver who acts as if he's in the Grand Prix.'

'It's right. You tell him, Rick,' urged Pete.

'Who rattled your cage, you bloody parrot?' Alun snarled as he turned to glare at Pete. 'I got you there and I got you back. And I was on time. So if you're thinking of shopping me to the boss—'

'We never said that, did we, Pete?'

Pete shook his head.

'Feel free if you want.' Alun shrugged. Attack is always the best means of defence, he thought. 'Though there's one thing you has to remember.' He smiled slyly. 'Grassing works both ways.'

Rick stared at him, then his gaze slipped away. 'Forget it, eh?'

'Yeah,' Alun said, 'it would be best. So,' he then said briskly, 'now you two had better get yourselves sorted; someone's bound to drive up here at any minute.'

The two men nodded, got out and went to the boot of the car. Once it was opened, they removed their gloves and trainers. Soon both men were dressed in business suits. Then they reached into the boot, brought out suitcases and stuffed their earlier clothing into them. To any casual passer-by, it would seem that both men had recently returned from a business trip.

Through the rear-view mirror Alun watched Rick with narrowed eyes; up until today he had always been a quiet lad, a bit dim. He'd never had much to say unless he got onto the subject of wrestling; then he was like someone obsessed, but otherwise…Alun looked at Rick again as he combed back his blond hair and put on his designer glasses. He'd need to watch him carefully in future. If there was any more trouble he'd have to tell the boss.

They closed the lid of the boot and Alun leaned out of the car. 'Got everything?'

They nodded.

'Call you later, then.'

With a casual wave, Rick and Pete strolled off towards their vehicles.

Alun watched as the respective tail lights of Rick's and Pete's cars disappeared down the ramp. He thought about Rick's attitude again and scowled. The problem was that whatever Rick said, Pete would go with, and if those two should gang up together against him…?

Alun sighed; he mustn't let stuff get to him. Only one more job to do and then came the payout; then came the gravy. He tugged at his collar; he felt warm. Leaning forward he peered at his reflection in the mirror, and noticed the tiny beads of sweat that had formed on his upper lip. The strain was showing. With a curse he reached for a tissue and scrubbed at his mouth. He was Mr Cool, wasn't he? Showing signs of stress would never do. Angrily he stuffed the damp tissue into his pocket; he had to get a grip on his nerves.

He got out of the car, pulled a large grey holdall out from the floor of the passenger seat and, removing his gloves, strolled down to a lower level of the car park. His van was there, loaded up with the garden deliveries, as had been promised. He unlocked it, pushed the bag amongst the other deliveries on the floor and got in. Closing the door, he sprawled on the seat and let out a long sigh of relief.

After a minute or two he took off his rolled-up balaclava cap, pulled his ponytail out from under the back of his shirt and grabbed a brown overall from behind the seat. Slipping it on, he fished a packet of cigarettes from the breast pocket. He lit one, inhaled gratefully and, leaning back, thought through today's raid.

In spite of a rotten start with lateness, traffic jams and his attack of nerves, the job had been successful. As voices and accents were a giveaway in this game, both Rick and Pete had learned to do their work without naming names, or speaking in front of their victims. As for Rick's outburst just now, he would have to find a way to cope with him, at least until the other job was completed.

With a tight smile Alun switched on the ignition. The engine responded immediately, and he relaxed as he drove out of the car park. Practice always makes perfect, he thought, as he headed for the open road.

It was only when he approached the motorway that he remembered, and for a second his smile was replaced by a frown: he'd forgotten to report in to the boss. Quickly he reached towards the glove compartment where his mobile was kept, but then he hesitated and looked at the traffic ahead of him. The motorway was busy, and any overtaking police car might spot him using the mobile. Should he pull into a service station and phone from there? he wondered. No, best be patient and wait until he found a more convenient spot.

The rain began to beat heavily on the windscreen and Alun groaned. He wanted to press down on the accelerator, but discipline ruled. His stomach rumbled; he was hungry. He'd taken a bite or two from a sandwich at lunchtime, but no more than that. He always felt queasy before going on a raid. Now it was over he needed a hot meal inside him. He looked up ahead and saw the turn-off for Selwich. He knew that Selwich was an 'A' road, and that there was sure to be a roadside café along the route from where he could eat and phone in his report.

Alun thought about what he'd tell the boss; all he needed to say was he had the cash and all had gone well; the boss wasn't interested in anything else. Of course, there'd have been hell to pay if any of them had been caught, but this hadn't happened. He looked back at the grey holdall; what he needed now were the directions for delivery.

A signpost for a café loomed up on the side of the road: 'All-Day Breakfasts, 200 yards ahead,' it stated. Alun grinned. 'That'll do nicely,' he laughed as he drove on, turning into the café car park.

Ten minutes later he switched off his mobile and made his way back into the café. As he sat down the waitress approached with the breakfast that he'd ordered. 'Thought you'd got lost.' She smiled.

'Had a phone call to make,' Alun apologized, 'bit of trouble getting through.' He eyed the plate of bacon, eggs and sausages hungrily, and murmured his thanks. Picking up his knife and fork he began to eat.

Later, having finished his meal, he pushed away his plate and drank his coffee. Now to pay the bill. Again he thought back to the call he'd just made, and his smile faded. Something niggled at him. He'd been told to report everything…but this time? He scowled; there was one outstanding incident that he would describe as 'something and nothing'. Surely it would be best to sort of 'forget' it? Perhaps he could mention it to the boss at a later time—after all, who would know?

The trouble was that if he told the boss about the woman, he'd have to own up to his own carelessness of not wearing his sunglasses, and to the tardiness of Rick and Pete. Had the woman noticed him whilst he was waiting in the car? Had she really seen what he looked like? He tried to reassure himself; was it likely? That shopper was probably far too busy thinking about the special offers. And yet....Alun's scowl deepened as he recalled the getaway from the hypermarket yard. The woman had stared right at him.

'More coffee?' asked the waitress.

Startled, Alun shook his head. He paid the bill and walked to the exit. His mind felt fuzzy, and he knew that after all the tension, tiredness was setting in. All he needed to do now was deal with the deliveries, then get back to his job, work until closing time, then head for home.

He went to the car park, leaned against his van and lit up a cigarette. He remembered what the woman looked like; mousy hair, brownish coat. Old, must be at least forty.... And? He felt sure he'd seen her somewhere before. He should tell the boss, shouldn't he? He sighed; he didn't even want to go there.

# FOUR

*Tuesday, late afternoon*

EMILY PICKED UP the binoculars, looked out of the window and watched the events taking place outside, then she pulled her notebook towards her and began to write. When she'd finished she looked out again and decided to add more details, then stopped in irritation when she noticed her biro had run out. She tossed the pen aside, muttered, 'Stupid blooming thing,' and fished in her cardigan pocket. 'Should have another one here somewhere,' she grumbled, but no pen could be found. She sighed and put her glasses on again. 'I'll remember to tell her when she comes in,' she sighed.

Hours dragged by and Emily remained on watch at the window. Looking out she could see the row of houses opposite, all with their nice big gardens; you didn't get houses built like that these days, she thought. Nowadays they were all crammed in like boxes. How different it had been when she was a lass; then there'd not been a house in sight, just fields and more fields, then the golf course and lower down the hill, the woods.

She smiled as she thought back to the times when she and her brother Jimmy used to go mushrooming in those fields on a Saturday morning. Up at the crack of dawn, they were, looking for the good ones. Then one day they'd got chased by some curious cows. They'd had to run like the clappers and she'd torn her skirt in her rush to climb over the stile and get out of the way. Emily grinned; her mum hadn't half given her what for 'bout that, but now.... She looked out at the street again; no fields for the young ones to play in. The powers that be had turned it all into suburbia. She sighed; time moves on, she supposed.

With a worried glance at the clock her thoughts returned to Christine. She got hold of her stick and went into the kitchen. The girl had been gone for over four hours—where on earth had she got to?

Emily made herself a drink and wondered if she should start on supper. She hesitated as she recalled that Christine had said something about making a Spanish omelette. She peered into the fridge, although she knew for a fact that there were not enough eggs in there. She'd make do with a biscuit until Christine got back. Just one or two, else she wouldn't want her supper, and Christine would whinge again.

She stood at the sink, dunked her biscuit into her mug of tea and for the umpteenth time wished that Christine had been happily married off with a good husband, instead of being lumbered with that rotten Charles.

The divorce was absolute now but the scars remained. Emily frowned. Christine had come back home to live with her, and although she was a good and dutiful daughter, it wasn't right that she should spend the rest of her life caring for her, an invalid. Life's short and after such a lousy marriage she should have the chance to get out and about and have a bit of fun. The problem was that up until now Christine had been scared of life. At least yesterday's row with Harry had made her angry enough to venture out as far as the hypermarket.

Emily peered into the biscuit tin again, thought about it, then replaced the lid firmly. She just hoped that because of her nosiness Christine hadn't managed to get herself involved in yet another argument; her daughter had the gifts of curiosity and obstinacy in abundance. It seemed a pity the good Lord had not given her common sense and discretion, to even the score.

She heard a car door slam, the sound of footsteps coming up the pathway, the grating of the key in the lock. She felt relief flood through her and, limping into the living room, she sat down.

CHRISTINE SHOULDERED HER way through the door and put the shopping bags down carefully.

Emily looked up at her. 'I thought you'd got lost. Did the bus break down or something? You've been gone over four hours. I tried ringing you but your phone was switched off.'

Christine stood in the doorway and took a deep breath. 'All in good time, Mother.' Easing the bags to one side she flopped into the nearest armchair. 'Just let me get my second wind—that lot was heavy.'

'I thought I heard…did you get a taxi? You'll do your back in if you keep on lifting like that.'

'A taxi? Yes,' Christine said thoughtfully, 'it might have been better if I had.' She looked at her mother, swallowed hard and wondered how to explain the afternoon's events without frightening her. Should she be casual and report the robbery in an offhand manner? She dismissed the thought. That wouldn't do; the old girl was far too shrewd to be taken in by that. She still felt nervous; she looked down at her hands and saw they were shaking, so she pressed them firmly against the arms of the chair. Was that the effect of carrying heavy groceries, or was she still in shock?

'Don't just sit there staring. Go on, then, tell me.' Emily leaned forward and glared across at her daughter. 'Where've you been and what kept you? I've been worried.'

Christine thought for a moment then blurted out, 'I suppose you may as well know the lot. Listen, Mam, I don't know how to put this.... Something dreadful happened whilst I was at the hypermarket.'

'You had a row with the checkout girls?'

Christine looked distracted. 'No! No, not that.'

'Kay Whelan, then? You're overdue for another one with her.'

'Will you just shut up and let me tell you? I'm trying to explain it to you.'

'Oh, do get on with it.'

'It was like this, see. I'd finished my shopping but it was too early to catch my bus. I remembered there used to be a shortcut through the back of the hypermarket to the bus stop, so I had a little wander around—'

'Well you would, wouldn't you, you just might miss something.'

Christine continued determinedly, 'I'd found the old footpath and I was all set to go to the bus stop when this car zoomed into the yard—'

'Aw! You've not gone and shopped some poor motorist for illegal parking—'

'No!'

'Then what have you done? Come on, spit it out.'

Christine took a deep breath as she felt the anger grow within her. Here she was, trying her best to be calm and tactful and her mother kept jumping to conclusions. 'Are you going to listen or not?'

Emily nodded, stone-faced.

'I didn't report anybody, and no, I didn't get nicked for shoplifting.' She paused, eyed her mother and then said, 'About that car.' She drew a deep breath. 'I witnessed a robbery!'

Emily put her hands to her head. 'Oh Lord, she's at it again!'

'Mother, you've got to believe me. It's true.'

Emily stared at her.

Christine sat stiffly in the chair. 'Don't you look at me like that. I have not imagined it.'

'But you've imagined everything else,' protested Emily. 'UFOs, aliens, parallel universes. You've seen them all.'

Christine felt her face flush. 'This is for real, Mother. Look, if you won't believe me, just phone the police.' She got up, marched over to the television and switched it on. 'The local evening news will be on in a minute. It should be on that.'

Her mother stared at her again, then turned pale. 'Then you really did?' She swallowed hard. 'Tell me what happened.'

Christine walked back to the carrier bags and looked down at them. 'All I was doing was putting a tin in a bin, you see. A bit of tidying up. Then three men in a car drove up and did a robbery. The store's takings, it was. Anyway, I've given a statement to the police. I've told them all I could remember. It was over in minutes.' She pushed some stray hairs back from her face and said worriedly, 'I don't know what more I could have done.'

Emily stood up. 'You did what you had to.' Her expression softened. 'You look all in. Will I make you a drink?'

Christine waved her back. 'You stay there. I've had enough tea to float a battleship. That and the endless questions.'

'Let's hope they catch them, then.'

'When they do, the police will call me as a witness.'

'Then you'll do your duty.' Emily limped towards the carrier bags. 'Let's hope nothing's melted.' She picked one up and said briskly, 'So come on now, let's get this lot unpacked.'

Christine hesitated, then picked up the other bags and followed her mother into the kitchen. 'Only…'

Emily turned and stared at her daughter's worried face. 'You've not told me everything, have you?'

Christine leaned against the sink and gazed out of the window. 'I haven't told the police everything, either.' She looked at her mother; she would have to tell her. She had to tell someone. She took a deep breath and said slowly, 'I told the police what the driver looked like but there was something else. Something that's really bothering me.'

'Out with it.'

'I didn't tell the police that I knew his face.' She tried to stop her voice from trembling. 'You see, in the seconds before the two masked men got back into the car, I saw the driver. He was wearing a black cap, too, but it was rolled up across his forehead. As he drove off he looked straight at me. I just froze.' She paused and looked at her mother in frustration. 'I know his face, but I just can't place him!'

'Why didn't you tell the police that?'

'You don't understand, Mam. I didn't want the police to think I was stupid. I feel a fool, but I can't put a name to that driver's face. I've seen him somewhere before, I know that.'

'Christine, you have got to remember.' Emily touched her arm. 'Think back, love. Could it be some local lad? Someone that lives in the village? Come on now, you've always had such a good memory for faces.'

'I've tried and I can't. It's there, but it's like an itch I can't scratch.'

'Perhaps when the police show you the photos, something might click into—'

'Oh no!' Christine put her hands to her mouth.

'Now what?'

'The police. In a police car.'

'Yes? So?'

'They dropped me off earlier, but Harry Myers and Kay won't think that when they see them, they'll—'

'Think you've reported them again.'

Christine stared at her mother and tried not to panic. 'What'll I do?'

'Get on the phone and tell them.'

'They'll never believe me.'

'Then start with Harry,' Emily said. 'At least he does try to listen.' She looked thoughtful. 'Yes, phone him now and ask him round.'

'What about Kay?' Christine folded her arms tightly against her chest. 'I'm not phoning her. She can think what she likes.'

Emily looked at her warily. 'Take it easy. Let's try and get Harry here first.'

Christine hurried into the hall and picked up the phone.

Emily watched her. 'After all,' she murmured, 'we don't want to start a neighbourhood war.'

# FIVE

*Tuesday, late afternoon*

ALUN WENT TO his van, took out the grey holdall and placed it on the floor beside the driver's seat, then leapt back in the van and continued his journey. He had to take care of this last special delivery, then get back to work at the garden centre before the manager got suspicious. After that, it was home to a nice hot shower and a change of clothing.

He still felt tense; he glanced down at the grey bag and knew that he'd not be able to relax until he got rid of it. Cheer up, he told himself. He forced a grin and beat a nervous tattoo on the steering wheel. It was all going well, in spite of the few hiccups of this lunchtime. He thought about that and ran his fingers through his thick brown hair. Be positive, he thought. Why was he worrying? All had gone brilliantly. He nodded in approval at his renewed, positive choice of words.

The traffic ahead of him became denser, forcing him to ease off the accelerator and focus on his driving. He cursed out loud and gripped the wheel tightly as he watched some idiot show-off cut a reckless zigzag through three lanes of vehicles, regardless of the other motorists. 'You stupid sod,' he yelled as he braked. He felt the sweat break out again on his upper lip and he licked at it anxiously. Calm down, he told himself; don't get involved in road rage roulette, this cargo is far too precious for that. His gaze strayed again to the grey bag and he frowned; this delivery was the last and most important part of the raid. If he were to be stopped and the bag examined, all would be lost, for in spite of all the planning, the contents of the bag would need a lot of explanation.

He shifted nervously in his seat and, leaning forward, peered through the windscreen at the signposts ahead. Only another five miles to go, then he could hand over to Don. Don? He grinned wryly. He didn't know what the man's real name was; he didn't want to know anything more about him, except that he'd be at the pick-up point, which was different every time. That was the man's job, wasn't it, transporting 'goods' from one place to another?

As he approached the turn-off for Faulton, Alun fished in his pocket and brought out a crumpled bit of paper. He nodded to himself as he re-read the instructions that the boss had given him over the phone; as usual, the directions were finely tuned down to the smallest detail.

Slowly he eased the van down the high street of the market town; he'd already spotted the meeting place so now he must find somewhere to park. He found a space, got out, picked up the holdall and, after locking the van, hurried back to the high street.

The heat and the smell of detergent greeted him the moment he opened the door. He hesitated, assumed a nonchalant expression and strode forward, his gaze flicking from left to right.

Through the steam he could see that the place was crowded; people all around were absorbed in feeding the machines. His pulse quickened as he looked about him. Above the rumble of the machines and the smell of damp washing, some reggae music blared loudly. All seemed well.

Alun moved on to where a bald-headed man was seated,

reading *The Sun;* by his side, on a chair, was a grubby grey holdall full of laundry.

As Alun approached, the man glanced up, then returned to looking at page three.

Alun put his bag on the floor. 'Aren't there any machines free?'

The man shrugged. 'Nope, and I've been waiting for over an hour.'

'I'll come back later, then.' Alun picked up the holdall from the chair, zipped it up, then walked towards the door. 'See you,' he called over his shoulder.

'See you,' Don replied. He shoved the holdall under his chair and returned to reading the paper.

## Tuesday

HARRY MYERS FELT irritable. He'd spent a restless night worrying about how to deal with Christine. Had he been too harsh? He hoped not but he'd been really embarrassed when the police had come round and questioned him like that. He felt hurt that she could do such a thing to him.

He'd spent most of the day cutting his lawn. Now, as he looked out of the window at the well-groomed result he felt a great sense of satisfaction. He grinned to himself; one good thing about anger was that, in his case, it made him feel energetic, and for once he'd had the sense to put that energy to good use.

He walked into the kitchen, opened the fridge, got out a can of lager and had a quick swig. He was on the point of going to switch on the television to watch the rugby when the telephone rang.

He looked at his watch as he hurried to answer it. It was too early for his son Martin to call—he usually rang about seven. Besides, he'd only spoken to him three days ago. Unless there was an emergency. He picked up the receiver. 'Hello?'

'Harry?' a woman's voice inquired.

'Yes.'

'It's Christine from over the road.'

Harry almost dropped the receiver. He felt the blood rushing to his head and the anger returning. He said tersely, 'I know who you are. What's the problem?'

Christine's voice sounded shaky. 'There's something I need to explain to you.'

'Get on with it, then.'

'I can't talk about it over the phone, it's too complex. I don't like to ask but could you possibly come over here? Please,' she added.

Harry stared at the receiver. Was that a plea or a command? What on earth could she want from him after yesterday's shenanigans? He hesitated; she did sound troubled. Maybe she'd decided to apologize after all, but what if she was going to start another row? 'Give me five minutes,' he growled, and he put down the phone.

He walked back into the living room and stared at the clock on the wall. He had no intention of rushing. Ms Christine Brett could wait. He'd told her five minutes and five minutes it would be. He watched as the hands of the clock moved round, and his mind went back to the time when he'd first met her.

It had been three years since Susie's death when he'd bought this house and decided to make a new start. When he was moving in Christine had been most helpful; she'd always had a smile for him, and given him friendly advice about the local amenities. He'd been surprised when he'd heard about her divorce and her return home to look after her mother, and at the time he'd thought that it wouldn't be too long before a pleasant-looking woman like her found a new partner.

Harry sighed, for over the last six months, since her return, something had changed Christine into the prying busybody of the neighbourhood, and yesterday's row had brought it all to a head.

He looked at the wall clock again; one more minute to go. Then he remembered the rugby match. He rushed into the living room and switched on the TV recorder. He thought about his dinner and hurried back to the kitchen and hauled the nearest two packages of ready meals from the freezer. He looked down at them: which one was it to be? Decisions, decisions. Hastily he unwrapped both of the meals and shoved them into the oven. If he was going to have another row with Christine he'd soon polish both of them off. He'd be bound to be hungry when he got back.

As he walked across the road he wondered just what the hell it was that Christine had not wanted to discuss on the phone. He snorted. Was he some kind of fool, obediently trotting towards her house like a puppy answering its owner's command? He stopped in his tracks. 'Which one of us is the daftest, then?' he asked of no one in particular.

He was about to turn back when he realized he'd reached her garden gate. He saw that it was still propped up against the wall, having been torn off its hinges, and he felt a sense of remorse as he remembered who the culprit was. That would have to be fixed; there was no doubt about it. He took a deep breath and strode up the path to the front door.

A few minutes later Harry sat on the edge of an armchair in Mrs Brett's living room and, with a sense of disbelief, watched Christine pace up and down as she told him about her recent escapade. Whilst he listened, his gaze shifted from Christine to her mother, who sat watching the TV with the sound turned down. He searched the women's faces, looking for anything to confirm his suspicions that this whole story was unreal and that he was being set up for some weird private joke. There was nothing. He shifted uneasily. What were they up to? Christine's voice reached him.

'That's exactly what happened, Harry. It's also the reason why I asked you round here in case you thought I'd been reporting you. So if you saw a police car outside, it's because they were driving me home. It had nothing to do with you.'

He could restrain himself no longer and his polite smile turned into a burst of laughter. He stood up. 'All right, all right, you ladies, hold it right there. Police driving you home indeed. So the joke's on me. Come on, be honest. You're spinning me a yarn because I lost my temper with you yesterday.'

Christine looked confused. 'No, Harry, this really happened. You can't think—'

''Course I do,' interrupted Harry. 'Come on, own up, you've gone and invented this.' He gave her a puzzled look. 'You really do like to get attention, don't you?'

From the depths of her armchair Emily said, 'Seen tonight's local news yet?'

He looked at her. 'I did, as a matter of fact, and the only thing of interest was that raid at the...' He broke off and looked from Emily to Christine in consternation. 'You can't mean the hypermarket raid was...?'

'It most certainly was,' said Emily.

Harry sat down again and this time he stared at Christine in awe. 'You got the registration number?'

'If only. I could kick myself.' She looked embarrassed. 'I just froze.'

He tried to reassure her. 'Probably a good thing you

did…but about this driver. Are you sure you've seen him before?' He leaned forward. 'What I'm trying to say is that a lot of people look similar. Maybe he just reminded you of someone?'

Christine folded her arms across her chest and began to pace again. 'It's like having an unfinished jigsaw, only I can't find the one piece that fits.'

'Go over his description again,' said Emily.

'Yes', Harry said, 'height, hair, build.'

Christine looked annoyed. 'I keep telling you I didn't see any of that. He was seated in a car, wearing some kind of black woolly cap.'

She hesitated, remembering. 'What I do know is that he was clean shaven, no glasses, pale thin face.' She touched her forehead. 'And thick, dark eyebrows.'

'That could mean his hair was dark as well,' said Harry.

'And his age?' asked Emily.

Christine stared at the wall, thinking back. 'About twenty-five to thirtyish.'

Harry shrugged. 'That could fit anyone, like the post-man or such.'

'Now, Harry, you know full well our postie is fifty if he's a day and besides, he's got a face like the full moon,' said Emily.

'The milkman, then, or the window cleaner.'

'Don't you notice anything?' Emily said. 'Our window cleaner's a woman; has been for the last three months.'

'What happened to the bloke, then?' Harry allowed himself to be diverted.

'*He* developed vertigo. *She's* his missus.'

Harry looked surprised. 'That seems odd, a window cleaner with vertigo.'

'Brought on by stress,' said Emily. 'Well, that and his liking for gin.'

Christine said impatiently, 'I don't know why you're going on about window cleaners; ours has made a fortune since she started cleaning windows in shorts—'

'Wearing shorts, was she?' Harry interrupted. 'How did I manage to miss that?'

Christine stared at him disdainfully for a moment, then continued. 'And we can eliminate the milkman with his soft hands, blond hair and creamy complexion.'

'You could learn from him,' said Emily. 'Yogurt does wonders.'

'Mother!' Christine blurted. She scowled at both of them. 'Will you stop rabbiting on! Don't either of you understand? You keep chattering on about milkmen and window cleaners and I'm scared, shit scared, of what might happen.'

Emily sank deeper into her armchair. She jabbed fiercely at the remote and a succession of pictures zapped across the TV screen. 'So am I, love,' she said quietly, 'so you're not alone.'

Harry felt uneasy; he got to his feet and moved towards the door. He felt sorry for the two women and embarrassed because he'd misjudged their situation. He tried to make amends. 'I'm sorry I thought you were joking, Christine. You must be worried sick. Look, if you feel frightened or you feel the need to talk again, I'm only over the road.'

Christine looked at him anxiously. 'Do you believe me now?'

''Course I do.' He saw the fear in her eyes and reached out and touched her arm in a comforting gesture. 'Don't be afraid. I'm sure it'll be all right.'

Christine's face reddened as he touched her. She faltered, 'I just didn't want you to think that this time....'

Harry tried to reassure her, saying gently, 'I know. This

time it's for real.' He looked down at her. 'If there's any way I can help...?'

'What you going to do about Kay Whelan, then?' interrupted Emily.

'We'll have to tell her,' said Christine. 'She's bound to have seen the police car.'

Harry frowned. 'Kay works for that big finance company up the road, doesn't she? Is she some sort of secretary?'

Emily chuckled. 'Nothing as brainy as that. She's "a horticultural assistant".'

'Sounds posh.'

'It isn't,' said Christine. 'She looks after the plants in the offices. She feeds and waters them and makes them look fabulous.' Christine's voice turned icy. 'And as Kay always looks glamorous, the job suits her to a tee.' She walked over to the window and peered out at the house on the other side of the road. She glanced over her shoulder at Emily. 'She home yet?'

'I think so,' Emily said. 'Just check with my notepad, it's there on the table.'

Christine picked up the pad and read out loud. 'Kay home 5.13 p.m. Let cat out 5.15 p.m. Put out empty milk bottle 5.40 p.m.'

Harry gaped at her. 'Do you always take such detailed notes about everyone?'

Christine blushed. 'Only the folk we can see—it gives Mother something to do.'

Harry's mouth dropped open. He swallowed hard and said hastily, 'Well then, what's happening about Kay?'

Emily leaned round the arm of her chair and smiled up at Harry. 'I was thinking, it might be better if someone, such as you, were to explain to Kay what has happened.'

She glowered at Christine. 'If she were to go see her that might well be the start of World War Three.'

Christine looked as if she was about to argue, so Harry said quickly, 'Yes, I can see that. It might be better if I were to have a discreet word.'

Emily eyed her daughter. 'Especially after last Saturday.'

'All right, Mother, that's enough.'

Harry frowned; it seemed as if yet another row between mother and daughter was brewing. He edged nearer to the living room door, searched for the door handle and opened it. 'I'll go and speak to her now.'

'Thanks, Harry,' Christine called. She went over to the window and watched him as he strode across the road towards Kay's house.

'He's gone straight there, then?' asked Emily.

'Yes, he's at her front door right now.'

'Nice man,' Emily said. 'One of life's gentle giants.'

'Except for when he's roused.' Christime smiled. 'But he was really kind tonight.' She stood gazing out of the window. 'Oh look, she's asked him in.'

# SIX

*Tuesday evening*

HARRY WALKED OVER to Kay's house and rang the doorbell. No answer. He looked at the front window and saw a light on. 'She must be in there,' he muttered. 'She's probably got the TV on too loud.' He rang the bell again. He tried to dismiss his embarrassment. He should never have offered to act as a go-between. He was about to turn on his heels and beat a rapid retreat when the door opened and Kay, silhouetted by the hall light, stood in front of him.

Although she was discreetly dressed in a navy sweater and skirt, her voluptuous figure was impossible to hide. She looked annoyed and Harry felt even worse. Then she recognized him and her mouth curved into a fetching smile. 'Oh my goodness, Harry! Long time no see. And there's me keeping you waiting.' She opened the door wider in a welcoming gesture. 'Please, come on in. I really am sorry but my friend was on the phone and believe me, that woman would not stop talking.' She broke off, ushered him into the living room, gestured towards the sofa, then sat down and looked at him. 'So Harry, what can I do for you?'

Harry perched on the edge of his seat. 'I'm sorry,' he began, 'I didn't want to disturb you. Is your friend…?'

Kay dismissed the question. 'I'll call her back later. Now, Harry, how can I help?'

'Where to start? That's the problem.'

'At the beginning, that's what all the experts tell us.'

Harry took a deep breath. 'Well then, it's about Christine Brett, one of our—'

'You don't need to tell me who Christine is,' Kay snapped. 'She's the nosiest woman in Britain. She's always making trouble for me.'

Harry nodded in sympathy. 'You're preaching to the converted, Kay. We've all had problems with her, but'—he looked thoughtful—'well, this time, she might—'

'Might what?' She leaned towards him. 'You did hear about her reporting my party to the police?'

He nodded again and said quickly, 'But that's not why I came.'

Kay stared at him, then got up and marched over to the window to look out at Christine's house. 'When I came here after my husband…well, all I wanted was peace and quiet. This place seemed ideal; suburban, a through road, not in any way noticeable.' She laughed bitterly. 'But then I'd reckoned without "dear Christine".'

'Now, Kay, don't be like that. Come back here and sit down. At least listen to what I have to say.'

Kay returned to the sofa, sank down onto it and sighed. 'Go on then, though I warn you, nothing will surprise me if it's about her.'

'Surprise wasn't quite the word I was looking for,' said Harry. 'Y'see, what happened today was that, well, Christine witnessed a robbery in town.'

Kay's expression froze, then after a second she laughed. 'So that's her latest shot at getting your attention, is it, Harry?'

He felt his face redden, but he carried on determinedly. 'She was the only witness and the police drove her home. The thing is, she has asked me, you see…she didn't want you to think the police might be interested in you again, so to speak.'

Kay jumped to her feet and said indignantly, 'Why on earth should the police be interested in me?'

Harry was startled. 'Of course the police aren't interested in you, but Christine was worried you'd jump to conclusions...because of the rumpus about your party the other week.'

'I see. So now she says she saw a robbery. And you believed her? You men!' For a second she turned and looked out of the window again at Christine's house and then she dashed into the hall and grabbed her coat.

He hurried after her. 'Kay! Will you listen? I think it's true. It was on the news.'

Kay sniffed. 'And I'll bet that's where she got the idea from.' She pulled on her coat and opened the door.

'Where are you going?' Harry asked as he followed her.

'Where do you think?'

EMILY LEANED ON her stick, looked out of the window and watched as Kay, followed by Harry, marched towards her house. Emily's jaw tightened and she glanced towards the kitchen. 'Enemy sighted,' she called. She returned to her chair, folded her arms across her chest and watched the door with anticipation.

There came the sound of furious hammering on the front door and Christine hurried to answer its summons.

Emily raised an eyebrow. 'Happen folk don't know we've got a doorbell.'

Kay pushed past Christine into the living room. 'Might I ask, where did this latest fantasy of yours come from? So now you've gone and seen a robbery, have you?'

Christine stared at her in silence. She said icily, 'Good evening, Kay. Won't you come in?'

'Don't you start being sarcastic with me,' muttered Kay. 'Are you up to your old tricks again?'

'I beg your pardon?'

'You know what I mean. Have you been playing silly beggars and gone and reported me to the police again? Because if you have, you bitch—'

'No!' shouted Christine. 'I haven't. Why else do you think I sent Harry to talk to you?'

Harry cleared his throat and eased his way between the two women. 'Ladies, ladies,' he began. He looked at Kay in reproach and turned to Christine. 'I did try to tell her, but she wouldn't believe me. She just marched straight over here.'

Christine sighed. 'Kay, it's true. It was all as Harry said.'

Emily chuckled quietly. She felt sorry for Christine, but no one could say she hadn't asked for it. 'That's the trouble with crying wolf, girl. Now it's at the door no one will believe you.'

'Of course they won't,' snapped Kay. 'She makes it up as she goes along.'

'I am not lying,' Christine said unsteadily, and Emily hoped she wouldn't break down in front of Kay. You could say what you liked about having sympathy for young widows, but to Emily's mind this young widow was as hard as nails.

'All by yourself, were you?' goaded Kay. 'Or was your mother with you?'

'I was alone. I saw this green convertible—'

'So the convertible did the robbery then?'

'No, there were three men in it. They were wearing balaclavas.'

Kay raised an eyebrow. 'Three masked men? So you didn't see their faces?'

'No.' Christine faltered. 'Two of them were wearing balaclavas, but the third one wasn't.'

'You got a good look at this man, then, and you took the car registration number?'

'I didn't get the car number, but—'

Kay turned to Harry, rolled her eyes and smirked. 'You see! Some witness.'

'I did see what the driver looked like,' Christine added determinedly. 'I swear I'd know that driver if I saw him again.'

For a moment Kay stared at her blankly, then her gaze shifted to Harry and her expression softened. 'Well, if what you say is true then I suppose I'm sorry, Christine.' She turned to Harry and, rubbing her hand along his arm, smiled up at him coyly.

Emily watched her. Sly little minx, she thought.

'I've been rude and I overreacted,' Kay added. 'It's just…since the loss of my husband, my nerves are in such a state.' Then she said, 'I'm sorry I doubted you, Christine. Only I did think you were making….' She dabbed at her cheek with a tissue. 'I'd better go. I'll leave you in peace.' She moved towards the door.

Emily watched as Harry looked between the two women and silently willed him to at least stay long enough to reassure Christine.

Harry looked embarrassed. 'I'd better see Kay home. Goodnight,' he muttered and he hurried after her.

Emily saw them leave and shook her head. 'Typical of a man. Never can see what's right in front of them.'

Christine sniffed defiantly. 'I don't know what that's supposed to mean. He certainly noticed Kay; he couldn't take his eyes off her.'

HARRY WAITED UNTIL Kay's door closed behind her, then made his way back down the path. He looked across the road to where Christine stood at the window, and waved.

She smiled, waved back, then drew the curtains. Harry walked on towards his house. He felt tired and hungry and remembered his oven meals would be ready by now so he quickened his pace and hurried indoors.

Half an hour later as he watched the recording of the rugby match, his thoughts drifted back to Christine. She must be worried sick. True, she had given as good as she got when Kay had barged in on her like that, but he'd seen how anxious she was and he knew she was trying hard not to frighten her mother. He looked at his watch—not quite nine o'clock. Should he go across the road and reassure her? It might be a good idea. He could mention that he'd mend the broken gate. And as for the damaged dahlias, well, he'd see to them first thing tomorrow.

# SEVEN

CHRISTINE SAT IN an armchair and stared at the TV. She'd hoped there would be further reports on the robbery, but so far there'd been nothing; she'd have to wait until the ten o'clock news came on. She shouldn't expect instant results; the police couldn't work that quickly. However, those robbers seemed to be very experienced, and if they did have a record it would be easier for the police to trace them. She hesitated; easier to trace perhaps, but as two of the men had been masked she wouldn't be able to identify them. She could only recognize the one man, the driver.

She shivered and rubbed her arms as she remembered how he'd stared right at her. Did he know her? That was the question. She was the one witness who stood between him and prison. And she knew his face. What if he was to track her down and find out where she lived; he could break into this house and threaten her.

Alarm filled her. She stood up and looked around the room. Her mother's house was old. In fact she couldn't remember when they'd last had the locks checked. There were none on the windows; that much she did know. The window frames were sturdy but they held plain glass. A single brick or stone could smash straight through them. She went into the hall and checked the front door lock. As she'd thought, it was an old-fashioned Yale one. It must be at least forty years old, and anyone could pick it. She thought about her mother and her fear increased as she realized just how vulnerable they were.

She must do something. She walked through the hall to the foot of the stairs and wondered how she could convince her mother that they needed new locks. Was there a way to do it without frightening her? Her mother's argument had always been that she needn't worry about security, as they had nothing worth stealing. Now the circumstances were different; Christine was the one person who could identify the getaway driver and that made them vulnerable.

Christine stood silently and listened to the muffled groans and yells of a wrestling match on the TV coming from her mother's bedroom, and she couldn't repress a smile. Earlier, Emily had said she felt tired and that she was going to have an early night because of all the excitement. Christine knew this was an excuse for her mother to go upstairs to watch her favourite American Wrestling programme, and her beloved hero, the Undertaker. As Christine listened a muffled cheer rang out; it seemed the Undertaker had won yet again. She wandered back into the living room; perhaps she could buy some locks and fit them herself. It would be less expensive.

She thought about Harry. He had been so helpful and kind today and had said he would help in any way he could. Maybe she could ask his advice or even ask him to fit the locks. Doubt entered her mind: but then men said a lot of things they didn't mean. She thought about her shattered marriage, the endless promises her husband, Charles, had made. All of them had been broken. Her doubts strengthened; maybe Harry hadn't really meant it, either. She had seen the way Kay had fluttered her eyelashes at him, and how eagerly he'd escorted her home.

She bit on her lip. Kay was an attractive woman and if Harry thought so as well, then she'd better not keep asking him for help. Anyway, why would Harry be interested in the likes of her? She'd never been glamorous like Kay. These days she hardly ever bothered to look in the mirror.

Her gaze strayed back to the windows; it would be wiser to get the job done properly. She remembered that there was a locksmith who lived nearby, if he'd not retired. She hurried back to the hall, picked up the telephone directory and leafed through it. Finding the firm's number, she picked up the phone. As she did so she checked the time. It was well after business hours; still, she just might be lucky.

HARRY PULLED UP his collar against the rain and pressed the Bretts' doorbell. As he'd crossed the road he'd seen there were lights on in an upstairs room and the living room. He hoped that the two women had not already gone to bed; it was only just after nine.

'Who's there?' Christine's anxious voice came from behind the closed door.

'It's me, Harry.'

'Oh, hold on a mo'.'

She opened the door cautiously; Harry thought that she looked surprised. 'I've just come over to make sure everything's okay,' he said. 'I've not got you out of your bed, have I?'

'No.' Christine smiled. 'Mother's upstairs watching her idol on the telly. Come in, won't you?' She ushered him into the living room. 'Is Kay all right now?'

Harry sank into an armchair. 'Let's hope so. That little lady has a very quick temper. Still, I think she'll have calmed by now. How about you?' He nodded towards the TV. 'Any more news yet?'

Christine shook her head. 'No, nothing.' She looked at him and said, 'I know you'll probably laugh and think me a coward, but I've just been on the phone to ask a lock-smith to call round first thing tomorrow.'

'I don't think you're a coward, Christine.' Harry was surprised at how much he wanted to smooth the fearful look from her face.

'Anyway I know I'm overreacting but I've realized that anyone could force these locks.'

'I think you're very wise,' said Harry. 'Not just because of what's happened to you,' he added quickly as he saw the fear return to her eyes, 'but making sure the house is secure is a good investment for insurance purposes. You might even get a discount.'

Christine's face brightened. 'Yes, you're right. I think that's what I'll tell Mother.'

Harry went into the hall and examined the front door. He turned to Christine and said gently, 'You know, I would have done this for you. What you need is a mortise lock on here. I could have fitted it for you in no time.' He grinned at her. 'And I don't charge.'

He saw her face turn pink. 'Oh, I couldn't,' Christine said. 'You've been more than kind to us already and after what I did.... I was just going to make a drink. Would you like one?'

'I could murder a cup of tea.' He went into the living room and sat down as Christine bustled into the kitchen. She returned shortly carrying a tray and some biscuits.

'I thought you might like some of these, they're home-made.'

'I shouldn't, but I will,' said Harry, as he reached eagerly for a biscuit. 'I'm being greedy, though. I've already eaten two oven-ready meals tonight.'

'Two? Surely that's not good for you. Don't you make your own meals?'

Harry shook his head. 'Me? No, I'm far too lazy. I usually get a takeaway or a pizza. My late wife, Susie, was a good cook, but when I try to make anything it ends up as a UEO.'

'What's that?'

'Unidentified Edible Object. So I've surrendered, and I'm eternally grateful to the freezer and the oven, even though the food starts to taste the same after a while.'

Christine laughed. She hesitated then said shyly, 'Do you like casseroles?'

'What? Stew and dumplings? I love 'em. But when I tried to make them before they ended up looking like walnuts with blobs of flour. I can't figure out what went wrong. I cooked the meat slowly like the book said. You'd have thought after six hours it would be tender, wouldn't you, but no.'

Christine giggled and held out the plate of biscuits again. 'Have another.'

'As long as you don't mind?' He bit into one. 'They're delicious.'

'I was thinking,' Christine said, 'I'm making a casserole tomorrow. I could always make a bit extra. You wouldn't be offended, would you?'

'Not at all. As long as it's not too much work. I can hardly wait....' He looked at Christine and felt grateful for the offer but also wished that she'd invited him to eat with them. Of course, if Christine made a meal for him maybe she'd consider letting him take her out to dinner. It might take her mind off things. He smiled at her, then added, 'But the real reason I came here was to ask you if it would be all right for me to mend your gate in the morning, weather permitting. After all, I'm the one that broke it.'

'I'd be glad if you did, and let's not go into the whys and wherefores any more,' Christine said. 'Just look at where it got me.'

Harry leaned forward and gazed at her earnestly. 'Christine, as I've said before, if you feel worried or frightened don't hesitate to call me. You have my number. If there's anything I can do, I'd be only too pleased.' He got to his feet.

Christine walked with him to the door. 'Thanks, Harry,' she said quietly. 'It's good to know there's someone on my side.'

He touched her arm and to his surprise felt her flinch slightly. 'Try not to worry,' he said, 'I'm sure the police will catch those men in no time.'

She smiled. 'Let's hope so.'

As he walked down the path Harry heard the door close behind him and the sound of the key being turned in the lock. He frowned as he thought about the way that Christine had reacted when he touched her arm. She'd seemed so afraid. Surely she wasn't scared of him? He crossed the road and found himself wondering just what her husband might have done to her to make her react like that.

# EIGHT

*Tuesday*

THAT EVENING ALUN bounded up the stairs to his flat, closed the door behind him and felt relieved that all of the day's work was done. He'd delivered the cash, then driven like a madman to get to his job at the garden centre on time. He'd been a few minutes late, but again his luck had held as his manager had been at a meeting. Alun smiled; it had been a day of near misses, but fortune had been on his side. Everything that had to be done had been done; there was nothing more to worry about.

He walked over to the fridge, got out a can of lager and took a long swig from it. Ah, that was better; he'd been looking forward to that all day. He stank of sweat and soil—best take a quick shower, then perhaps grab a bite to eat down at the Angel. He thought about the blonde he'd seen there last Friday. His smile deepened; he hoped she'd be there tonight. He definitely felt the need for some female comfort and relaxation.

He stripped off his clothes and thought about the next job. Things had been going well for so long it might be better to go over a few details again. No, he dismissed the thought irritably, what was he worrying about? The lads knew what to do, and most people noticed nothing even when they were only a few yards away. As for the one percent that did see something, they usually got the facts wrong—even the cops would tell you that.

Stepping into the shower, he flinched as the hot jets of water beat down on him and he stretched and felt his muscles relax. He should be grateful that he belonged to a nation of people that prided themselves on minding their own business, he thought. It was at that moment that the phone rang. He cursed and ignored it. Whoever it was would have to call again. He was out of the shower and drying himself when the ringing stopped, but a nagging suspicion entered his mind. It couldn't be the boss, could it? As he pulled on his jeans the phone rang again. He struggled towards it and answered breathlessly, 'Hello?'

'Alun?'

With a sinking sensation Alun recognized the voice. 'Yes. What's wrong?'

'You reported earlier that everything went according to plan.'

'It did...well almost.'

There was a long silence.

Alun swallowed hard. 'You still there?'

'Yes.'

'I thought we'd got cut off for a minute.'

'I'm waiting, Alun.'

'For what?'

'To hear what the bloody hell happened today. Why did you lie to me?'

'I don't know what you're on about...oh, I see. You mean about that woman.' He thought again about the woman he'd seen as he drove off. He wondered why her face seemed so familiar. 'She only saw me for a second... how did you know about her, boss?'

'I have sources. Why didn't you tell me?'

Alun forced a laugh. 'But it was only this woman.'

'She's a witness. She could ruin everything.'

'What are the odds on her recognizing me?'

'Don't argue. I want her dealt with. I want her house cased. I've been told a Mrs Brett lives there. Here's the address. Have you got a pen?'

'Oh, bloody hell!' Alun swore as he put down the receiver and scribbled the address on the corner of a newspaper. He felt surprised when he wrote down the details. He wondered how the boss had managed to get this information, and why it should ring a distant bell in his memory. Then he remembered! He'd seen the woman when he'd delivered some goods to one of the garden centre's customers. She lived on the same street, in fact almost opposite his customer's address. He thought about her and his lip curled. That bitch was always pottering around in her front garden. A right nosy cow she was. He snorted in disgust. And there was an old woman that lived with her. Talk about sod's law! He felt the fury build inside him and cursed under his breath. It was no use. He picked up the receiver again and gave a deep sigh. 'Boss,' he said. 'It was like this....'

When he put the receiver down, he finished dressing and scowled. He'd been looking forward to a good night out and now it would be ruined. He'd have to find a team who'd do a good job on casing the house. He searched his memory; he needed someone who'd be thorough. Sam's lot was quick and reliable. Irritably he pulled on his jacket, grabbed his keys and strode out of the flat. Now he'd have to spend his evening scouring the town, searching for Sam.

Alun found him standing near the poker tables watching the action. After searching most of the pubs in town he'd remembered one of Sam's 'little hobbies', and he'd headed for the casino. He gave a wry smile as he approached the chubby figure and felt relieved that he'd guessed right. After all, leopards never change their spots.

He tapped him on the shoulder. Sam spun round at his touch and for a split second his ice-blue eyes were as piercing as lasers, then his round face creased into a cheerful grin as he recognized Alun.

'Hi there, stranger!' He spread out his arms in a welcoming gesture. 'What brings you to these foreign parts?'

'I've been out all night looking for you,' Alun grumbled. 'Don't you ever switch your bloody mobile on?'

Sam chuckled. 'Not whilst I'm…relaxing, and never ever in this place.' His gaze drifted longingly to the poker tables. 'I'm waiting to join in on the action. I take my pastimes seriously, I'll have you know.'

More than any other bloody pastime, Alun thought as he looked around with distaste. You could smell the hunger for money in here. He felt uncomfortable and his headache returned as the so-called upbeat background music played relentlessly on; that and the stench of stale beer and sweat, and the constant *ker-chink* of the slot machines nearby. He watched as the machines gulped down the cash that was fed to them by the eager players, and his foul mood deepened. He didn't need this; he'd had enough tension for one day.

'Don't stand there looking miserable.' Sam's voice broke in on his thoughts. 'What brings you to me then?'

'Business, what else?' Alun replied. 'Is there some place where we can talk?'

'Here's the safest place in town.' Sam nodded at the punters surrounding them. 'As you see, these guys have other things on their minds.'

'Well then,' Alun said reluctantly, 'there's a job needs doing, and it's urgent.'

Sam's eyes became hard as stone. 'If it's urgent I take it there's a bonus?'

'Agreed.'

Sam got out his notebook and pen. 'Who? What? Where? And when?'

# NINE

---

NEXT MORNING, HARRY stood at his front window and peered down the road. It was a fine sunny morning after last night's rain. Earlier he'd seen the locksmith's van arrive and the man go into the Bretts' house; minutes later he'd seen Christine come out and hurry along the street.

Harry frowned; it was not like Christine to be in such a rush. The police had probably phoned her and asked her to go to the station. He wandered back into the kitchen and looked down at the toolbox that stood in readiness near the back door. He'd been about to go over to make an early start on the gate when he'd seen Christine leave. Now it might be best to wait until she returned. He wanted to find out what was happening at the police station; besides, it would be a good excuse to have another chat with her. He went to the front door again and looked out. From across the road he could hear the intermittent sounds of a drill. It seemed that the locksmith was already busy at his work. Further along the road he could see the distant figure of old Brian Sharpe and his dog. Harry grinned. The old boy was forever walking the poor creature along the street; said it was to keep the animal's claws from getting too long. Harry thought the dog was just a good excuse for Brian's nosiness; he knew the old boy was retired. He squinted at the dog again. He was sure its legs had been straight when Brian had first bought it; now they were decidedly bandy. Harry chuckled to himself as he closed the door and went back to the kitchen. In his opinion that dog was exercised so much it was buckling at the knees.

HALF AN HOUR later Emily also peered out of her front room window. The street was deserted. She sighed and hurried back into the kitchen. Why hadn't Christine told her that she'd decided to have new locks fitted instead of dashing off to see the police again without so much as a 'by your leave'? Couldn't she have waited instead of yelling up the stairs, announcing that Fred Hamlin the locksmith was here?

Now here she was with a man in the house who insisted that he'd got to follow Christine's instructions. Whose house did he think it was anyway? The wretched man had been fiddling with the lock on the back door for ages, as well as doing his best to smoke his head off.

Emily sniffed and walked towards him, waving her arms in an exaggerated manner at the smoke. She stopped and glowered down at him for a while whilst he worked. 'You could be a burglar, or a con man, even. How was I to know who you are?'

Fred Hamlin looked up at her. 'You should know me by now, Ma. I've lived round here for the last twelve years and I've always done locks and odd jobs, you know that.'

'So you say, but money's tight these days. For all I know you might have converted to the mugging profession and have designs on robbing frail old ladies.'

Fred Hamlin chuckled. 'Give us a break, Ma. Don't keep making me laugh.'

Emily sniffed. 'I don't think it's funny, and stop calling me "Ma", I'm not your mother.'

She looked at the living room clock and wondered how long Christine would be at the cop shop. A vision of her daughter staring at a video screen came into her mind. Knowing her daughter well enough by now she'd have the SAS on standby, and Interpol on red alert. Anyone else would have thought Christine would love all the attention she was getting but, although the girl hadn't said much, Emily knew she was worried sick.

What annoyed her was the fact that there was nothing that she could do except wait at home, and keep an eye on the dratted locksmith. She glared again at the workman with undisguised annoyance. She knew that Fred Hamlin was aware of her disapproval but he worked on stoically. Having measured and fitted a lock to the door, he tested it to make sure that it functioned smoothly. Satisfied with his efforts he tightened up the screws. When he'd finished he pulled out a packet of cigarettes and looked at Emily with a hopeful expression.

'Any chance of a cuppa, Ma? Whoops, I mean Missus.'

Emily bristled. 'You've had two mugfuls already. This is not a Lyon's Tea House, I'll have you know.' Then she went off to put the kettle on.

Fred Hamlin called after her, 'Soon be finished, Ma. Just got the front door to do.' He lit his cigarette, ambled into the hallway and squatted down to examine the lock.

Five minutes later Emily handed him a mug of tea and scowled, wafting a hand in disapproval. 'And who said you could smoke? Haven't I told you before that our house is a smoke-free zone?'

Fred looked wistful. 'I could open the door, like I did with the windows earlier?'

'No, you can't. It's freezing in here already.' She saw his glum expression and relented. 'Well, all right, if you're an addict there's not much I can do about it. So just this once you can puff your smoke through the letterbox. That should keep both of us happy.' She turned and limped back into the living room before Fred could think of a reply.

Ten minutes later Fred came into the kitchen carrying his empty mug and a bunch of keys. He handed them to her. 'All done now, Missus. Want to take a look?'

Emily shook her head. 'My daughter will check it all when she gets back.' She looked at him with speculation. 'How much did all this lot come to?'

'Don't you worry about that. Your daughter will get the bill.' He got out his receipt book. 'If you'll just sign here?'

Emily scanned the invoice. 'I'm not Christine Brett, as you well know.'

'Just put pp in front of your signature,' said Fred. 'It's just to say the job's been done. Oh, and tell her I'm all out of door chains, but as soon as they come in I'll nip round and fit one.'

'Just so long as you do remember. She's not paying for stuff she hasn't got.'

'Right you are, Ma.'

Emily put the receipt book on the table and signed it, steadying it clumsily with her impaired left hand. She wrote some more. 'I've compromised; I've signed and put "work unexamined, door chain still to come".' She gave him back his pen.

'Whatever you say, Missus. Would you tell her she'll have the bill in the next few days and if there's any problem she's to phone me?' Fred headed for the door then stopped in his tracks. 'Hang on a minute. I forgot to check those bolts.' He squatted down behind the front door, with yet another smouldering cigarette in his hand.

'Just you make sure that they don't fall off before you're halfway down the drive,' said Emily acidly. 'And what did I tell you before about where you've got to puff that smoke?'

'THAT'S THE LAST of them,' Sergeant Farrell said as he switched the screen off. 'Didn't you recognize anyone?'

Christine shook her head. 'No, nothing. No one at all.' She sat back in her chair and stared at the blank monitor. 'So what do I have to do now? I've told you everything.' Her gaze shifted anxiously towards the door. She'd been here for close on two hours, staring at the mug shots until her brain went blank. She wanted to go home, to make sure that Fred Hamlin had followed her instructions, and that Mother hadn't managed to declare war on the poor man.

Sergeant Farrell looked at the woman seated across from him and tried hard not to think of the notes he had on her in his file. Hopefully this time what she claimed might be genuine. He had to give her the benefit of the doubt. But, given her past record of making frequent reports of litter louts, suspected peeping Toms and, last week, reporting one of her neighbours as being the getaway driver of a robbery (on investigation it turned out he happened to be driving the same colour car), the stirrings of doubt crept into his policeman's mind. He sighed and got to his feet. 'Then we'll have to call in the police artist, Miss Brett, so that you can describe the man to him.'

'I keep telling you, I've told you all I remember.'

'But you said that you felt that you knew him?'

'Yes, but I don't know from where.'

The sergeant picked up her statement and read through it again. 'I see that you didn't get the registration number? Not even one or two letters?'

'I was watching the man, not the car.'

He gave a wry smile. 'That's unusual for you, Miss Brett, you're normally so observant. When I think of the times you've reported suspicious activity in this neighbourhood, and you've been...very emphatic.' He leaned forward, his gaze intense. 'Can you at least remember if it was a new car, or an old one?'

'How many more times? It was a green convertible.' Christine sat upright and glared back at the police officer. Did he think she'd imagined the driver? 'You've imagined just about everything else,' her mother's words echoed in her mind. She shifted uneasily in the chair. 'Look, I've told you what I saw and if you don't believe me—'

Sergeant Farrell got to his feet. 'No one has said that, Miss Brett, but you were the only person who saw the driver, and I'm sorry to have to say this, but lately when you've reported incidents to us, there have been some exaggerations.'

Christine stared at him. She knew he doubted her. Did he think she'd imagined seeing the driver? 'Well, I'm telling you now I didn't invent this,' she said. 'I saw the car and the driver, I've given you his description and it was all exactly as I told you. That car and those crooks are out there somewhere. If you've no further questions, I'd like to go home.'

'As you will, Miss Brett.' Sergeant Farrell went to the door and opened it. 'Thank you for coming in.' He hesitated then said, 'We'll call you again as soon as an artist is available.'

TEN TO TWELVE. Harry looked at the clock, then turned to stare out of the living room window; a sunny autumn day like this yet hardly a soul about. Where had all the neighbours gone? He opened the window and looking down the road, listened carefully. He smiled; faintly he could hear the distant hum of lawnmowers. So that's where they were, in their back gardens, cutting the grass whilst the sun still shone. He glanced down at his own neatly clipped lawn with satisfaction; all he needed to do in the garden now was to get the compost and those wood chippings down before winter came. He thought about that; Mr Longley, the manager down at the garden centre, had said he'd phone him once the wood chippings were due to be delivered. But as for today, he could make a start on washing his car.

He looked down the road again, hoping to see the distant figure of Christine returning, but there was still no sign of her. There were two men at the far end of the street, though, and Harry's interest deepened. He looked closer. They were smartly dressed and carrying bulging brief-cases. They seemed to be deep in earnest conversation. 'Aha, the Jehovah's Witnesses have decided to honour us with a visit,' Harry muttered, but as he watched he saw the men separate and begin to canvass the houses on either side of the street. He shrugged. 'Rule out Jehovah's; they always work in pairs. They must be double-glazing sales-men.' He watched as the men rang each doorbell briskly, then without waiting for anyone to answer, posted their brochures through the letterboxes and moved on.

Harry's curiosity increased. Why weren't the men wait-ing for the occupants to open the doors? Were they leaflet distributors? If so, then why ring at all? He closed the win-dow. 'Pull yourself together, man, you're getting as nosy as Christine. Best get on with cleaning the car.'

CHRISTINE HURRIED DOWN the police station steps and tried to blink back the tears. She didn't want the police to see how upset she was. Besides, she needed to walk in order to think clearly, to put into mental boxes the thoughts that were frustrating her. She had tried her best to tell the police everything, yet still they pressed for more. Just because in the past she'd made one or two mistakes in reporting peo-ple, that didn't mean that she'd got it wrong this time. The point was that the getaway driver's photo had not been on file, so it was clear the man had no previous convictions. That wasn't her problem. Doubtless they were a gang of amateurs, but they were clever, for their getaway had been well thought out.

She frowned and wondered what had made her decide to search for the old shortcut at the back of the hypermarket on that particular day. Just look at where it had landed her. She swallowed hard; that driver had seen her, she knew that. What if he did know her? She considered the implications and her pulse quickened. Her mind leapt ahead to her mother at home. She increased her pace as she thought about the work that she'd ordered, and hoped that by now Fred Hamlin had completed his task.

She thought about the new locks and winced as she calculated the expense, but in view of what had happened she knew they were essential. Mother would whinge about the money. It would be her favourite theme from now until Christmas; but Mother had been through enough hard times to make her always worry about money.

As she turned into the street she shivered and pulled her coat tightly about her. In spite of the autumn sunshine the wind had turned colder. For a moment she stopped and looked up at the trees, but there was no increase in the movement of the leaves. Maybe it was stress that was making her imagine things? She tried to conquer her unease as she looked about her and her gaze scanned the road. At the far end she could see a man with a bulging briefcase and an armful of leaflets making his way through the garden gates to the houses. On the other side of the road was another man, intent upon the same thing. They were promoting some product; this road must be their target for today.

She saw the men walk briskly from house to house, then, glancing at her watch, she realized it was almost noon. Mother would be hungry; she would also need to take her medication.

SOME MINUTES LATER as he washed his beloved Vauxhall Corsa, Harry watched one of the men approach the Bretts' house. To his surprise the man walked past the parked van in the driveway, completely ignored the front door letter-box and hurried round to the back of the house. The man returned within seconds. He glanced briefly up at the windows and door, and then strode down the pathway to continue with his canvassing.

Harry was puzzled; why had the Bretts escaped the delivery of the brochures? If any house cried out for double glazing it was theirs. And why had the man gone round to the back? Harry peered at the Bretts' front door and saw that it was not quite closed.

'So maybe that's....' He stared at the door again and saw smoke trickling through the letterbox. He blinked, rubbed his eyes, and looked once more. There was no doubt about it; greyer than before, the smoke continued to billow out!

'My God! The house is on fire!' he yelled. He got his mobile from his pocket, keyed in 999 and asked for the fire brigade, then, grabbing the bucket of water, he raced across the street.

'I'm coming,' he shouted. 'Don't worry, Mrs Brett, I'll rescue you!' Kicking the door open he flung the contents of the bucket through it. 'Stay calm, Mrs Brett,' he roared.

AS CHRISTINE APPROACHED the house she saw that Fred Hamlin's van was still there. Good, she would have time to inspect the locks before he— She started in surprise as she saw Harry Myers charge across the road with a bucket. He seemed to be heading straight for her front door. What on earth? She raced after him into her driveway....

'I'VE CALLED THE—' Harry stopped in mid-sentence and gasped as the door swung wide and a soaking wet Fred Hamlin glowered at him. From Fred's mouth dangled a sodden cigarette. 'What the devil's going on?' Fred spluttered as bubbles formed on his lips and lather slid down his chin. 'I've heard of folk that are anti-smoking but this is bloody ridiculous!'

'But I thought...' Harry stammered.

'Would you mind telling me what you're doing?' said Christine from behind him.

Harry spun round. 'I thought the house was on fire.'

'So you tried to drown Mr Hamlin?' Christine's voice was demure but Harry could see that she was trying not to laugh.

'But it wasn't like that.' Harry felt his face go red as he heard the fire engine siren. He'd never felt such a fool in all his life.

# TEN

*Wednesday*

AN HOUR LATER, Christine stood at the window and tried not to move the net curtains as she watched a still red-faced Harry stoically fix the hinges on the garden gate. Her shoulders shook and she laughed out loud as she thought about what had happened earlier, and she turned away from the window in case he should hear her. She didn't want to embarrass him still further, but this was the first time that she'd laughed in months. Once more the mental picture of 'Hero Harry' galloping to the rescue with, of all things, a bucket of soapsuds, crept into her mind and she giggled again.

'Don't know why you're stood sniggering. I'll bet you've not heard a word I've said.'

Christine started. 'Yes I have, Mother. Now mind you don't slip on the hall floor, it's not quite dry yet.'

'Never you mind the flaming floor. What I want to know is why did you leave me in the house with a strange fella? Got the shock of me life, I did, when I came downstairs. Besides, does it take all morning to look at a few mugshots?'

Christine felt defensive. 'A few? There were thousands, and they're not all on the same database. Seems to me we've got wall-to-wall crooks in this country. As for you calling Mr Hamlin a "strange fella", you must remember him; he's lived around here for years.'

'He'll remember us all right,' Emily snorted. 'He'll want paying danger money before he comes in here again.'

'I left you a note. Didn't you read it?'

Emily drew herself up to her full five feet. 'Yes I did, but then I wasn't to know that you'd rush off like that. And I sure didn't think that you'd expect me to be kept in here like the prisoner of Zenda, not knowing what the hell was happening.' She walked over to the window, struggled to unlock it and called, 'And I've been trying to open this damn thing for ages.'

Christine forced herself to stay calm. She went over to her mother, released the lock and pushed the window open. 'There you are. I'll show you again, shall I? Or better still, you have a go.'

Emily scowled but managed to open the window after a few false starts.

Christine nodded in approval. 'You see? All it needed was a bit of patience.'

Emily gave a disdainful sniff and seated herself in an armchair. She sat in silence whilst she watched Christine walk around rechecking the locksmith's work, then said, 'Just how much did these so-called "improvements" cost, then, if I might be permitted to ask?'

'Did you not see the invoice?' Christine asked slyly.

'I've signed it "unexamined",' Emily said. 'He said he'd send the bill in the post.'

Christine let out a soft sigh of relief. 'Shouldn't be all that much, he's quite reasonable,' she said airily.

Emily's mouth turned down and she gripped the arms of the chair. 'It's not that it matters to me. I know as far as you're concerned I'm only the lodger in this house.'

'Mother! Will you stop that? This is your house and it always will be.'

'That's what I thought, but then you go haring off and

ordering work-people to come here without talking to me about it, and I have to stand here like some prize idiot and watch them do things I know nothing about.'

'Calm down, will you? What's been done, this work, it's the best thing for both of us.'

'He who pays the piper calls the tune,' Emily shouted. 'Why wasn't I told beforehand?'

Christine looked at her mother's flushed face and tried to keep her voice calm. 'It's like this. When we joined the Neighbourhood Watch, they did recommend extra security, and the insurance companies are all for it. These extra locks will knock the premiums down.' On seeing her mother's thoughtful look, she said quickly, 'Now, whilst I remember, did you take your medicine this morning?'

Emily nodded.

'Good, then I'd best get started on lunch.' She hurried towards the kitchen.

'Not so fast, lady,' Emily called. 'Just you hang on a minute. Two things I want to know. How much, and why?' She eased herself to her feet and watched her daughter closely.

Christine hedged. 'I can't be sure about the exact price; sometimes the VAT's different on maintenance jobs. It shouldn't be too much and those locks will last for years.' She edged nearer to the kitchen door.

'You still haven't said why.'

'I just told you, the insurance.'

'Don't give me that waffle, I want the truth.'

Christine refused to meet her gaze.

'Why won't you tell me?'

There was a long silence. 'Think about it, Mother. You must know why.'

'Don't tell me you're scared of burglars?' Emily sniffed. 'It isn't as if we've got anything worth taking.'

'Mother, you're missing the point.'

'What other reason could there—'

'Let me finish, will you? Do I need to remind you that I know the getaway driver's face, and if I know him, he'll know me?'

'What has that got to do with my house and fitting locks to my windows?'

'Mother!' Christine shouted. 'Won't you understand? Have I got to spell it out?' She looked at Emily and wondered if this mood of stubbornness was a side effect of the stroke.

Emily's mouth turned down. 'What I want to know is how much is that locksmith going to charge you?'

'Sod the bloody locksmith. I've just said I'll tell you when I get the bill. Just listen. If that getaway driver knows me, he might come here.'

'Then you'll need to keep your eyes peeled.'

Christine snorted in exasperation. 'If he comes, he might not be alone. There were three of them, if you remember.'

'You deal with that, then, it's got nothing to do with my house.'

Christine's patience snapped. Tact and diplomacy were useless when her mother was in this mood; only the truth would do. She strode up to her. 'Mother, if I'm in danger… then so are you!' She regretted her words the minute she'd said them. She watched as her mother's face turned ashen and she stood by helplessly as Emily sank back down into the chair.

Emily stared up at her with stricken eyes. 'I didn't think….'

Christine saw the trembling of her mother's hands and bent to reassure her. 'That's why we need the extra security,' she said softly. 'Don't worry, Mam, I'd never let them hurt you.'

'It's not me I'm worried about. But if they really were… to get at you?'

Christine leaned over and gently squeezed her mother's shoulder. She brushed her lips against her wispy white hair and said, 'Nothing's going to happen to either of us.' She glanced out of the window and forced a smile. 'Least not whilst we've got Hero Harry to protect us.' After a moment she straightened up. 'You must be starving, I'd best get you your lunch.' She paused as she reached the kitchen doorway, 'How would a bit of poached salmon suit you? You know it's good for you.'

Emily eyed Christine then said craftily, 'Can I have treacle pudding instead of fruit for afters?'

Christine smiled. 'Don't you start your wheeler-dealing with me…but just this once. Now, I've got to hurry, I've got that casserole to do for dinner and I've promised Harry I'd make a bit extra for him.'

Emily leaned forward and looked out of the window. 'He's going to need something substantial after the way he's been hammering at our gate. What time's he coming, then?'

'Coming where?'

'Here, of course. You have asked him?'

'I didn't like to. I thought he might think I was being pushy.'

Emily shook her head, clicked her tongue and eased herself to her feet. 'I'll ask him whilst he's still out there.' She walked towards the door muttering, 'In this house if you want anything doing you've got to do it yourself.'

With a bemused smile Christine watched her mother go out of the door. She didn't mind that she was interfering. She'd wanted to ask Harry over for dinner, but she'd have been embarrassed if he'd made an excuse and turned her down. For all she knew he might have a date with Kay. She'd seen the way that the glamorous blonde had ogled him last night, and what man could refuse her advances?

Christine got the sponge out of the freezer, popped it into the microwave and made a start on the salad stuff. Her thoughts returned to Harry and she felt her face flush as she realized how caring he'd been, rushing to her mother's rescue like that, even if he had got it wrong. She giggled; Harry was funny and outspoken, but there was something so heartwarming about such a straightforward man. Quite a good catch for someone such as Kay.

She dried the lettuce and sliced the tomatoes swiftly, then picked up the table mats and cutlery and went into the living room. She might not be able to compete with Kay in the looks department but she did have one or two things in her favour; she was an excellent cook and a good housekeeper. She pulled a face at her reflection as she passed the living room mirror—and if she could just find the time to get her hair done, she could be quite presentable. After all, not every man wanted a glamour-puss as a girlfriend, or even as a w— A faint spark of hope ignited in Christine as she thought about this, and a breath of confidence returned. She liked Harry and deep inside she was almost sure that he liked her, in spite of the fact that she always managed to upset him. She straightened up. 'Stop daydreaming, woman,' she said out loud and continued setting the table.

*Wednesday 7.50 p.m.*

HARRY LOOKED IN the hall mirror. He'd combed his unruly dark hair for the third time and he peered at his shoulders to see if there was any sign of dandruff. He smiled in satisfaction; his jacket remained immaculate. He checked his hands; his fingernails were clean and short and he knew that his shoes were well polished. 'In fact you've scrubbed up nicely for a middle-aged bloke,' he told his reflection. He took a deep breath, pulling in his waist, then muttered, 'But your belly could do with being a bit thinner.' He sniffed. 'And you've been a bit gung-ho with the aftershave. Otherwise, though, for a man in your fifties, you're not that bad at all.'

He wandered back into the kitchen and eyed the tray of dahlias, the box of chocolates and the bottle of wine that were on the table. Should he take them all to Christine's house? Or should he take the wine and leave the chocolates in case Mrs Brett was not allowed to eat them? If Mrs Brett wasn't allowed chocolates he wouldn't want to upset her. After all, she'd been the one who'd invited him.

He picked up the box of chocolates and looked at it; shouldn't he put some ribbon on it or something? He shook his head; he'd never been good at tying those fancy bows. He felt sure that Christine would like them and he guessed that Mrs Brett would like a glass of wine. Red wine was supposed to be good for convalescents, wasn't it? As for the dahlias, they were going with him; that much was certain.

The problem was that it was a long time since he'd been invited to someone's home for dinner. Not in the three years since Susie's death, in fact, and she'd always known what to take and what to do. He scratched his ear in frustration—decisions, decisions, why was he always plagued by them? He glanced up at the kitchen clock. If he didn't watch it he was going to be late, and that was all he needed. Not after that fiasco of this lunchtime. On an impulse he got out a cardboard box from a cupboard and placed all three gifts in it. There, it was time to go.

*Wednesday 7.55 p.m.*

SAM WAS LATE! Alun paced the floor of his living room, looked at the clock again and cursed out loud. Sam had said he'd report in at 7.30…or thereabouts. Now 7.30 had been and gone and it was close on eight. What the hell was keeping him? Alun got a can of Coke from the fridge, and drank from it. Nervousness always made him thirsty but he didn't want to start on the beers when there was business to be done. He was already in the boss's bad books because of that bloody woman; he daren't make any more mistakes. He walked to the window and looked down onto the street into the night. There was no one about. He fingered the white envelope in his jeans pocket. It seemed to him to be one hell of a lot of money to pay Sam for his services, but again he hesitated; he didn't want to argue with the boss—that might be pushing his luck too far.

There came a soft knock on the flat door and Alun started. He'd not heard anyone climbing the stairs. He hurried to open it and sighed in relief to see Sam standing there.

'Come in. Where the hell have you been?'

Sam slid past him and went into the living room. He turned to Alun and smiled apologetically. 'Had to wait until it got a bit darker—wouldn't want your neighbours spotting me. What they don't see can't worry them.' He looked around the room appreciatively. 'Not a bad place, this. You lived here long?'

It's only temporary,' Alun said defensively.

'Ah!' Sam sank down on the sofa and leaned back. He tapped his nose. 'Enough said. Take my advice, though, and look for somewhere quiet…without too many neighbours.'

Alun tried to curb his impatience. 'Did you do what I wanted?'

'Sure thing.' Sam looked around again and said cautiously, 'Nobody else here, is there?'

'I'm not that stupid.'

'Always best to be certain.' Sam pulled his notebook from his pocket, unfolded a slip of paper that was inside it and read out loud. 'Target's house is straightforward. There's no way in from the back, although that's where the kitchen is so it's simple to get in once you've got past the driveway at the front of the house. No sign of a burglar alarm, either false or genuine. No sign of a dog, which is great, but then there's no trees or bushes at the front of the house, and that's always a problem.' He looked up at Alun. 'Now, if there was, you could move an army in there and not a soul would notice.'

Alun tried not to get irritated. Was he ever going to get his night out on the town? 'So go on, then, once you've got past the front driveway and into the back garden, then what?'

'A doddle! There's a large shed and a hut. No exterior lighting and a good thick hawthorn hedge all round the back, so you'd not see a bloody thing at night.' He looked again at Alun and raised his eyebrows questioningly. 'You did know that the owners were having locks put in today?'

'Would that cause a problem?'

Sam chuckled. 'Nah, that's them locking the stable door after the gee-gees have done a runner.'

'What about this shed and the hut?'

'Padlocks. One of them might take a bit of handling; it's a heavy-duty one on the shed, but with a good bolt-cutter, shouldn't be a problem.'

'No bolt-cutters. I don't want it to look as if it's been tampered with.'

'Then you'll need a good locks man…could take a few

minutes.' He handed Alun the piece of paper. 'You got anyone for that? I could supply—'

'No need.' Alun stared down at the paper thoughtfully. 'I'll deal with it.' He looked at Sam. 'Anything else?'

Sam shook his head. 'Nope, except, of course, for my fee—plus the agreed bonus.'

Alun gave him the envelope.

Sam smiled and got to his feet. 'I take it it's all there?'

'Check it if you wish.'

Sam raised an eyebrow, tore open the envelope, counted the notes, then looked up with satisfaction. 'All as promised. Best to be sure, you see. I can't trust anyone these days, no matter how long I've known them. So we're straight, then?'

Alun nodded and walked with him to the door.

Sam turned to him and looked hopeful. 'Any further work, you'll let me know?'

'Yeah, but we've got what we need here, Sam.' He opened the door. 'Thanks again.'

Alun felt annoyed as he stood in the doorway and watched as Sam's chubby form glided soundlessly down the stairs and out into the night. With reluctance his thoughts turned to Rick—he was good at locks. He'd have to send him in tonight to fix that padlock; he didn't want the job botched at this stage, and he wasn't going to pay Sam any more than was needed. He pushed the slip of paper into his pocket and went to get his jacket; there was yet more work to be done, and no time to lose.

He reached for his mobile and called Rick. 'Hi, it's me, Alun. Where are you?' Alun listened to Rick's reply then said, 'I'm sorry mate, but there's a job…. Yeah, I know it's your night out, but this can't wait.' He held the mobile away from his ear whilst he listened to a string of expletives coming from Rick. He waited for a pause. 'Look, Rick, it'll be well worth your while, I promise. Can you make it to my place by midnight? Sober? Well, at least you've got four hours, see you.' Alun put his phone back in his pocket and headed for the door. He sighed as he hurried down the stairs. Now he'd have to go and find a car to borrow.

# ELEVEN

*Wednesday 7.58 p.m.*

HARRY CROSSED THE road and rang the doorbell at Christine's house. Whilst he waited for her to open it, he balanced the cardboard box on his arm and looked about him. No sign of life on the road; all his neighbours were probably safe at home watching the telly. The front door opened and Christine was there, smiling at him.

'Hello, Harry, come on in.'

'Not too early, am I?' he said as he wiped his feet and thrust the cardboard box of goodies at her. 'I brought you these. Well, they're for you and your mum, I mean.'

'Harry, thank you, but you shouldn't have.'

'My pleasure.'

She took the box from him and placed it in the kitchen. 'Let's go into the living room.'

Emily looked up from her newspaper as they came in.

'Harry's brought you some lovely red wine, Mam,' Christine said. 'It'll go well with the beef casserole.'

'That's kind of you, Harry. Thank you.' Emily smiled. 'Come and sit down.' She gestured at the electric heater. 'It's nice and warm over here.'

Harry joined her; he took a deep breath and sniffed the air. 'I hope this casserole is as good as it smells,' he said. 'I'm starving already.'

'It's not that special,' said Christine. 'It'll be ready in a few more minutes.'

'Could we have a sherry before dinner?' Emily said swiftly. She winked at him. 'I'm sure Harry would like one.'

Christine looked flustered. 'I'd not forgotten, Mam. I was coming to that.' She headed back to the kitchen.

Emily looked at him. 'I'm glad you could come.'

'I'm glad you asked me. It's nice to be popular.'

'That wasn't it.' Emily eyed the kitchen door, leaned forward and whispered, 'Y'see, when we have company she always makes a trifle with lots of cream on top.'

'Are you allowed to have trifle, Mrs Brett?'

Emily chuckled. 'Oh no.' She looked at the kitchen door. 'But let her try and stop me!'

He grinned at her. 'They do say a little bit of what you fancy….'

'Christine's a good girl,' Emily interrupted, 'but she's a bit on the strict side. "Orders is orders," if you know what I mean.'

'I think she means well, and I'm sure she'll let you have a chocolate.'

Emily's eyes lit up. 'Did you bring chocolates? She never said.'

Harry felt guilty. He thought he knew the reason why Christine hadn't mentioned them. 'I've brought you some dahlias as well,' he said, by way of changing the subject.

'That'll please her.'

'What'll please me?' asked Christine as she returned with a tray of sherry glasses.

'I think your mother meant the plants.' Harry held up his glass. 'To friendship.'

Christine looked at her mother. 'To good health.'

Emily took a large gulp of the sherry. 'To happiness, and to have the guts to grab it whilst there's a chance.'

She looked at her near-empty glass and eyed the sherry bottle hopefully.

Christine said quickly before Emily could speak, 'Now, let's have dinner before it spoils.'

An hour later after an excellent meal, Harry sat at the table playing a game of Scrabble. At that moment, in spite of Emily's blatant attempts at cheating, Christine was winning.

He sat back, sipped his coffee and felt a sense of contentment as he watched the two women gently bicker about the rules of the game. He looked at Christine as she carefully placed the letters on the board. For the first time in a long while she seemed to be relaxed and mellow. The wine had brought a glow to her skin and he remembered how pretty she looked when she was enjoying herself. Quite a change from the aggressive, tight-faced woman that she'd been a few days ago. But then, stress changes us all.

At that moment Christine looked across at him. He saw her blush deepen as she smiled. His pulse quickened. Did she find him attractive? Or, was she just being polite and friendly?

'It is a word!' Emily's voice reached him.

'Mother, it is not. You can't keep on inventing words like this.'

Emily's jaw tightened. 'WXYZ is a word. I know it is because it's in that song.' She trilled shrilly, 'A, you're adorable, B, you're so beautiful, WXYZee. It's fun to wander through the alphabet with you. See what I mean?'

Christine groaned and held her head. 'Now we're going back into the fifties, Mam. That song's ancient history, and it's still not a word.'

Harry tried not to laugh. He stared fixedly at the Scrabble board.

Emily shrugged; she seemed to realize that she'd lost this battle and that it might be wise to bow out gracefully. She gave an exaggerated yawn and got to her feet. 'Ah well, I'm too tired to sit here arguing with you.' She turned to smile at Harry. 'So I'll say good-night. I'd best be off to my bed.'

Harry stood up. 'It's time I was going, too.' He watched as Emily went out of the room, then turned to Christine and asked quietly, 'How did your mother react to the new locks?'

'Not very well, I'm afraid. At first she was angry about the cost, and then when she knew the real reason, she was quite shaken. But Mam is Mam, and she's one tough lady. Within an hour she'd bounced back to her old self again.'

'As long as she knows the truth.' He smiled at Christine as she walked with him into the hall. 'Tonight was one of the nicest evenings I've had in a long time. The food was great, almost as good as the company.... But I won't outstay my welcome, in case you don't invite me again.'

Christine's face turned pink. For a moment she seemed tongue-tied, then she stammered, 'I...I mean we, have been glad of the company, and thanks again for the plants, the chocolates and everything.' She opened the door.

Harry pulled up his jacket collar as he looked out and saw that it was raining heavily.

'I'll get you an umbrella,' Christine said. She turned towards the hallstand, and as she did so, she brushed against him. On an impulse Harry kissed her cheek.

Christine stiffened and stared at him, then her mouth curved into a smile.

He pulled her close and kissed her softly on the lips. 'Goodnight,' he whispered, 'I'll see you tomorrow.' Then, forgetting the umbrella completely, he dashed through the rain across the road to his house.

CHRISTINE CLOSED THE door and leaned back against it. Her heart was pounding and she found it difficult to swallow. She could hardly believe what had happened. It had been so long since any man had kissed her. Harry liked her. He really liked her. She drifted back into the living room, cleared the coffee things and went into the kitchen. What exactly had he meant by, 'I'll see you tomorrow?' Was he going to ask her out on a date, or was that just his way of saying 'Goodnight'? She touched her lips. She really should get some new lipstick, perhaps some of that glossy stuff, or was she too old for that? No, she was not, she told herself. You're never too old.

AS HE ENTERED the house, Harry brushed the rain from his shoulders, then took off his jacket, hung it up and strode into his living room. Although it was late he didn't feel the least bit tired, in fact he felt excited and wide awake. His thoughts returned to Christine and he smiled; she must have liked him, otherwise she would never have let him kiss her, but…the doubts returned. She could hardly have shoved him away, there wasn't that much room in the Bretts' hallway. But even so, if she'd really hated him for it, she would have thumped him. He grinned; she wasn't the type to be timid.

He sat down in the chair, then, still restless, jumped up again and began to pace the floor. He stopped to switch on the TV, only to stare at the screen, his mind a blank. He should have seized his chance, and asked Christine out, but then he'd only managed to mutter a daft 'Goodnight,' and 'see you tomorrow'. Just how wimpish was that? But he would see her tomorrow and he'd— He stopped. He'd forgotten all about his shift with St John Ambulance. He was due to be in Otley at the Shire Horse Show tomorrow morning, and it wasn't as if he could get out of that. It always drew a big crowd with lots of kids running around, and St John Ambulance needed all the help they could get. He glanced at the phone, then shook his head; it was too late to phone her now. He would just have to see her when he got back. His gaze drifted to the TV recorder that was near the TV and he brightened as he remembered the rugby match he'd recorded. He pressed play, then, returning to his chair, turned up the sound and sat back to watch the game.

# TWELVE

IN THE EARLY hours of Thursday morning an old blue Volvo estate car drove silently into Poole Road and parked three doors down from the Bretts' house. Alun switched off the engine and the car lights, and looked along the road. All was still.

'Which one is it, then?' Rick asked.

Alun pointed at the house. 'That one there, but it's not the house I want you to check, it's the padlock on the shed in the garden.'

Rick gaped at him in disbelief. 'A padlock? I can soon crack a padlock, most anybody can. Why the hell did you bring me here for this?' He made as if to get out of the car.

Alun grabbed his sleeve. 'Hold on, hold on—when will you learn to listen?'

'You're making me miss a good night out for the sake of a bloody padlock?'

'And you're being well paid for it, so just shut it, and let me finish.' He stared at Rick for a while. 'Have you calmed down yet?'

'Get on with it.'

'Right then, the garden shed is at the top of the driveway to your right. I want you to look at said lock and unlock it…without forcing it. Then return it to its original position so that it still looks to be locked. Have you got that?'

'Yeah…but why? Don't make sense to me.'

'Never mind why. That's my problem. Just do what I've told you. Don't light up any fags while you're working, and don't move anything more than you have to. Got that?'

'Right, but it would have been dead easy with bolt-cutters,' Rick protested. He reached inside his jacket pocket, and checked he'd got his tools, torch and gloves, then, opening the car door, he slid off into the night.

Alun eased the door closed and glanced along the road once more. Nothing stirred. He took a deep breath. *I can't screw up again,* he thought, *if anything else was to go wrong at this stage, how the hell would I explain it to the boss?* He sighed, leaned back in his seat and told himself: *It's no use worrying; make your mind go blank and think,* 'So far so good, so far so good….'

SLEEP DID NOT come easily to Christine. She felt happy and excited and her thoughts kept drifting back to Harry. She lay there listening to the rain and for once felt confident that things would work out. After a while the rain stopped and she closed her eyes determinedly and tried to sleep.

But it was not to be. After a few minutes' dozing, she was wide awake, listening to the sounds coming from Emily's room. Mam was off on a midnight prowl again. Christine lay still as she heard the click of lights being switched on and off, a sharp blast from Mam's TV, hastily muted, then the closing of the bathroom door. She waited patiently and a few minutes later the figure of Emily appeared in her doorway.

RICK CREPT UP the DRIVEWAY and tried to control his anger. There he'd been, down at the pub, drinking Coca-Cola until it nearly came out of his ears, thinking he'd got to stay sober, that he'd got to do an important job tonight, and what had it turned out to be? Fixing a bleeding padlock! He reached the shed and shone his torch down on the lock—easy enough to force, but to make this look as if it were still locked, that would take a bit longer.

He tried to make sense of Alun's instructions, but he couldn't. But there was no good in worrying about things like that, it only brought on his headaches. Silently he began his task. After a while he grunted and looked down with satisfaction at the newly arranged padlock. Well pleased, Rick was tightening up the hasp when from inside the house the lights came on.

'IT'S ALL RIGHT, Mam,' Christine called, 'I'm not asleep.'

'I think I might have left the oven switched on,' Emily said innocently. 'I thought I'd just go downstairs and check.'

Christine started to get out of bed. 'Do you want me to make you a hot drink?'

'I can do that myself, thank you very much,' Emily said briskly.

'You stay where you are.' She went off down the stairs.

Christine sat up in bed and listened. She heard the creak of the living room door as it opened, and suspicion dawned. That was not the kitchen door. What was Mam up to? She strained her ears and listened again intently. After a few seconds she heard the faint crackling of cellophane and she flopped back against the pillows in relief. She should have known. Mam was raiding the chocolates that Harry had brought. She ought to be cross with her; she wasn't supposed to have sweet stuff except on special occasions. Christine thought about this, but tonight had been special and Harry had brought the chocolates for both of them. She smiled to herself as she got out of bed and hurried down the stairs to the living room.

Emily looked up guiltily as Christine came in. 'I was

just having the one,' she said, as she tried without success to shove the lid back on the chocolate box.

'We all know your idea of "one", Mam. Now, I'll make us both a drink, and whilst I'm doing that do you think you can manage to save a few coffee creams for me?' With that, she went into the kitchen.

She'd finished making the hot chocolate when she heard a noise outside like the sound of metal against concrete. She stood still and listened, but hearing nothing further she switched off the kettle and was about to put the mugs on a tray when she heard a thud, quite loud this time. It was coming from the garden. Christine froze. Could it be next door's cat? No, it sounded far too loud for that. She lifted the Venetian blinds and tried to peer out of the kitchen window into the blackness, but could see nothing; besides, she could hardly go out there in her nightie....

RICK FROZE AND looked around; a light was coming from a downstairs room. He felt his heart race as he tried not to panic. Clumsily he shoved the screwdriver into his pocket...and missed. The screwdriver clattered loudly on the driveway and as he bent to retrieve the tool he stumbled and banged hard against the shed door. Panicking and muttering, 'Gotta get the hell out of here,' he pounded down the driveway, bashing against the gatepost as he turned into the road. Glancing back he saw more lights come on and, increasing his speed, he ran full tilt towards the Volvo estate.

'Move it,' he yelled as he climbed into the car. 'I think they heard me.'

'DID YOU HEAR that, Christine?' asked Emily from the kitchen doorway. 'I'm sure I heard someone running.'

Christine fought back her own fear and tried to reassure her. 'Probably some cats or a dogfight or something.'

'Dogs don't wear shoes,' said Emily. 'I think we'd best call the police.'

Christine hesitated. 'Should we?'

Emily stared at her and snorted, 'My goodness, you've changed your tune.'

'Only it seems a bit rash, it could be something or nothing,' Christine protested.

Emily gave an indignant sniff, limped into the hall and picked up the phone.

TIGHT-LIPPED, ALUN swung the car round and raced back into town. He parked and glared at Rick. 'You bloody idiot! What have you done, you moron? If you've buggered this up…. What the hell did you do?'

A COUPLE OF hours later two policemen arrived at the Bretts' house.

'I'm glad we didn't hold our breath until you got here,' Emily said acidly as they came into the living room. 'We could have been raped and pillaged and they could have emptied the house by now.'

'We're not the flying squad, Madam,' said one of them. 'It is the early hours of the morning.'

'Ah. We must remember that,' said Emily, looking at Christine. 'In fact, you'd better make a note of it, then if we want to kill somebody or do a bank heist, we'll do it in the early hours of the morning.'

The older policeman looked at Christine helplessly. 'Is she always like this?'

Christine glanced at her mother; she looked tired and pale. She'd tried to make her go back to bed whilst they waited for the police, but she should have known better.

Mam had set her jaw determinedly and refused to move out of her armchair. 'It is half past three,' Christine protested, 'and we have been worried.'

The policeman consulted his notebook. 'It seems you reported some prowlers, Miss Brett?'

'We heard some noises in the back garden.'

'And I heard someone running,' Emily added.

'Best have a look,' the policeman said. 'Come on, Jack.' They went outside to the garden.

Five minutes later they returned. The older policeman shook his head as he looked at Christine. 'Nothing to report, Miss Brett. Everything seems to be in its place, no sign of any damage. Probably some yobbos having a running battle with each other, when they've got p—' He broke off and looked warily at Emily. 'Er, I mean drunk. Anyway, there's no sign of anyone.' He stared again at Emily and said loudly, 'You sure you did hear something, Mrs Brett? It wasn't perhaps a neighbour's back door slamming?'

'She knows what she heard, and I do, too,' Christine said as she showed them to the door.

'Yes,' the older policeman said, 'although the smallest sounds can seem loud late at night.'

Christine bit back her tongue. She stood in the doorway and watched the two policemen stroll towards their car. 'Need we do any more?' she heard the young one say.

'Nah, just the usual report,' the older one replied. 'Waste of time; women of that age are all the same, y'know.' He lowered his voice. 'And this one here is forever reporting folk. They know all about her down at the station.'

Christine slammed the door shut. She tried to control her anger and humiliation.

'Try not to worry,' said Emily as she joined her in the hall. 'I heard the noise, too.'

'Mam, they think I'm crackers!'

'And I know you're not.' Emily took hold of Christine's arm and guided her back to the living room. 'Come on, then, it's almost daylight. Let's polish off the rest of these chocolates before we go back to bed.'

KAY WAS ABOUT to climb into bed when she heard the car doors slamming outside. She peered at her alarm clock: 3.20 a.m., probably some late-night party-goers. Even so, that was late for this road. Kay grinned to herself as she wondered what Christine Brett would make of this distur- bance. 'I'll bet she's on the phone calling the cops already,' she muttered. She strolled over to the window, looked out and saw to her surprise that a police car was parked out- side the Bretts' home. Kay stood in the dark, watching. After a while two policemen came out of the front door and walked round the side of the house towards the back garden, then they returned and went back inside the house.

Some minutes later the policemen came out of the front door again and went towards their car. From what Kay could see they seemed to be sharing some private joke. The front door slammed shut and the cops got into their car and drove away.

Kay allowed the curtain to fall back into place and, crossing the room, got into bed. She'd felt tired earlier, having had to work late into the night to catch up on some paperwork, but now she wanted to know what had hap- pened out there. Why had the police been called to Chris- tine's house? She could hardly go over and ask Christine. Who else was likely to know? She thought for a while about this then realized there was only one person who was friendly towards the Bretts these days, and that per- son was Harry Myers.

Kay laced her hands at the back of her neck, lay back

and thought about Harry. So, what did she know about him? He was quite handsome for an oldie; he must be about fifty, tall, a bit beefy, but a friendly, open type of man. Rumour had it he'd inherited money. No one knew how much, but it was enough to leave him comfortably off and not to have to work any more.

She pondered over what it would be like to have tons of money; to have so much cash that you didn't know what to do with it. Her smile deepened. In her case that couldn't happen; she knew exactly what she would do with every penny—she could never have enough.

Her mind focused on Harry and she smiled. He was a widower and not a bad catch for someone. She would pay him a visit, the question was when. She was owed a day off work so she would phone the boss first thing in the morning, and if he okayed it she might be able to see Harry later today. With any luck she'd be able to find out more about what happened at the Bretts' house—she felt sure she could persuade Harry into telling her. She stretched sensuously under the duvet as she thought about how she would do this. It shouldn't be too difficult; after all, Harry was a man, wasn't he?

# THIRTEEN

*Thursday afternoon*

'THAT'S THE TROUBLE with workmen these days,' Emily muttered as she limped round the back garden with a dustpan and brushed the wood shavings off the windowsills. 'They spend years learning their trade, yet they never learn to tidy up after themselves.' She went round to the front of the house, inspected the newly repaired gate and nodded in approval at Harry's handiwork. A good, neat job.

Whilst she rested against the gate she looked about her. The day was fresh and sunny after last night's rain and Emily wished that Christine hadn't been called in to see some artist bloke at the cop shop. It would have been nice to go for a little stroll down the street.

Further along the road she could see Brian Sharpe walking his dog. Emily watched them and pulled a face; it wasn't that she'd anything against dogs or any other animal, after all they were all God's creatures, but that mutt was forever slipping its lead and darting off up driveways and rummaging in dustbins. She wondered whether the dog slipping the lead was in fact 'accidentally on purpose', for it gave Brian the perfect excuse to chase after it into the neighbours' driveways and their back gardens, and to snoop around. Then again, maybe she was being too suspicious, for, to be fair, Brian always caught the dog before any damage was done. Come to think of it, it was amazing how fast Brian was for a man of his age; he could run like a hare, although with that dog he'd got no choice.

Emily gave a wistful sigh, looked down at her feet in frustration and thought back to the days when she could run—they were long gone. Her gaze drifted back towards Harry's house; such a kind man, and those had been good chocolates he'd brought last night. There was no sign of him or his car today, though, and it didn't look as if he was in his back garden, either. She saw that the sacks of compost were still neatly stacked at the top of his driveway where the driver had left them on Tuesday, just before Christine got back and all the trouble started. She looked again along the road and smiled as she saw her daughter approaching.

BRIAN SHARPE STRODE along Poole Road and tried hard not to look over his shoulder because he knew that would make him appear to be furtive. He'd noticed Mrs Brett standing at her gate and he could feel her eyes watching him, almost burning a hole in the back of his neck. 'Heel, Scamp!' he shouted as the dog strained on its lead in front of him. Scamp took not the slightest notice of its owner's command and Brian was forced to increase his pace. He saw Mrs Brett's daughter coming towards him and felt uneasy; 'Miss Busybody', as he privately called her. She knew everything that went on in this road, or at least she thought she did, though she didn't know everything about him. He was sure that she saw him as a slightly eccentric pensioner obsessed with walking his dog and that suited him to a tee. He nodded politely as she passed him and received a brief 'Good morning,' in return. The problem with that girl was she was inquisitive and observant. It was wise to be wary of her. An old quotation came into his mind, 'You can fool some of the people all of the time and all of the people some of the time but—' He nodded to himself as he strode along. Live up to your name, he thought, stay sharp!

'THAT'S THAT ALL done with,' Christine said with relief as she approached her mother. 'The police say they'll only call me in again when they find a suspect.' She looked at Emily and took her arm. 'Been tidying up the window ledges, have you? If you like we can have a cup of tea, then go for a little walk down to the park.'

'That'd be nice,' Emily said. They went inside, Christine made the tea and they sat down in the living room.

Emily looked at her daughter. 'How were the policemen, then? Were they civil to you? There was no need for them to be so offhand with us last night.'

Christine sighed. 'Well, you did warn me about crying wolf, Mam.'

'*You* might cry wolf, but I don't. Anyway, what was this police artist like?'

'He was quite pleasant. It was interesting. They do it all on computers these days.'

'They use them for everything,' Emily said. 'I reckon we've all been programmed onto a giant computer. Did they give you a copy of what they've drawn?'

'Yes.' Christine rummaged in her handbag. 'Well, I asked for one. Here, have a look.'

Emily put her spectacles on, took the paper and stared down at the likeness on it. 'Oh my Lord! I know this man! I swear it's the lad in the grey transit van who brought the compost sacks to Harry's house. He sometimes delivers heavy garden stuff round here.'

Christine stared at her mother; the second she'd said 'the lad in the grey transit van,' she'd remembered. It was as if the last piece of the puzzle had slipped into place.

'That's him, all right,' Emily continued. 'Would you credit it? I saw him on Tuesday. I was going to write down his van number and then me blooming pen ran out.'

Christine shrank deeper into the chair. She could hear her heart thudding; she felt more scared than ever, but she tried to keep her voice steady. 'Mam,' she said quietly, 'I think that man is the getaway driver.'

'You can't see his ponytail on here,' Emily said accusingly as she scrutinized the drawing. 'Straggly thing it was; looked more like strands of old rope than anything else.'

'The cap he was wearing covered that,' said Christine tightly. She gripped the arms of the chair, watched her mother and wondered how she could stay so calm.

'Best get on to the police, then.'

Christine felt a surge of panic. 'I don't know, not after last night, they'll think I'm nuts. I mean, I don't know his name or anything.'

'So what are you going to do?'

What should she do? Christine felt the fear grow inside her. She'd have to do something. With a sense of relief she heard the sound of Harry's car as it turned into his driveway. She jumped to her feet. 'I'm going to see Harry.'

'Good idea,' said Emily. She got up and went over to the window. 'Off you go.'

Christine rushed out of the door and across the road. 'Harry!'

He got out of the car and turned towards her. 'Christine, what's wrong?'

She ran up the drive to him but the words wouldn't come. She burst into tears.

HE STEPPED TOWARDS her and enfolded her in his arms. 'Whatever's the matter? Tell me.'

'It's the man,' she blurted. 'The man. The driver of that car.' She sniffed and wiped away her tears. 'Harry. I'm sure; no…I mean I think…I know who he is.' She became aware that Harry's hands were around her and she took a backward step.

'You certain about this?' Harry said urgently. "Cause if you are we can hop in the car and drive straight to the police station.'

'Well, I'm nearly one hundred percent sure, unless he's got a twin brother.'

'What?' Harry gaped at her in astonishment. 'Oh, Christine! Now you're not…?'

'Harry, I'm not making this up. The man that delivered those sacks of compost to your house last week, and some garden fencing the week before…well—' he felt her begin to tremble '—I'm just about certain that he's the getaway driver.'

He guided her gently across the road to her home. 'If you say so, Christine…as long as you are absolutely certain? Come on, we'll ask your mum to make you a nice sweet cup of tea, then we'll go over all of the facts together.'

KAY WATERED HER plants on the windowsill for the third time whilst she watched Christine Brett talking agitatedly to Harry. She was irritated; she'd been ready to visit Harry with her peace offering when she'd seen Christine run across the road. She waited to see what would happen, then clicked her tongue in annoyance as she saw Harry put his arms round Christine and walk back with her to her house. Why did Harry need to reassure Christine? And why had he gone back into her house with her? She scowled, picked up the watering can and walked back into the kitchen as curiosity gnawed at her. What had happened last night and just now out there? What was it that had upset Christine so much? *Patience,* she told herself. *Wait until Harry returns, then go find out.*

# FOURTEEN

*Thursday*

'MAM SAW THE man delivering those sacks of compost on the day of the robbery; that was on Tuesday,' Christine insisted half an hour later, as she drank the last of her tea. She looked at her mother, then at Harry and said, 'She didn't put it in the notebook because then I would have remembered—'

'I'm sorry, love,' Emily said. 'I was going to but then my biro packed in.'

'But how could he do the delivery and do the robbery on the same day?' Harry asked.

'That's not impossible,' Christine said. 'The police were questioning me for close to four hours on that day.'

Harry looked doubtful. 'But that delivery driver is always so pleasant. As far as I know he's been working at that garden centre—' He paused, thinking back. 'Well, for quite a while, at least.'

Emily leaned forward in her chair. 'How long is quite a while, Harry?'

Harry stared at her. 'I don't rightly know. He's delivered all sorts of garden stuff for me, so he must have been around for about six months, if not longer.' His gaze strayed over to Christine. He saw that her hands were clenched and she looked pale, but she spoke calmly.

'As I said before, I'm almost hundred percent certain, but then I wouldn't want to accuse anyone without being absolutely sure.' She gave a rueful smile. 'After what's happened over these last few days, I've learned my lesson.'

'Yes,' agreed Emily, 'after last night's incident nobody seems to believe us.'

'What incident?' asked Harry. 'Did I miss something?'

'About one o'clock, it was,' Christine said. 'I'd come downstairs to make us both a hot drink, when we heard someone prowling around outside.'

'She thought it was a dog or something,' interrupted Emily, 'but I thought "burglars", and I got on to the police straight away.'

'Not that it did much good,' Christine said. 'The police didn't get here until after three in the morning, and then they didn't believe us.'

'There was someone out there,' insisted Emily. 'For two pins I'd have gone out and sorted them myself. If they come again—'

'Don't even think about it, Mam,' Christine said sharply, 'you're not going anywhere.'

'Why didn't you phone me?' Harry said—he was already feeling guilty about sleeping so well. 'I'd have been here in minutes.'

'You've done enough, and here we are again, asking for your help.'

'Is there some way we can find out more about this delivery man?' Emily said.

Harry leaned forward. 'I happen to know the manager of the garden centre where he works. I ought to; I spend enough money at his place. His name's Longley, he'll sometimes stop and have a chat when I'm in there shopping. I'm one of his best customers.'

'But what if I'm mistaken?' Christine interrupted. 'The man could lose his job if the police go charging in there. I could be wrong.'

Harry looked at her and in spite of his growing attraction to her a dark thought came into his mind. What if she really is neurotic? Is she doing this because she's seeking attention? From what she and her mother had told him about last night, the police had certainly been sceptical. He stood up and tried to mask his sense of doubt. 'I tell you what, I've got my son and his family coming to visit at the weekend and I've got one or two things to sort out, but if I can manage it, I'll drive down to the garden centre either later today or tomorrow, and see what I can find out.' He edged towards the door.

'Oh Harry, would you?'

He saw the gratitude in Christine's face and immediately felt guilty. 'I can't promise that anything will come of it. I'll just make a casual inquiry, that's all.'

'It's more than enough,' said Emily. She glanced at her daughter.

'We're grateful for any help we can get.'

*Thursday*

KAY WATCHED HARRY come out of the Bretts' house, cross the road and return to his home. She glided back into the hall, scrutinized her appearance in the full-length mirror, then smiled with satisfaction. She looked glamorous in a carefully understated manner. Her sweater was of a soft pink shade, low cut and just a tad too tight; the skirt that she wore was pale lilac, flaring gently from the hips; her shoes were navy with modest kitten heels. She nodded in approval at her reflection and checked her make-up once more; not too much eyeshadow and just a touch of lip gloss. Had she got it right, was this to Harry's taste?

She went into the kitchen and opened the fridge. Now for some insurance, she thought as she got out a cardboard box and peered at the cream cakes therein. 'These ought to clinch it.' She smiled and headed for the door.

HARRY SCOWLED IN irritation as the doorbell rang. 'Who the hell is it now—am I to have no peace?' he muttered as he went to answer its summons. Surely Christine hadn't remembered something else about the deliveryman? He'd only left their house a few minutes ago. He opened the door and gaped in amazement to see Kay standing there.

'Hello,' he said. 'What a pleasant surprise.'

Kay laughed. 'Don't look so astonished, Harry, I've come to apologize after Tuesday night's temper tantrum.' She edged in over the threshold, smiled and fluttered her eyelashes at him. 'And I've brought you a peace offering.'

He caught the faint scent of jasmine as Kay squeezed past him; he took a backward step and stared down at the white cardboard box that she held. 'Are those what I think they are?'

Kay nodded. 'For you.'

'How kind of you.' He took the box, peeked at its contents and beamed at her. 'Come on in to the living room and sit yourself down whilst I make us a drink. Tea or coffee?' he called as he headed for the kitchen.

'Coffee, please, but if you don't mind I'll come with you, it'll be nice to have a cosy chat.' She perched herself on a stool and gazed up at him. 'Now tell me all about what you've been up to. Are you having any more problems with the Bretts?'

Harry hesitated as he made the coffee. 'Er, no, everything's quiet.'

'She's not gone and reported you for anything else, has she? Christine, I mean. Only I saw her with you earlier on and I wondered.'

This nosiness must be contagious, thought Harry. Now

*she* wants to know everything. Aloud he said, 'Oh, that was nothing.'

'But I saw the police car outside her house, last night,' Kay insisted. 'She must have called them out for something. They don't do courtesy visits at three in the morning.'

'Sorry, love, I slept like a log last night,' Harry said truthfully as he offered Kay a cream cake, 'so I can't help you there.' He watched her nibbling at the cake and wondered why she was visiting him instead of Christine. If anyone had earned an apology and cream cakes it should be Christine and her mother. 'Perhaps she'll tell you about it when she sees you,' he added.

Kay sipped her coffee. 'Yes, she might,' she said thoughtfully, 'only I didn't want to ask her—she still might take offence after Tuesday night.' Her blue eyes gazed up at him again. 'It might be more tactful to ask you, as you're always so friendly towards everyone.'

*Oh no,* Harry thought, *I'm not into tale-carrying, especially between two women. I'd end up being pig in the middle.* He smiled and said firmly, 'Really, Kay, it's best if you ask Christine yourself, if it's so important.'

Kay frowned, but she finished her cake, brushed the crumbs from her sweater and stood up. 'It's not that important, I just wanted to…' She hesitated then said quickly, 'Yes, I suppose you're right, Harry, you men usually are.' She looked at her watch and gasped, 'Heavens, is it that late already, and I've so much to do. I took a day off to catch up on the backlog of paperwork I've got, and I'm still miles behind.' She stroked his arm and squeezed past him into the hallway. 'It's been so good to have a chat with my handsome neighbour, even if it's only a short one.' She pouted. 'But now I've got to dash.' She trotted along the hall and after opening the door, turned and blew him a kiss. 'Byee…see you soon,' she called.

Harry strode after her and watched her hurry along the path. Such a bonny girl and she smelt so nice and flowery today. Must be a new perfume; it was certainly different from that overpowering stuff that she'd worn on Tuesday night. But what was the real reason for her visit? he wondered, as he closed the door. Why did Kay want to know what had happened last night? For that was all she'd talked about. Why this sudden interest in Christine when they hated each other? He sighed and dismissed the questions; he'd given up on trying to understand the female mind years ago.

He walked back into the kitchen, finished off the remaining cream cakes and tried to think of what he was going to do next. He should start preparing for his son's visit, but thoughts of Christine, and the garden centre driver, kept creeping into his mind. Was Christine imagining all this? Surely not. He picked up his keys, went out and got into his car. 'Never put off until tomorrow what you can do today,' he muttered. He started the car and drove to the garden centre.

# FIFTEEN

*Thursday, early evening*

ALUN STOOD IN the garden centre garage and turned the hosepipe on to the delivery van. Over near the entrance he could see a red Volvo parking up and Mr Longley getting out of it. The manager stood for a moment and looked in his direction. He seemed about to cross the yard to talk to him, then changed his mind and walked quickly towards the entrance. Alun let out a sigh of relief; he'd thought for a moment that old Longley was going to have a go at him and he'd enough worries already.

The water from the hosepipe continued to splurge in a stream onto the windscreen and spatter down onto the concrete floor. Alun watched it for a while, then, picking up a sponge, vigorously began to wash the van. As he did so he felt some release from the resentment that had been building within him during the day. The root of the resentment was Rick.

What a stupid bloody idiot that guy was. How could anyone be so brainless? He'd really wanted to sort him out last night and give him a right kicking for messing up the job. But no, he'd got him home, shoved him out of the car and kept his fists firmly clenched by his sides. For the fact of the matter was the boss needed Rick—they still had work to do. As he thought about that Alun's lips tightened and he gave the sponge a vicious twist. He was finished with Rick, he wouldn't forget what had happened, and when this was over, he would get the bastard…. His mobile rang; he wiped his hands on his overalls and answered it.

'Hello?'

'Alun?'

'Yeah, it's me.'

'How did it go last night?'

'All right.'

'No trouble?' The boss's voice was insistent. 'You didn't arouse any suspicion, then?'

Alun hesitated. *Think quickly,* he told himself. 'Well, not really…bit of a hiccup, but I sorted it.'

'You sure 'bout that?'

'Count on me, boss, I always come through.'

There came a slight pause. 'Until now.'

Alun felt nervous. Did the boss know something he didn't?

'About tonight,' he said quickly, 'everything's to stay as planned?'

'Yes.'

'Do I need to take Rick with me? I can easily manage to—'

'Stay with the plan!'

Alun sighed. 'Okay.'

'And call me as soon as stage one is completed.' The phone went dead.

Alun stared at his mobile, shoved it in his pocket, then returned to washing the vehicle with renewed fury.

# SIXTEEN

*Thursday evening*

ALTHOUGH HARRY HAD spent the last ten minutes prowling around the garden centre looking at the plants on the chance of meeting the manager, there was no sign of him. He stopped and looked around, then he noticed that a new assistant was staring at him suspiciously, 'Bet she thinks I'm a shoplifter,' he muttered, then smiled and approached her. 'I'd like a word with Mr Longley, if he's available.'

The girl looked startled. 'The manager? Was it important?'

'Sort of,' Harry replied.

'Only, he's in his office, and I'm new. He said not to disturb. It's my first day here, y'see.'

'Can I see him?' Harry interrupted, aware that this conversation was getting him nowhere.

The girl nodded. 'I'd best take you there, then, although I'm not rightly sure where it is, it's such a big place, y'know.' She looked at him helplessly. 'And I keeps getting lost.' She hurried on in front of him.

Harry strode after her. *Looks like we're on the scenic route,* he thought as he followed the slim figure of the girl through various departments of the garden centre. So that's the 'casual approach' plan gone for a Burton, and he'd only intended to ask Longley a few questions about the van driver.

Having finally reached their destination, the girl rapped

on the glass door of the manager's office, opened it and whispered nervously, 'A gentleman to see you and I don't know what about.' She smiled timidly again at Harry and, holding the door open, allowed him to enter.

A harassed-looking man with a thin face and lank blond hair was seated behind a desk and scrawling his signature on several letters. He looked up, smiled tightly and said, 'Would you take a seat and bear with me one moment, please?' and continued to sign the letters.

Harry sat and watched him. He felt trapped, like some poor soul about to ask his bank manager for a loan. He was about to say, 'I'll come back later,' when the man pushed aside the papers and forced his face into a 'customer-friendly' smile.

'Well, sir,' he said, 'how may I help you?'

Harry said firmly, 'Oh, do come off the "sir" business, Longley, you know me. There's no need to be formal, I haunt this place.' He looked around. 'In fact I almost live here.'

Mr Longley's smile became warmer. 'Yes, of course I know you, Mr Myers, and we're grateful for your custom, but when the girl ushered you in I thought you might have some reason for comp—' He broke off. 'I'm sorry, Mr Myers, looks like I got my wires crossed. Now really, what can I do for you?'

Harry felt uncomfortable; after a bad start like this, how was he to get information from Longley when one wrong question would make him suspicious? 'The thing is,' said Harry, 'I thought I'd come here on the off chance. Y'see, I buy just about all of my garden stuff from you, because the quality's good, your prices aren't too high and your delivery driver is always helpful.' He hesitated. 'Well, I wondered whether your lad would be interested in doing a bit of part-time work for me.'

'By "your lad", I take it you mean Alun Rhodes? He delivers goods to your area.'

'If he's thin with a ponytail, he's the man I mean, yes. He's always efficient and polite, seems a nice sort of lad.'

Mr Longley nodded. 'Yes, he's good and he's reliable.'

'Has he worked here for long?' Harry asked.

'Less than a year, more than six months I guess, but I'd have to check my records to be sure. He's one of our flexitime workers.'

'Perhaps he'd be glad of some extra work, then,' Harry said, 'but what I wanted to know was…has he got references and such?' He lowered his voice. 'You know what I mean, Longley, I'm often away during the day, and I don't want him working on my property if he's been in any bother.'

Mr Longley looked annoyed. 'Of course he's got references. My company wouldn't employ anyone without them.'

'Can I see them?' Harry said eagerly.

Mr Longley leaned back in his chair and stared at Harry.

'Surely you know, Mr Myers, I cannot allow that. Such information is strictly confidential.'

'Then how do I…?'

'If you write to our firm and tell them you're thinking of offering Alun Rhodes further employment, I'm sure they'll be only too pleased to supply you with his references.' He picked up a business card from the desk and gave it to Harry.

Harry took it then pushed back his chair and stood up. 'Can't you tell me a bit about him, I mean, is he short of cash?' He felt himself floundering; he knew he'd gone too far. He said desperately, 'And if he is, do you think he'd be interested in more work?'

Mr Longley looked wary; he got to his feet and joined

Harry at the door. 'I don't know what other little jobs he's got, although knowing the hours he puts in here he'd have the time to do other work.' He stared again at Harry, then said guardedly, 'Have you any reason to think he could be working elsewhere?'

Harry shook his head. 'I would have thought if he was, you'd be the one to know about that.' Harry watched as the man opened the door. *Why does he seem so keen to be rid of me?* he wondered.

Mr Longley sighed politely. 'I'm sorry, I don't have the answer to that either, I only wish I could be of more help.' He opened the door wider and said, 'Now, if you have any other problem, I'll be only too pleased to....'

Harry shook his head and walked through the doorway.

'Then if you'll excuse me. Pressure of work, you know.' Longley looked at his watch pointedly. 'And time is passing.'

'Thanks anyway,' Harry mumbled, and the door closed quickly behind him. 'Alun Rhodes,' he muttered. 'Well, at least I've got a name.'

IAN LONGLEY CLOSED the door firmly behind Mr Myers and stood for a while thinking about the man's request. 'Alun Rhodes,' he mouthed silently, and he went back to his desk as he thought about his employee. The question was, why hadn't Mr Myers gone straight to Alun and asked him if he wanted to work for him on the side? Why had Mr Myers chosen Alun Rhodes? There were plenty of other members of the garden centre who would be only too pleased to take on extra work these days. Could Mr Myers have another reason? He hesitated; maybe he was being over-cautious, but just in case. He reached for the office phone, then changed his mind, got out his mobile and keyed in a number—better to be sure than sorry.

HARRY LOOKED AROUND at the array of plants that surrounded him and remembered that he wanted to buy some Christmas cacti; it would be nice to have some flowering plants throughout the winter. He turned again towards the office and was about to rap on the door and inquire about them, when he saw that Longley was speaking urgently into his mobile. Harry couldn't hear what he was saying, but from Longley's agitated body language, it looked to be important. He thought it wiser not to interrupt him again and decided to have a quick look round the showrooms and search for the Christmas cacti himself. If he couldn't find any then he'd order them whilst he was here. Soon he was wandering through the showrooms lost in admiration at the beautiful plants that surrounded him. For a while he lingered over the new selection of barbecues that were on display; he wondered whether he should buy one at the ten percent discount that was offered, or whether to wait until winter came when they might be offered at an even better price.

He drifted further along to where the patio roses were displayed and stood trying to decide whether to buy some now, ready for planting next month. He glanced around, hoping to catch the eye of an assistant, but there seemed to be no one about. In fact there were no other customers anywhere. The place seemed strangely silent. Harry started to feel uneasy. He hurried in the direction of the tills, then noticed that the till drawers were open and empty.

Where was everyone? Panic grew in Harry as he hurried from department to department, only to find it deserted. He turned back and headed towards the manager's office; Longley might still be at his desk. As he reached the office he saw that it was empty. He tried the door and found it was locked. He looked at his watch, 8.30 p.m. Of course, this place closed at 8 p.m., but surely...? He ran towards the exit and hammered on the locked doors. Racing back towards the outside area he reached the glass doors, which he knew overlooked the car park but it was no use, they too were locked. Climbing unsteadily onto a stack of bricks, he could see the car park outside. He pressed up against the glass. Yes! Enormous relief swept through him as he saw there were some people still there. A young couple with a pushchair were quite close by. They were about to get into their car.

Harry pounded frantically on the glass and yelled, 'Help!' as loud as he could.

The couple looked up and saw him. 'Hi, man!' the man yelled back and they laughed and waved at him as they drove away.

His hopes plummeted as he watched the car drive off. In desperation he scanned the car park; in the distance he could see his own car, but otherwise…nothing. 'Stay calm,' he told himself as he clambered back down from the bricks and tried to stop his heart pounding. Surely there must be CCTV cameras here, there had to be…but if there was no one monitoring them? He walked back to where there was a display of garden furniture and sat down. There had to be some security here, he thought, but where were they? A darker thought came into his mind: was this 'lock-in' accidental…or deliberate…? Was it a warning? *Don't be so bloody stupid,* he told himself, *stop imagining things, try to relax and think.*

He thought again about Longley talking agitatedly into his mobile. By golly the man had seemed— Stop! That was it! *Try your mobile, man.* Quickly he fished in his pocket, brought out his phone and keyed in the number for the local police. One good thing about working for St John Ambulance was that he knew such numbers by heart.

# SEVENTEEN

*Friday morning, early hours*

HARRY LAY IN bed and stared into the darkness. After a while he squeezed his eyes shut and tried to sleep. It was no good. Although his body was tired, on the inside of his skull it was 'Why?' time. His mind had tuned into overdrive, thinking and rethinking the day's events. So many questions and no answers, and they all began with 'Why?' Why had he, a mature man, managed to get himself involved with those two ladies from across the road? Why hadn't he minded his own business? Why had he been so bloody impulsive and offered to speak to the garden centre boss about that van driver?

None of this was his business, yet off he'd gone and a fat lot of good it had done him. All he'd got from the manager was the van driver's name, Alun Rhodes. As for his other questions, they'd been stonewalled, and then to cap it all he'd had to suffer the embarrassment of being locked in the bloody garden centre and having to call out the local police and the key-holder before he could get out. Doubt clouded his mind once more. Had that lock-in been deliberate? And had the key-holder really just nipped off to buy some cigarettes? 'Will you stop being such an idiot,' he told himself again, 'your imagination's gone into overdrive.' But as he thought through what had happened, another 'What if' joined the queue in his mind.

He lay on his side and punched his pillow yet again.

Could the garden centre boss be involved in all this? If he was, he'd certainly made him suspicious. Longley might even send someone to sort him out. Strange things did happen when people asked the wrong kind of question. He could end up as fertilizer, or even supporting a bridge on the M1. 'Don't be so bloody daft,' he told himself firmly. 'Think of something else.'

Think of something pleasant; think of something to look forward to. He remembered that his son and his wife and grandson were due for a visit tomorrow and he smiled. It was always a joy to see little Liam, and of course he'd need to get his train set set up for him again. Yes, he'd do that first thing in the morning. The bin men were due and— He sat bolt upright. The dustbins! He'd forgotten to put the bins out again. Should he leave his warm bed for the sake of the dustbins? If he got up early he could put them out before the bin men arrived. In the end discipline won. He tossed back the duvet and groped for his slippers. As his feet touched the floor the beam of a car's headlights shone through a gap in the curtains and lit up the room. Must be some late-night party-goers returning home. Harry sat on the edge of the bed and waited for the expected 'Good night' calls and the sound of car doors slamming. They did not come. Walking over to the window he pulled back the curtain. Down below, a few yards opposite his driveway, Harry could see a red estate car. He tried without success to see its number plate, then he shrugged. 'Stop being so nosy,' he muttered as he pulled on his dressing gown and went downstairs.

Once outside he shivered against the cold night air as he wheeled the dustbins to the collection point. He looked again down the road at the parked car and couldn't restrain his curiosity. Was there a young couple in there having it away? The car wasn't rocking, so it seemed unlikely. He tiptoed to the end of the path and peered along the road. What he saw made him stand as if rooted. He watched as a hooded figure got out of the car, opened the boot and removed something—it looked like a box. The driver of the car joined him and together they made their way silently up the driveway to Christine Brett's house.

Harry frowned; he couldn't see any lights on in the house. Perhaps they were visitors? Maybe heavy traffic had delayed them? But it seemed to have been a box he'd been carrying, not suitcases. He felt his unease grow as he thought back to what Christine had told him about the prowlers of last night. Surely they wouldn't dare to return tonight? He crept back up the driveway, leaned against his house wall and pondered; everything was in darkness at the Bretts'; shouldn't they have put the light on by now? Should he take a stroll across the road and have a look-see? He looked down at his dressing gown, hesitating, then, in the next second, shrank back into the shadows. He saw the men hurry down the drive, get in the car and drive off.

CHRISTINE LAY IN bed and stared up at the ceiling, wondering if she would ever be able to sleep again. She thought about the thieves, and the artist's picture of the driver kept running through her mind. She knew she was right about the driver—well, she was ninety-nine percent sure anyway, it's just that if she was wrong— She stopped in mid-thought. Was that the sound of a car outside? She rolled onto her side and peered at the luminous dial on her alarm clock: 12.45 a.m.; probably some party-goers. Christine snuggled back into the pillows as the silence returned; even the rain seemed to have stopped. There it was again! Abruptly, a car engine started up and she listened to the sound of it moving off. It was probably a taxi, she thought, she was worrying over nothing. But now she lay in the dark, eyes wide open. Perhaps she should read something. She switched on the light, reached for a book from the bedside table and tried to read but it was no use. A minute later she heard the 'click' of the garden gate. There was no doubt in her mind, it was their garden gate. She knew that sound so well. She got out of bed and, putting on her dressing gown and slippers, crept down the stairs, unaware that a short, slight figure was standing on the landing watching her.

EMILY HAD BEEN en route to the bathroom when she'd seen Christine's light come on. She watched as Christine went downstairs, then, pausing only to get her dressing gown, she switched on the landing light and with a sigh went downstairs after her. She didn't know what the lass was up to but, sure as hell, she was going to find out.

SOMETHING WAS WRONG! Harry was sure of it. He hurried down the driveway in time to see the tail lights of the car disappearing at the end of the road. He took a deep breath and squared his shoulders. It was no good; he would have to investigate. He ran across the road to the Bretts' gate and as he came nearer he saw a light shining through an upstairs window. He thought about ringing the bell and telling Christine what he'd seen, then decided against it— there just hadn't been enough time for the men to commit a burglary. That being so, whatever they'd carried up the driveway must still be here. Somewhere in this garden. Somewhere close by.

He went into the back garden. Where would they have put it? He peered into the darkness, though even without a light he should be able to find it. The biggest danger was that he might trip over it. He heard a door slam and he froze. He listened again, yet heard nothing more.

Pulling his dressing gown collar up tightly around his neck, he moved forward; if only he'd brought his torch with him. Cautiously he eased his way around what he could make out of the flower beds. If he could find that damned box and remove it, then tomorrow in the clear light of day he'd be able to tell Christine what had happened without frightening her....

What was that? There! Over by the conifers something moved. Could it be a cat, or a fox? With narrowed eyes Harry regarded the conifer. It couldn't be either of those men...or could it? Had one of them doubled back, or, perish the thought, had they brought reinforcements?

The conifer rustled again, this time vigorously. Harry crept towards it; that was never a cat. Memories of his Territorial Army training rushed into his mind. He was not going to be intimidated by a conifer! 'When in doubt, attack,' was his commanding officer's motto! Taking a deep breath Harry charged at the tree.

At that precise moment the kitchen window opened and a voice yelled, 'You'll catch your death out there, Christine.'

Harry spun round. Something hard and heavy hit his neck. Daggers of pain shot through him and he sank to the ground.

Some time later he became aware of the distant murmur of voices. He shivered; he was freezing. His bed felt cold like ice and his hands searched for the comforting warmth of the duvet. Slowly, the murmured voices became clearer.

'Shall I get the whisky, Christine? I keep a little bottle in the back of my wardrobe.'

'He's concussed, Mam. You don't give concussed people alcohol.'

'You'd best give him something. He can't stay there all

night. Besides, he's right on top of your pansies. If he stays there much longer they'll never recover.'

Silence returned and with a shudder Harry groped again for the duvet. Must be some awful nightmare. His fingers touched soil and he opened his eyes. He groaned as realization and the pain in his neck got worse.

'Harry, ah. You're back with us.'

Harry squinted up in the direction of the voice and a beam of light shone back at him. Christine's face was inches away. 'Get that light out of my eyes, you're blinding me,' he groaned.

She leaned over him again and grabbed his arm. 'Oh, I'm so sorry. I didn't mean…. Think you can stand? 'Cause I can't lift you.'

Harry struggled to his feet. For a while he swayed whilst the universe rotated around him. There was a throbbing pain around his neck and his ear. He fingered it gently.

Christine tugged on his arm. 'Harry, honestly I didn't know it was you.' She eased him down onto a garden seat. 'Are you all right? What are you doing here?'

'What happened?' he said. 'I saw the conifer rustle and—' Looking down in the gloom he saw something large and round. Something that glinted evilly in Christine's hand. 'What the hell have you got there?'

'A frying pan.'

'It's cast iron, too!' said the voice from the window.

Harry gasped. 'You mean you hit me with…how could you?' He clutched his neck.

'I thought you were a burglar, how was I to know? And after all the bother of last night!'

Harry stared up at her in disbelief. 'You could have killed me with that thing.'

'You were lucky,' said Emily. 'She used the skillet 'cause she couldn't find the rolling pin, and that's marble.'

He took hold of Christine's arm. 'I had thought that you and I…. Are you crazy? Attacking folk like that.'

'No, I am not! How many more times must I tell you I'm sorry? I saw this figure in the dark, I didn't recognize you and…you are just about the last person I would hurt—' She choked back a sob then said determinedly, 'But you were trespassing in our garden.'

'Just tell us what happened, Harry,' said Emily quietly.

Harry's gaze shifted from Christine's face to the skillet and back again. He cleared his throat and looked at Emily. 'I saw someone; that is, some men. One of them carried something into your back garden. It looked like a box. I thought their behaviour was suspicious, so—'

'But so was yours,' Christine blurted.

Harry rubbed his neck. 'Christine, haven't you noticed? I'm on your side.' He saw that she was close to tears, and he added gently, 'Do you want to hear me out, or don't you?'

She didn't answer, so he said, 'They drove off before I could get over here. I saw your upstairs light go on, but I didn't want to frighten you.'

In the half light Christine looked at him. 'All I can say, again and again, is that you should understand why,' she gulped. 'So, where is this…box, then?' She turned to her mother at the window. 'Can you pull the blinds back so we can have more light?'

Emily obeyed and the garden became lit by a yellow glow. Both Harry and Christine looked around, but they could find nothing.

Harry said, 'I think it was a box, I could have sworn they brought something. Maybe we should check round the shrubs and bushes?'

'Can't that wait until daylight?' Emily wailed, 'My sleeping pills are kicking in.'

'Go to bed, Mam, before you get dizzy.'

'Not with you cavorting around out there, I'm not. Besides, Harry's neck needs seeing to.'

Christine looked at him. 'You'd better let her look at it; I'll get no peace otherwise.'

Harry followed her into the kitchen and sank gratefully down onto a chair.

'Let's see your neck then,' Emily said.

He eased off his dressing gown, and looked up at Christine. 'For heaven's sake, will you put that skillet down?'

Christine looked down in surprise at the frying pan that she still held and she felt herself blush as she placed it on the cooker.

Emily leaned over him and peered down at his injury. 'You've got a couple of scratches there. I'll put some antiseptic cream on them.' Having smeared on the cream, she said, 'Just touch it with your fingers and tell me if you feel anything cracking.'

Harry did as she asked. 'Just feels sore, that's all.'

'She's not got your collarbone, then, so I don't think anything's broken, but you'll need a cold compress for that.' She turned towards the freezer.

Red-faced and embarrassed, Christine leaned against the back door and watched these proceedings. 'Harry, if you'd try to see it from my point of view, how I felt after what happened last night.'

'Christine, there was something,' Harry insisted.

Emily intervened. 'It'll be much better once it's morning.' She turned away from the freezer. 'It'll have to be mixed veg, Harry; we've run out of frozen peas.' She wrapped the packet in a towel, placed it on Harry's neck and tried to stifle a yawn.

'Mother! Will you go to bed? I can look after Harry.'

Harry got to his feet and said wearily, 'I thought you

two ladies were in danger.' He eyed Christine. 'I didn't reckon on being set upon by you.'

'Someone was lurking in my garden, what else could I have done?'

'You could both stop arguing,' Emily said in a voice like ice.

Both Harry and Christine turned to stare at her.

'For years we've lived here and hardly a soul has bothered to speak to us,' she said. 'And now, because of you, "Miss Busybody", this house is like King's Cross Station, with folk coming and going at all hours. And all I get to hear is non-stop rows.'

'But you like arguments, Mother, you've always said it exercises the—'

Emily snorted and headed for the living room. 'Not when it's open warfare, I don't.' She paused in the doorway to stare at the kitchen window and they saw the fear in her eyes. 'Not when I think God knows what might be out there, waiting and watching us…just biding their time.'

The door closed behind her, leaving Christine and Harry looking at the window and at the blackness beyond.

# EIGHTEEN

A FEW MINUTES later Christine stood at the lighted living room window and watched Harry stride across the road to his house. She wanted to run after him, there was still so much she'd wanted to say, but he'd been so angry and upset. She walked into the hall, checked again that the door was locked and bolted, then leaned against it, trying to think things through.

She thought about the return of tonight's intruders and her fear deepened. This was their second visit. Why did they come here? Why were they interested in her garden? None of it made sense, and now she'd gone and hurt Harry.

He'd been such a good friend to her over the last few days, but then this afternoon she'd seen Kay go into his house and her confidence had plummeted. She'd wondered how she could compete against such a glamorous lady. With a sigh, she turned and went upstairs; how likely would it be that after tonight's fiasco, Harry would be able to forgive her?

*Friday Morning*

HARRY PUSHED OPEN the kitchen door and started to wipe his feet on the mat, then looked in disgust at the mud on his slippers. He kicked them off and watched as they skittered across the floor to the sink, then he padded barefoot into the hall and switched on the light. He paused to remove the towel and melted packet of mixed veg, and then examined the bruise on his neck in the hall mirror. Although it was now bright red it could have been worse; his dressing gown collar had deflected most of the blow. He went into the kitchen, got out a cold pack and taped it to his neck. That should ease the throbbing. Looking at his watch he saw that it was close to 2 a.m. and realized that it was Friday already. He felt a twinge of anxiety; his son and family would be arriving later and there was a lot to do. He thought about his daughter-in-law; what would she make of the bruise on his neck? He felt embarrassed; he didn't want to explain to them what had happened— well not just yet. Perhaps he should wear a cravat to cover it. He went upstairs into the bathroom and gulped down a couple of painkillers. There was no point in worrying; best try to get some sleep.

His thoughts returned to Christine. He'd been so sure that she liked him, but after this? He'd always admired feisty women, but it was a bit much when they whacked him and knocked him out cold—none of them had done that before. He fingered his neck. Christine had been right in trying to defend her property, but he sure wished she hadn't used a cast-iron skillet to do so.

As he flopped back against the pillows the painkillers kicked in and he began to feel drowsy, but then he remembered he'd forgotten to tell Christine about his trip to the garden centre; about the manager's reaction to his questions and that he now knew the van driver's name. His last waking thought was that first thing in the morning he'd talk to her about it.

*Friday 8 a.m.*

HARRY WIPED THE sweat from his eyes and struggled on, battling his way through the jungle of yucca plants and palm trees. He'd gotta keep going; he could hear the roar of the engine. It was too close. There was a constant ringing; what was that ringing? He staggered on; gotta tell Christine, hurry, gotta keep moving. The sound of the truck became deafening and he risked a glance behind him. His heart missed a beat as he saw a wild-eyed Mr Longley driving the cement mixer lorry. Too late! He was going to—

Harry tore the duvet away from his throat and sat up. His heart was thudding and he could feel the sweat on his face. He brushed it away and as he did so, felt the dampness on the dressing and the wetness in his hair. He took a deep breath. Phew! It must have been a nightmare. He bashed down on the button of the ringing alarm clock and peered at it: 8 a.m. It must have been the ringing that had woken him. He'd forgotten to reset it and he hadn't got back to bed until well after two. It was no use; he couldn't get back to sleep, not after that nightmare.

He sat on the edge of the bed, rubbed his eyes, then got up, showered and went downstairs. His neck throbbed and he rubbed at it wearily. *Must change the dressing and take a painkiller,* he thought, *but let's have some food first and deal with that later.* Having finished his breakfast and dealt with his first aid, he wandered into the hall and picked up the morning paper. *Just have a quick read,* he yawned, *find out what's gone on in the world overnight.* He sat down in the armchair and opened the paper, scanning the headlines. After a while his eyelids began to droop. *Just have a quick five minutes,* he thought, and his head sank onto his chest....

What was that ringing? Not that blooming alarm clock again. Harry sat upright with a start. It was the hall phone. He staggered out of his chair and answered it. 'Hello?'

'We thought there was something wrong, Dad,' said

Martin. 'We've been calling your mobile for ages. We couldn't get past your voice mail, are you all right?'

No wonder he hadn't heard it, thought Harry, his mobile was still upstairs on the bedside table. He picked up the phone. 'Hi there…where are you? I'm fine. Is there something wrong?'

'Just taking a loo break for Liam,' said Martin. 'We're on the M6, thought we'd call you as we're making good time, should be with you in about an hour.'

'My,' Harry was about to say, 'so soon,' but when he looked at his watch he saw to his horror it was close to twelve….' That'll be great,' he said, as he tried not to panic and think of all the things he still needed to do before they arrived. He put down the phone and looked around. 'First, make my bed,' he muttered, 'then check the spare bedrooms, and then there's the supermarket—can't disappoint young Liam, the lad really loves his mint choc-chip ice cream.' He tidied round quickly then went outside to the garage. *What else do I need?* he thought as he climbed into the car. *Yes, fresh bread, milk and that's about it, really.*

As he drove out onto the road he saw the figure of Christine on her driveway; he wondered if she was coming to see him but now there was no time to stop for a chat, so he gave her a brisk wave and drove on. When he glanced in the rear-view mirror he could see her approaching the gate. He wondered what she wanted to say to him. He'd have to tell her what happened at the garden centre at some time today, but for now, he had to think about getting to the supermarket and getting out the train set for young Liam.

# NINETEEN

*Friday morning, around midday*

WHEN EMILY CAME downstairs the next day she stared in disbelief at the living room clock: twenty to twelve! She'd overslept. She tutted in annoyance—she'd not done that in years. She looked around; the breakfast things had been set out, but of Christine there was no sign.

She went into the kitchen, switched the kettle on and wondered whether Christine was out on yet another errand. Pouring the boiling water into the teapot, she placed it on the table and thought about last night's happenings. As she did so she felt goose pimples rise on her arms and she rubbed them fiercely. She had to admit she was worried about Christine; she knew that in the past the girl had brought it on herself by reporting every Tom, Dick and Harry for next to nothing, so who could blame the police for being sceptical?

She opened the fridge and peered longingly at the bacon that was on the shelf. Picking it up, she was about to get the frying pan out when she looked out of the window and spied Christine in the back garden. Emily hesitated; her daughter was heading towards the house. She clicked her tongue in irritation, returned the bacon to the fridge and got out a tub of low-fat spread instead. She glanced again at the window; on any other day she'd have stood her ground and ignored Christine's nagging, but today she felt washed out. She sighed; gone were the days when she could stay up half the night and not suffer for it. She took a couple of rolls from the breadbin, got a packet of cheese spread from the fridge and returned to the breakfast table in the living room.

The back door slammed and a few seconds later Christine popped her head round the door. 'Hello, Mam. Surfaced at last, I see.'

'I overslept,' said Emily, 'you should have woken me—it's nearly midday now and half the day's gone.'

Christine brought a mug from the kitchen, sat down and poured herself some tea. 'You've had two late nights on the trot, you needed your sleep.' She smiled. 'And anyway it's your own fault if you will go mixing alcohol with medicine.'

Emily stiffened. 'Since when are you judge and jury? Besides, I only had one glass.'

Christine raised an eyebrow. 'How big was the glass, Mam? And how often did you top it up whilst I was outside?'

Emily felt her face flush. She got to her feet and began to clear the breakfast things into the kitchen. 'I had to keep the cold at bay, what with doors being flung open in the middle of the night, and you waltzing around in the back garden.' She glared at her daughter. 'Will you never stop your nagging?'

Christine followed her. 'I just think you should drink in moderation, that's all.'

For a second, doubt crept into Emily's mind. 'I've not been swinging from the lampshades, have I? Besides, I'm too old to be moderate. In fact I reckon I'm overdue for a rave-up, so you can stop your fussing.' She picked up the tea towel. 'What I want to know is what you've been up to, lady, 'cause if you've been and reported Harry—'

'I've reported nothing. In fact I've been out in the back garden…investigating.'

'Did you find anything?'

Christine chewed on her lip and eyed her mother. 'I might have,' she said cautiously. 'I'll tell you about it later. But for now we've got to get a move on, we've to be at the hospital for your blood test by half past two.'

Emily stared at her.

'Don't you remember?' Christine prompted. 'It's marked up in red on the calendar.'

Her mother pulled a face. 'Oh no! I've not got to go trailing up there again, have I?' She thought for a minute, then said, 'We can't go, 'cause I've already eaten, so you'll have to cancel. I'm supposed to fast for fourteen hours, see.'

'Wrong again, Mam.' Christine smiled gently. 'This is for a thyroid test, not cholesterol, so you'd better get yourself sorted whilst I phone up for a taxi.'

Emily tutted angrily as she hung the tea towel back on the hook.

'Well, you could still cancel. You could tell 'em I'm having one of my off days or something.'

Christine shook her head. 'No, Mam, you know very well we have to keep an eye on your health and it's not fair messing them about just 'cause you're not in the mood.'

Emily went towards the stairs. 'All this fuss, I just don't know why them medics don't siphon off a pint of my blood while they're at it, then they can do as many tests as they like without bothering me.' She looked at her daughter hopefully. 'You should tell 'em, save us a fortune in taxi fares, it would.' And with that, she climbed the stairs to get ready.

Christine shook her head as she watched her mother. There was no sense in arguing with her or even trying to explain the technicalities of a blood test when she was in this sort of mood. Besides, she thought, as she reached for the phone, there were other things she needed to deal with. Whilst she waited for the taxi firm to answer, her mind strayed to what she'd discovered in the back garden. *Don't go there just yet,* she told herself firmly, *try not to think about it. Just make sure Mam's okay first.*

'Terri's Taxis,' announced a voice.

Christine started. 'I'd like to order a taxi for 1.30 today, please, to go to St Martha's Hospital.'

Having ordered the taxi, Christine came out of the house and strolled towards the gate to check the front garden again. She hadn't seen any shoeprints on the driveway earlier but she thought she'd just make sure so that Mam wouldn't spot anything when she came out. She felt guilty about not telling her mother what she'd discovered, but she could see no point in upsetting her just before she was going to have a blood test; it would only make her give the nurses hell when they got to the hospital. As she approached the gate she saw Harry's car coming down his driveway and turning on to the road. She was about to hold up her hand to ask him to stop but before she could do so, he waved briskly and drove past. She watched him drive towards the end of the road, then walked back to the rear garden. She thought about Harry as she double-checked what she'd found and she sighed; she'd just have to go over and talk to him later on when he got back.

As HARRY TURNED out of Poole Road onto the Leeds road he thought about the incidents of last night and touched his neck gingerly. The sore patch still felt damp even though it was a fresh dressing, and the painkillers didn't seem to be working at all. He felt irritated; he had to stop thinking about it. He was becoming obsessed by thoughts of policemen and Longley, mysterious boxes and would-be burglars. And now he was getting nightmares. *Focus,* he told himself as he drove into the supermarket car park; *think about mint choc-chip ice cream, fresh rolls and semi-skimmed milk.* With that thought firmly fixed in his mind he grabbed a wire basket and hurried through the supermarket doors.

Some time later he dropped the groceries onto the front seat, got in the car and headed for home. It was easy enough getting into a supermarket, he thought, as he glanced at his watch, but getting through the checkouts could take forever. He smiled in relief; even so, he should be back at his house in time. He scratched at the dressing on his neck again and winced; should he wear a cravat? He thought about it and decided to pull on a polo-necked sweater once he got home. It would stop Martin noticing it and avoid the need for any embarrassing explanations. He didn't want to have to talk to Martin about prowlers and running around in the dark at one o'clock in the morning, nor was he anxious to tell his son that one of his neighbours had whacked him. Soon Christine and he would have to talk things through, but not today, there was no time.

He was about to turn into his driveway when he noticed the red Volvo estate parked outside Kay's house, and saw a man walking up her driveway carrying a tray of cyclamen plants. Harry did a double take as he identified the man as Mr Longley. He beeped the car horn in recognition, but Longley, on hearing the horn and seeing him, rushed up the driveway and into Kay's house.

Harry felt puzzled; he'd never seen Longley in this area before, and he'd never seen him delivering stuff, either, especially as he knew that the garden centre had plenty of staff. He picked up his groceries and went into the house. It must have been an emergency to bring Longley out, he thought. Harry paused as he put the ice cream into the freezer. It was weird; he'd only talked to him last night, so why the hell was the man blanking him today? He remembered the nightmare he'd had that morning. Was it some kind of warning, maybe a premonition? 'You're turning into a superstitious idiot,' he muttered, but still he shuddered as he slammed the freezer door shut.

Harry went upstairs, pulled on a polo-necked sweater and was about to go down and start setting up the train set when he heard the cheerful beep-beep of a car outside. He pushed all thoughts of Longley away and rushed down the stairs, opened the door and hurried down the drive to greet his family.

# TWENTY

*Friday 3 p.m., St Martha's Hospital*

'LET ME GIVE you a hand, Mam,' Christine said as she eased Emily back into her coat. 'There, you see, all done and dusted. Didn't take that long, did it?'

'Not when we finally got to the nurse it didn't, one quick jab and it was over. Mind you, they had to find my veins first and that took some doing,' Emily grumbled. 'But you know, when I was sitting in that waiting area and having to look at all those other patients I couldn't help wondering what they'd got.'

'They were here for blood tests, just like you.'

'Yes, but think a bit, Christine, why would they need a blood test?'

Christine looked at her mother. 'I don't know. It's not something I worry about.'

'Ah,' said Emily, 'that's because you don't think like I do.' She glanced over her shoulder at the patients still seated in the waiting area. 'I gets to wondering, I mean, you never know,' she said, 'one of them might have legionnaires' disease, or—' she stared hard at a bald-headed man who shrank back on seeing her gaze '—even mad cow disease. I mean, you just can't tell—'

'Mother!' Christine hissed as she tried to hurry her along the corridor. 'Will you shush. You can't go around saying things like that in hospitals. Come along now, there's a café on the ground floor, we can go get a cup of tea and a sandwich.'

Emily stopped in her tracks and looked at her daughter. 'I saw a nice little pub just before we came into the hospital, Christine. Couldn't we go there? They might still give us a late lunch.'

'Mam!' Christine looked at Emily in reproach, then smiled. 'Just so long as you don't mean a liquid lunch?'

'Well, I have to replace my bodily fluids somehow, after the lot the nurse drained off,' Emily said. She looked at Christine with innocent eyes. 'I could well be dehydrated by now, besides, I could right fancy a bit of Welsh rarebit.'

Christine thought again about what she would have to tell Emily once they got home. She knew that once she'd told her, neither of them would feel much like eating—best have something now. 'All right then,' she said. 'I'm getting a bit peckish as well. Come on, let's go treat ourselves.'

*4.30 p.m.*

THE DAY WAS fading as the taxi pulled up outside the Bretts' home and Christine and Emily got out. As she paid the driver Christine looked across the street and saw that two cars were parked on Harry's drive. She chewed on her lip; she'd intended to go to see him, but if he'd got visitors… it was probably best not to intrude. She hurried down the drive after her mother.

'Well,' said Emily as she limped into the hall, 'that wasn't such a bad trip after all. I right enjoyed having a nice lunch.'

'As well as having a large glass of Chardonnay?' teased Christine.

'You had one, too,' said Emily, 'you have to have something to help the food slide down.' She turned to look at

Christine hopefully. 'Can we go to that pub again when I have another blood test?'

Christine laughed. 'We'll see.'

'Well, it made the trip to the hospital worthwhile, and suffering should be rewarded.'

'Did the nurse hurt you?' Christine looked at Emily in concern. 'How's your arm now?'

'I was joking.' Emily smiled. 'My arm's fine, and no, the nurse didn't hurt me, she just said not to put any weight on it for a few hours.' She started to unbutton her coat.

'I should leave that on for a few minutes, Mam,' said Christine as she walked past her and into the kitchen. 'I want to show you something in the garden.'

'I'd forgotten about that,' said Emily. 'Did you find something? Was it "that box", as Harry kept calling it?'

'No, not the box,' said Christine.

Emily looked at her daughter. 'You don't think he could have invented that, do you, as an excuse for prowling around?'

Christine pursed her lips. 'Why would he want to? Besides,' she added brightly, 'yes, I have found something.' She put her shoulder bag on the draining board, hurried towards the back door and unlocked it. 'Come and see.'

Emily refastened her coat and reached for her stick. 'Wouldn't it be easier to bring it here?'

Christine smiled and stood at the open door. 'Not this, it wouldn't. Now watch out for the moss, it's still a bit muddy round the back.'

OUT IN THE garden Christine waited patiently for her mother to join her. She watched as the frail figure picked her way carefully towards her.

'What's there to see?' Emily asked as she crossed the lawn. 'It all looks the same to me.'

'That's because you're not looking properly. I'll tell you this, Mam, something very strange happened out here last night.'

Emily leaned on her stick and gave her daughter a sardonic smile. 'What? As well as you belting Harry Myers round the head, you mean?'

Christine's mouth tightened. 'Yes,' she snapped. She strode briskly over to the flower beds and looked down. 'There was more than me and Harry in this garden last night.' She looked at her mother defiantly. 'And I can prove it!'

'I bet Harry'll be relieved to hear that. That's what he'd been trying to tell you.'

Christine flushed and evaded her mother's gaze. Changing the subject she said briskly, 'Now come over by the shed and have a look at this. See? Down there by the begonias?'

Emily joined her daughter and contemplated the patch. She looked at Christine blankly.

'Those shoeprints in the flower bed,' prompted Christine, 'can't you see them? They weren't there yesterday, I know, because I raked all round this area.'

'It might have helped if you'd told me what I'm supposed to be looking at,' Emily said irritably. 'For a while I thought you'd found a leprechaun or something.' Emily peered at the shoeprints again. 'Happen they're Harry's?'

'No, Mam, they're not. Think back to last night. Harry was wearing slippers. If you look closely you'll see that these shoeprints are ribbed, like trainers.'

Emily lifted one foot and allowed it to hover unsteadily over the shoeprint for a while. 'Them's big feet,' she said. 'And they're not mine.'

Christine touched her arm. 'They're not mine, either. Come on, let me show you.' She guided her mother away from the shed to the grass in front of the kitchen window. 'See? Those footprints are mine and Harry's. You can see the scuff marks where we had…' she hesitated. 'Our difference of opinion.'

Her mother bit back a chuckle. 'Is that what you call it?'

'Anyway,' Christine continued briskly, 'I've checked the front garden, and back here, and the shed and the hut are both padlocked as always. I looked in the hut and the lawnmower is still there.' Christine frowned and stared into space….

Emily gave a deep sigh. 'Now what?'

'Why did they come? I've searched everywhere and I can't find any box, yet we know someone was here.'

'I'll bet you thought Harry had designs on your lawnmower, didn't you?'

'The lawnmower's the only thing of value. It is pretty new, but it's still there and as for the shed, that's got a heavy-duty padlock on it. I'd know if someone had tried to force it.'

'I'm amazed you can find anything in that shed, you've that much junk stashed in it. Any day now it's going to burst right through the roof.'

'Waste not, want not; I'm only doing what you've always told me to do.'

'I'll tell you another thing, I think you ought to go and apologize to Harry right now. He didn't nick your lawnmower, and as those shoeprints show, he was right about the prowlers.'

Christine looked at her in exasperation. 'But why did they come, Mam? And where is this so-called box that Harry thinks they were carrying?' Once more she gazed around the garden.

Emily shivered, pulled her coat collar up and turned

towards the house. 'I don't know, but it must be here somewhere.'

'Where? I've just told you the shed's locked. I always keep it locked. How could someone break in there and re-lock it again in that short time? It's impossible.'

Emily went towards the kitchen door then looked back at her daughter. 'I reckon you'd better check again.'

'Mam, why?'

'Well, as I recall, according to Sherlock, "If you elimi-nate the impossible, all that's left is the improbable," so you go and have another look.' She closed the door behind her.

*Friday, close to 6 p.m.*

EMILY STOOD AT the sink on tiptoe, leaned up against the window and tried to see what Christine was up to, then snorted in frustration. She realized it was hopeless try-ing to see into the shed from that window. She thought about pulling a kitchen chair up to the window and climb-ing on that, but then shook her head. If Christine spotted her doing that she'd have hysterics and it wasn't worth the aggro, so she limped back into the living room. One thing was certain, she was not going to stand at the back door and call Christine in for a cup of tea and a biscuit yet again. If the silly girl couldn't be bothered to come in and have something to eat and drink, then so be it!

Emily's mouth tightened as she picked up her plate and her cup and saucer and carried them into the kitchen. She scowled as she ran the hot water, gave a quick squirt of washing-up liquid into the washing-up bowl, then placed the crockery in it. As she washed the dishes and placed them on the draining board she saw Christine's bag and with an irritated swipe she pushed it out of the way. As she did so Christine's keys and mobile phone slid out and into the washing-up bowl. For a split second Emily stared at them in horror then quickly fished them out of the water. She picked up both the keys and the mobile and rubbed them vigorously with the tea towel until they were dry. Having done this she placed the keys back in the bag and then scrutinized the mobile phone. 'It looks all right to me,' she muttered. She gave it a quick shake just to make sure there was no more water in it but it seemed dry. 'Best tell her about it when she comes in.' Having reassured herself she put the phone back into the bag, then went into the hall and placed the bag on the hall table.

As she thought about her daughter, Emily's mouth tightened. Apart from the trip into the back garden and Christine's two brief forays into the kitchen, the first to get a Stanley knife, the second to get the high-powered torch, she had seen nothing of her since they'd got back from the hospital and that wasn't fair! She had questions and she needed answers. Frowning, she picked up the TV remote control and flicked a button. Why would Christine need a Stanley knife? Obviously to open something, but why a torch? It wasn't dark yet and it wasn't raining. If something had been put in the shed, or 'planted' as some folk called it, surely she should have found it by now?

Emily shifted uneasily in her chair. What if it turned out to be a bomb or something horrible? People had been known to dump stuff like that on other folks' doorsteps, just out of spite. She sank deeper into the armchair and tried to reassure herself. She'd been watching too many James Bond movies lately, and her imagination was running on overdrive. Could it just be that someone with something to hide had picked on their house at random? It might well turn out to be pure coincidence.

Emily flicked at the remote control again; she needed to take her mind off things. Perhaps there was something decent on the movie channel. An old Humphrey Bogart film appeared on the screen and Emily's interest deepened; yes, it was one of the all-time greats, *The African Queen*. She snuggled into her chair and relaxed. As she gazed at the screen and listened to the familiar dialogue her eyelids began to droop. She yawned, looked at the clock and realized that she was long overdue for her midday nap. Yes, she thought, she might just snatch forty winks....

A HAND TOUCHED her shoulder and Emily sat up with a start. She looked about her and saw that it was almost dark.

Christine bent over her. 'Sorry, Mam, didn't realize you were still asleep.'

'What time is it?' She rubbed her eyes. 'I only closed my eyes for a second.'

'It's well after six now.' Christine patted her shoulder. 'Still, you must have needed it.'

Emily yawned again and turned to her daughter. 'Did you find anything? Daft question, of course you must have found something—you've been out there long enough—and judging by the amount of junk you've got in that shed....'

Christine gave a nervous laugh. 'All in good time. I'll put the kettle on and get us a drink first.' She headed for the kitchen.

Emily watched her go and listened to the sound of the kettle being filled. She knew Christine had found something. She could hear it in the excitement in her voice. Fully alert now, she sat up straight and waited for her daughter to return.

Out in the kitchen Christine placed the coffee mugs on the tray, hesitated for a moment, then put an extra spoonful of sugar into her mother's mug. Sugar was good for shock, wasn't it, and Mam was going to need nerves of steel to cope with the discovery she'd just made. She stared at the coffee and tried to force her hands to stay steady and her mind to remain calm. Should she tell her? Yes, she'd have to; there was no way out of it. But *how* should she tell her? Should she just bring the box into the kitchen and yell, 'Surprise, surprise, Mam!' She checked herself; *now you're the one that's being hysterical. Calm down and remember, first things first. Yes, start with the box.*

She picked up the tray and, taking a deep breath, walked into the living room and handed Emily the mug. 'Would you like some biscuits?'

Emily shook her head. 'I've had a couple already, but you must be peckish by now.' She peered up at her daughter. 'Come on, tell me, what kept you so long in that shed?'

Christine sat down and tried to speak calmly. 'I've found Harry's "box".' She took a sip from the mug and eyed her mother warily. 'It was as he described it! It's the size of the boxes that you get when you order a dozen bottles of wine; you know, square and pretty deep.'

'Well of course, I should have known, I order cases of wine every day…' said Emily, her voice sharp with sarcasm. 'Huh, I'm lucky if we can run to just one bottle of plonk,' she muttered.

Christine looked at her and, deciding not to rise to the bait, she continued, 'They'd shoved it behind two boxes of Christmas decorations and a carton of wallpaper rolls, although I still can't figure out how they ever managed to get into the shed. I mean, I always keep it locked.'

'Let's deal with the whys and wherefores later,' Emily said. 'The thing is, there is a box, just as Harry said.' She looked at Christine expectantly.

Christine stared back at her.

'Go on then!' Emily urged, losing patience. 'Tell me what's in it! It's not a bomb, is it?'

'Why would it be a bomb, Mother?'

'That's all the rage these days; people get into a temper, and the next thing you know some idiot has dumped a bomb on some poor soul. They don't seem to have much time for talking things through—'

'You mean arbitration?''

'If that's what you call it. So, where is this box, then?'

'Still in the shed.' Christine glanced at the window. 'I'll bring it in once it's dark.'

Emily looked at her daughter in horror. 'What do you mean, "once it's dark"? What the devil's in that thing?'

'You'll see soon enough, I just don't want the neighbours or the police—' Abruptly, Christine jumped up, strode over to the windows, looked out and then pulled the curtains closed. She walked to the door, switched on the lights and turned to her mother. 'Whilst we're waiting I could make a start on supper. I'm not hungry but I suppose I'd better eat something.' She looked again at her mother. 'Until then…' Her voice trailed off as she went into the kitchen, switched on the light and closed the blinds.

With surprising speed Emily got to her feet and limped after her daughter. 'Never mind about supper, young lady!' she scolded. 'Will you tell me just what the hell is in that box?'

Christine turned to her mother. 'Can't you be patient? Just for a few more minutes?'

Emily's mouth turned down. 'I've been patient. All day I've been patient. I've been wandering around here like a lost soul. I can't do me crossword and I've binned me knitting. Christine…I'm worried!'

Christine tried to tease her. 'You managed a nap, though.'

'That's old age. It's got nothing to do with worrying. So stop stalling.'

'Aha, been watching Humphrey Bogart again, I see.'

'Will you go get that box? Please?'

Christine peered through the blinds. 'All right, but you go back into the living room because I'm going to have to switch the kitchen light off.'

'Why?'

'It should be obvious, Mam.' She sighed again and said slowly, 'In case someone should see me when I bring it into the house.'

Emily waved her hands in exasperation then limped into the living room. She dragged a chair over from the living room to the kitchen doorway and sat on it. 'I'll wait here.'

'Right then!' Christine switched off the light and, leaving the back door open, went out to the shed. After a few minutes she came into the kitchen carrying the box. She put it on the floor in the middle of the room, then, locking the back door, she switched the light on again.

Emily remarked from the doorway, 'You reckon it's going to make a bid for freedom?'

'What?'

'Locking the door like that. The box, I mean. It's not going to try and escape, is it?'

Christine said nervously, 'You can cut the sarcasm, Mam. What worries me is that someone may try to get in here.'

There was a silence whilst Emily digested this remark. She set her jaw, got to her feet and limped over to inspect the box. 'Let's get on with then, shall we?' She gave it a tentative kick. 'It looks harmless enough to me.'

Christine stared at her, moved her gently to one side, knelt down and carefully opened the box. She hesitated, looked up at her mother and, taking a deep breath, slowly withdrew a thick bundle of banknotes. For a moment she looked at the wad without speaking, then, swallowing hard, she held them up for her mother's inspection.

Emily gaped at the notes, then turned pale and leaned heavily against the sink for support.

'Before you start, Mam, this is not Monopoly money,' Christine said shakily as she waved the notes slowly in front of her. 'These are all tenners; the others—'

Emily whispered hoarsely, 'You've checked the serial numbers?'

'Yep, as far as I can tell they're used notes, they're not consecutive and they've got watermarks and silver thread.'

Emily stared at the money, mesmerized. She whispered, 'How much is in there?'

Christine shook her head, ran her hands through her hair and delved into the box again. This time she brought out several plastic bags full of pound coins. She gazed at her mother and in a voice tight with hysteria said, 'I dunno! I think there's fifty in each of these bags, but I've not got round to checking them all. I kept trying to add up these and all the notes earlier, but the more I looked at them, the more scared I got. Mam, my brain won't work, I can't count past nineteen.' She threw the notes and the coins on the kitchen floor and rubbed at her eyes. After a while she looked up at her mother, fighting to control her nerves. 'What are we going to do? I shouldn't have touched them, should I? Maybe I've left fingerprints on the notes or something, but then, they're used notes so there's bound to be fingerprints, aren't there, Mam? So how would the police know the difference between my fingerprints and the others—?'

'Christine! Slow down.' Emily looked at her daughter with concern. Taking a deep breath, she moved towards the packing case and poked at the bundles of notes with her stick. She said shakily, 'Well you've already touched them, love, so we can't go back on that. Even if you hadn't handled the notes your prints would still be on the box. The only thing we can do is find out how much is in there.'

'And then what? What about the police? I should ring them. Maybe now they'll believe what I've been telling them about the prowlers. Now I've got the proof, now they'll know I'm innocent.'

'But will they—?' Emily blurted, then pressed her hand to her mouth.

'Will they what, Mam? Go on, you were going to say something. Out with it?'

'I wondered what I'd think if I were a copper and some-one phoned me and said they'd found a load of money in their shed,' Emily said. 'They'd have to work hard to convince me they were innocent. Cash doesn't just appear in folks' garages, there's got to be a reason.'

'I *know* the reason, Mam. It's to do with that hyper-market robbery, and the crooks are trying to bribe me to stay silent.'

'Odd way of bribing someone,' Emily said. 'Looks more like a set-up to me.'

Christine fought back her tears. 'I'm sure they're watch-ing me.'

'Calm down,' said Emily, 'they can't watch you through a wooden door. It's locked and you've closed the blinds, so nobody can see us.' She stared again at the money, then tightened her jaw. 'But we can't leave that lot there.'

Christine sniffed and wiped her eyes. 'What do we do?'

'You know what to do, Christine. Pick up the money and get it on the table.'

'I've just told you, Mam, when I look at it I can't even think properly.'

Emily limped to the cupboard, got out a glass, went to the sink and filled it with water.

'Here,' she said as she handed it to Christine, 'drink this—slowly.'

Christine stood up and sipped the water. After a while she said, 'Sorry, Mam, it's just….'

Emily touched her daughter's arm. 'Christine,' she said softly, 'you can if you think you can.' She nodded at the box on the floor.

Without a word Christine picked up the box and put it on the table.

'Now,' said Emily, as she pulled out a chair at the table and sat down. 'First things first, let's get a bit of order here. All the plastic bags on one side and the notes on the other.'

'And then?' asked Christine.

Emily put her hand in the box and drew out a plastic bag of coins. 'We ought to count it; we need to know how much is there. There must be several thousand.'

Christine watched as Emily opened the bag, and saw that despite the calmness in her mother's voice, her face was drawn and her hands were shaking.

'Leave it, Mam,' she said sharply. She took the bag from her and placed it back in the box. 'I'll deal with it.' She closed the flaps on the box and leaned on the lid. 'Now you go and have a sit down whilst I find somewhere to put this.'

'You sure?' Emily looked at her. 'I mean, I can help…' Her voice trailed off.

'Just you go. I'll call you if I get stuck.' She watched as Emily went out of the kitchen, then stared for a long time at the box.

'Now where can I put you for the time being?' she said softly. She glanced at the back door. 'You're not going back into the shed, that's for sure.'

# TWENTY-ONE

*Friday 6.30 p.m.*

Rick had been about to nip down the road for a quick smoke when he saw the thin beam of light, shining on the pathway from the kitchen window at the rear of the house, go out. He'd heard the sound of the back door opening and through the gloom he'd watched as a shadow darted across the drive to the shed. Puzzled, he stood and waited. What was the woman up to now? With a sigh he fished in his pocket, pulled out a pack of cigarettes and a lighter and looked at them with longing, and then reluctantly, with a grunt, he shoved them back. What was she doing? She'd been in the shed for ages earlier, surely by now she'd have found the box.

Still keeping the driveway in his line of vision Rick strolled a few paces up the road; it would never do if the woman should spot him at this late stage. Without warning he heard the sound of a door banging and he stood stock-still, his eyes still focused on the driveway. He listened again as he searched the darkness. Yes, now he could just make out movement. It must have been the shed door he'd heard. He waited. After a second or so he heard the back door close and the sound of a lock being turned.

Rick let out his breath slowly and smiled in relief. Now they were all safe inside the house—the woman, the old lady and the box. He could relax for a while, but should he? He felt puzzled; he was sure that it was not part of

Alun's plan that the woman should find the box tonight.
Alun hadn't said a word to him about that. Perhaps he
should phone him and tell him what had happened. Rick
thought about this, then shook his head. Orders were orders and he wasn't going to give Alun another chance to
tear his head off, he'd been given enough of an ear-bashing the other night. Alun had given him strict instructions
to phone him at nine, so he would tell him then and Alun
could deal with it; that was his job. Meanwhile he had a
few hours to kill. As for the rest of the night he'd have to
keep an eye on things in case the women decided to do
something daft like going for walkabouts in the direction
of the cop shop.

Rick studied the house across the road. The narrow
shaft of light, which he knew came from the kitchen window, shone down on the path once more, so all was as it
should be. His gaze moved upward towards the gables of
the house where the telephone lines were situated and he
felt a bit uneasy. Earlier he'd suggested to Alun that perhaps the wires should be cut. 'Just you do as you're told,'
Alun had snarled. 'I know more about fixing telephone
lines than you've had girlfriends, so shut it and keep your
brainwaves to yourself.'

Rick shrugged as he thought about Alun's reply. He was
a right bastard, but he wasn't going to argue—not until he
got his money. Best leave the thinking to the brainy ones;
all he wanted was his wages. His wages…. He turned and
ambled back to the car that was parked further down the
road. What about his wages? He was due for them any day
now, only one more job to do and then, once that was taken
care of…. He grinned as he thought about how he would
spend the money. First a gut-buster of a meal at the poshest
place in town, then some new gear, decent designer stuff.
His grin widened. Then, the cream of the cream: a trip

to America to watch the wrestling live, and see for himself how the real pros worked. For a moment he scowled as he tried to remember whether he'd set the TV recorder right for tonight's match. Recorders were stupid things, he would never understand them; all those instructions in Japanese and even in English, but the writing was so tiny, he'd spent three hours reading the instruction booklet and he was still none the wiser. He sighed. All being well he'd take a day off tomorrow; just phone the factory and report in sick, then when he'd crashed out for a while with any luck he could spend the afternoon watching the wrestling.

A picture of the ice-cold cans of lager and the pizza in his fridge came into his mind and his mouth watered in anticipation of the hard-earned supper that awaited him when he eventually got home.

He reached his battered old car and looked at it with contempt. One day soon, very soon if he could help it, he would have a new one. Rick's expression softened as he thought about his dream car. It would have to be something smart, something sporty. Something like the convertible that they'd used on the last job, only not quite so big and not so old. It would definitely have to be a sports car, one that would impress the women; a two-seater, though, big enough for him and some bird—he didn't want to be forever giving lifts to his pals, let them buy their own cars. He lit up a much-needed cigarette and pondered. As for colour, well that would have to be red or black. On reflection he nodded and climbed into the old Ford. Yes, black would be the colour, much more sophisticated.

Closing the car door he flopped back in his seat, took another drag from his cigarette and peered out of the window. In the distance, over to his right, an energetic-looking old bloke strolled along the road with a dog in tow, out for the nightly walk. Rick straightened up. At last! A real live living soul out and about on this street, but then, it was only because he had to exercise the dog. His lip curled as he watched both man and dog wander off down the road.

He hated old people. In fact he shuddered at the thought of growing old. That TV film had got it right, he thought. What was its name? *Logan's Run,* that was it, where everyone got bumped off at the age of twenty-nine. He nodded in approval—solve a lot of problems that would. Then he remembered that he was twenty-seven and he frowned. He scowled down at his half-smoked cigarette and after some consideration decided that perhaps thirty-nine might be the right age to leave the planet. Yes, that would be much better. People should take care of their bodies, though. That was the trouble with old folk; they didn't bother about their bodies or keeping fit. As they got older they just used their minds a lot more. Rick's scowl deepened as he thought about this and he nodded in confirmation. And that's where all the troubles started 'cause they just turned into busybodies like those two old dears up the street, who spent their lives spying on others and making extra work for poor sods like him. If folk minded their own business all would be well…ouch! His glance fell again on the cigarette stub that was now burning his fingers and he stubbed it out in annoyance; he was smoking too much.

Looking through the windscreen Rick saw that the old man and his dog had turned around and were heading back towards him. They were walking slowly now and the old guy was peering at the number plates of the car. As they reached his car the man stopped and looked at him through the car window. *Here we go,* thought Rick, *here's another nosy old git that can't mind his own business.* The man rapped on the glass and Rick pressed the button opening the window and scowled up at the man.

'Just wondered if you'd got lost or something,' the old man said, ''cause you've been parked here for ages.'

'I'm waiting for someone,' Rick muttered gruffly. He started to close the window.

The man looked apologetic. 'Oh, then I'm sorry to have bothered you, only it's easy to get lost round here. It's these street names, y'see; I mean, you can't see 'em in the dark. I've made loads of complaints to the council, but they never listen.'

'Right,' said Rick, easing the window up further. He scowled at the man and said nothing.

'I'll be off, then,' the old boy said, then he winked and whispered, 'Let's hope she hasn't stood you up.' He strolled away, dog in tow.

Rick grunted and started up the engine. He watched the old man walk away, then turned the car round and drove to the bottom of the road, where he waited until he saw the man opening his garden gate and going into his house. Five minutes later Rick turned the car round again and drove back up the street, parking this time on the opposite side of the road.

Having parked he pulled over a plastic carrier bag from the passenger seat, brought out a can of Diet Coke and glared at it. This was no substitute for lager. He took a swig from it and pulled a face. He fished again in the carrier bag and got out a sandwich, tore the cellophane wrappings away and took a bite from it. He chewed for a minute, then examined the contents of the sandwich. Tuna? He swore loudly; he thought he'd bought chicken. Nevertheless he chewed on stoically; it seemed a bit dry and it was not as tasty as chicken, but he had to eat something, his body needed the fuel.

Having finished his snack Rick crammed the wrappings back into the carrier bag and checked his watch once more. Still a while to go before he had to phone Alun. All was as before. He switched on the radio and leaned back. He felt sleepy but dared not close his eyes. There was no telling with Alun, he might decide to come along and do a spot check, and if he were to be caught napping.... Rick wound down the window, turned the music down low and let the night air seep in. Shivering against the chill he sat upright and let the damp air cool his skin, then he grinned; he was alert once more. Taking a deep breath he stretched his arms out in front of him. All he needed to do now was watch and wait.

# TWENTY-TWO

*Around 8 p.m.*

CHRISTINE SAT AT the kitchen table and stared at the neat piles of notes in front of her. She listened; there were no sounds, not even from the TV. She got up and tiptoed into the living room. As she suspected, Emily was dozing. Christine looked down at her mother; her face was still drawn and there were shadows under her eyes. As she watched Emily rubbed at her eyes and looked up at her.

'I wasn't sleeping, you know,' she said, 'I was just resting my eyes a bit.' She yawned, then said, 'Go on, then, tell me how much is out there.'

'Haven't finished counting yet, Mam,' Christine lied, 'but I think you should go rest for a while. I'll bring you up a sandwich and a nice glass of wine, and later when I've finished counting I'll come and tell you what we've got.'

To her surprise Emily struggled to her feet and stretched.

'I think you're right. Two late nights on the trot is making me drowsy.' She looked at Christine. 'Although a nice beef sandwich would be good if you'd bring it up.'

Christine watched as her mother climbed the stairs, then called after her, 'I'll be up in a few minutes.' She went back into the kitchen and made the sandwiches. When she'd taken the tray upstairs she went into the kitchen, sat down and stared at the money on the table.

All this money! She'd never seen this much money in

real notes before. There were thousands of times when she'd added these kinds of figures up in her bookkeeping job, but to see the actual notes spread out in front of her, that was different. She smiled as she looked at it; now if the money actually belonged to her, just what would she do with it? There were so many things, she thought, perhaps a scooter for Mam? Then she could get around a lot more. Perhaps a holiday? Maybe in Scarborough, or even in the Channel Islands. People said they were wonderful and neither of them had ever been there. She stared again at the stacks of notes and pondered; if the money were hers they might even be able to buy a car—not a flash one, just a little runabout would do. She stretched out her hand towards the nearest stack of notes and stroked it, letting her fingers feel the texture. Then she picked up the wad and looked at it thoughtfully. Who would miss a few thousand? she wondered, and how would anyone prove that she'd taken anything? After all, the money would be insured, the hypermarket would have made sure of that. She and Mam deserved it, really, after the stress they'd been through. She could give some of it back, of course, and swear blind that that was all she'd found in the shed. Who could prove otherwise? Only the thieves would know differently and it would be her word against theirs. *'But then you would be a thief too,'* said a little voice in her head. Christine felt her face flush; she sat up straight and dropped the notes back on the table as if they were on fire. No, this would not do! She got to her feet and looked around. To take even a fifty pound note would put her on the same level as the thieves; she knew she was a more honest person then that.

*Focus,* she told herself, *stop daydreaming, you've got to find a hiding place for this...stuff, just in case the thieves come back tonight.* She paced up and down in the kitchen; where would it be safe until morning, until she could call the police— She stopped in her tracks; she could call them now. She thought again about the previous night and when the police had arrived in the early hours only to find nothing; and she felt her face burn with embarrassment. If she called them again tonight, they'd be think she was nuts; best wait until daylight came.

But where to hide the money until then? Her gaze drifted towards the pantry. She went towards it and opened the door. Immediately she caught the earthy scent of potatoes mingling with the tangy smell of onions. She walked inside; on either side of this long narrow room there were wooden shelves whereon a multitude of items were stacked. On one shelf were Mam's emergency rations (just in case World War Three broke out), tins of ham, peaches and pineapples; all were lined up neatly along with several jars of pickles, jars of red cabbage and tins of plums. Beside them was a selection of cooking pans; a huge one for bottling, an old pressure cooker minus weights, plus three ancient saucepans with dodgy-looking handles. ('They only need tightening up with a screwdriver,' Mam had said.) Christine smiled at the thought and turned around. On the other shelves were some shopping bags full of empty bottles, ready to go to the recycling bin when she had the time, and hanging from a nail on the shelf were also several long-life carrier bags from the local supermarkets. Below them, standing on the floor, was a nearly full sack full of Wilja potatoes (Mam's favourites). Christine smiled when she looked down at them. Honestly, how on earth were the two of them going to get through a large sack of potatoes like that before they went soft? But Mam had insisted; the greengrocer had promised he'd not charge for delivery, she'd said. So there they were. She turned around; on the shelf nearby was a tired-looking cabbage and a string bag half full of onions. Christine automatically squeezed the onions; they were still firm, and she moved on. As she came out of the pantry she faced the back door. She saw the new bolts that were across the door and felt a sense of relief; they at least would buy them some time. She thought about the locksmith Fred Hamlin and wondered if he'd ever return with those promised door chains. Her mind went back to the incident with Harry and Fred and she stifled a laugh. It was still funny. She looked again at the money on the table and at the box that had contained it earlier, now on the floor. Where could she hide it? Then she had it! But she must work quickly before Mam decided to come downstairs again to see what was happening. She set about her task.

Ten minutes later she resealed the box, then removed a shelf from the fridge and was about to place the box inside when she heard a thud followed by a loud wail from Emily upstairs. Christine's heart missed a beat as she shoved the box into the fridge then raced upstairs. As she burst into the bathroom she found her mother on the floor. Instinctively she rushed towards her but Emily said, 'No! Let me be. There's a right and a wrong way of doing this, them at the hospital said if ever we fell—'

Christine stood as if frozen whilst her mother rolled over into an all-fours position. She watched in horror as blood from a gash on Emily's eyebrow trickled down her face and she fought against all of her instincts to rush forward and pull her mother to her feet.

With aching slowness Emily put one hand on the bath rim and brought herself into a kneeling position. From there she grabbed the edge of the sink and finally stood upright.

'There.' She looked at Christine and said shakily. 'Y'see? Them hospital nurses always said that was the best way of doing it and they should know.'

Christine rushed to her. 'Mam, what happened?' She attempted to stop the flow of blood from Emily's eyebrow with a towel. 'I think that needs a plaster.' She reached behind her mother, opened the bathroom cabinet and took out the first-aid box. 'Mam, keep pressing the towel to your eyebrow whilst I get the plasters.'

Emily did so and leaned against the sink. 'Eyebrows and ears always bleed a lot...don't look so worried, I'm only leaking a little bit.'

Christine stuck the plaster over the cut and wiped her mother's face. 'Mam, tell me what happened. Did you go dizzy?'

'I did not.' Emily looked at the floor. 'I tripped over that thing there.'

Christine stared down at the offending bath rug and felt a huge sense of guilt. She'd unthinkingly left it there after her bath this morning. She'd forgotten to drape it over the side of the bath so that her mother wouldn't trip. 'Oh, Mam, I'm so sorry, it's my fault, I shouldn't have left it there.'

'Can't be helped,' said Emily, 'what's done is done.' She frowned at her daughter. 'And I wouldn't mind only I've not had a drop of me wine.' She peered down at the floor. 'Me glasses fell off as well...ah, there they are.' She bent to pick up her spectacles and tried to grasp at them but her fingers refused to move.

She looked at Christine, then tried once more to retrieve her glasses. Her fingers still did not move. 'Christine,' she said, her voice shrill with fear, 'my fingers won't work and my hand and my arm feel numb!'

Christine hugged Emily to her, fought back a growing suspicion and tried to say calmly, 'Let me see.' Whilst she examined her mother's hand, thoughts of what she'd been told about recurring strokes by the doctor grew in her mind. Surely not, she thought. It had been eight months since her mother's massive stroke. *Please God, don't let this be another one.* She looked closely at the hand; already there were some signs of bruising.

'I knocked it as I fell,' explained Emily, as if reading Christine's mind. 'I tried to get my balance and I lashed out. I think I caught the rim of the toilet base as I went down.'

'Mother,' said Christine, 'sit down and get your breath back.' She watched her mother ease herself onto the toilet seat; she said carefully, 'Just to be sure, I think I'll phone for an ambulance.'

Emily nodded and said quietly, 'I think you're right.' She stroked her injured hand.

Christine hurried down the stairs, went into the hall, picked up the receiver and keyed in 999. She listened, then glared at the phone. No ring tone. She banged hard against the phone rest in irritation; still no sound. The phone was dead. Furious, she slammed it back on its rest then got her handbag from the table and fished out her mobile. Once more she keyed in 999. She listened then stared at the mobile in horror. From it came a strange crackly sound.

'I'm sorry, love,' said Emily, who'd followed her downstairs, 'I thought I'd fixed it. It fell into the washing-up bowl, you see. It was only in there a second and I dried it as best I could—'

Christine was filled with panic as she gaped at her mother. What was she to do? Now she'd no way of getting through to the ambulance: both phones were dead....

'I forgot to tell you, I thought it'd be all right,' continued Emily.

Christine looked from her mother to the front door. She'd got to do something; she'd have to go over to Harry's, visitors or not, and ask to use the phone. With strokes, time was all important.

'Go sit down, Mam, I'll go see Harry.' She opened the front door and ran across the road.

HARRY HAD JUST reached the last page of reading *Mr Chuckle* to Liam, when he heard the doorbell. He smiled down at his grandson lying in his bed and was about to say, 'I'll see who that is,' when he heard Martin go into the hall and open the door. He heard Christine's voice and, closing the book, said, 'Back in a minute, Liam,' and went downstairs. When he reached the door a worried-looking Christine greeted him. 'Sorry to bother you, Harry, when you've got visitors, but it's my mother, she's had an accident and my phones aren't working.'

'Use mine.' Harry gestured at the hall phone and then hovered uncertainly while Christine dialled for an ambulance. When she'd finished he said, 'What's happened?'

Christine turned to him and he could see she was fighting back her tears. 'Oh Harry, she fell, and I think she's having another stroke....'

RICK WAS HALFWAY through his second tuna sandwich when the Bretts' front door opened and the younger woman dashed across the road and rang her neighbour's doorbell frantically. After a moment the door opened and she went inside. What's going on? he wondered. She'd not even bothered to lock her own door. He put the sandwich away and thought about the situation. Where was the old woman? What were they up to? Rick chewed on his lip and thought hard; the younger woman hadn't been carrying anything, so she couldn't be running away with the money. He pressed the button to wind down the car windows and sat up straight, his eyes now firmly fixed on the neighbour's door.

After a few minutes the younger woman came out of

the house and this time a man came with her. They hurried across the road and entered the house.

HARRY FOLLOWED CHRISTINE into the living room, where Emily was seated and saw that the old lady's face was grey with pain and fatigue. 'Hello, Mrs Brett,' he said. 'Christine tells me you've had a bit of a fall.'

'I'm shattered,' Emily said. 'I fell badly, Harry.' She held out her hand. 'But I'm lucky I only hurt this.'

'Do you mind if I have a closer look at it?' Harry asked. 'Only I do some voluntary work for St John ambulance.'

'Feel free,' Emily said as she looked anxiously at the door. 'I do wish them ambulance people would hurry up, Christine, I want to know what I've done with this hand.'

Harry touched her arm gently; it felt clammy and Emily was trembling. Although her hand was swollen and it was difficult to see if there was a fracture, he thought there was more danger of Emily going into shock. He tried not to show his concern but he knew that she really needed to see a doctor up at the hospital. 'I'll just go see if there's any sign of them,' he said gently, and walked towards the door.

RICK SHRANK LOWER in his seat as after a few minutes the younger woman and the man reappeared and stood talking at the garden gate. He hoped they hadn't noticed him; he didn't want to have to move the car yet again. He peered at his watch: nowhere near nine o'clock—he couldn't call Alun yet—so what should he do now? He stared again at the man. Was the bloke going to help the two women to make a run for it? Alun hadn't said anything about there being a man with them. That was typical of Alun, he never told him nothing, and if you asked a question he snapped your head off. Well, Alun had told him to keep watch, so that's what he was doing, right? But one thing he was sure of, it looked like the man and the woman were waiting for someone. Rick folded his arms across his chest. Why should he worry? This was not his problem.

HARRY STOOD AT the front gate waiting for the ambulance to appear. He tried to push back the thoughts that were flooding his mind and focus on Mrs Brett. He knew that although her injuries seemed minor, there was a possibility of a stroke and grave danger of her going into shock, so it would be best if the hospital kept her in overnight.

His thoughts moved on to Christine; there was so much he wanted to say to her, so many questions he needed to ask, but the poor girl had been through enough this week, and he knew they both must deal with this emergency first. He looked across the road at his own house; Martin must be wondering what was going on. He'd have some explaining to do when he went in, but he'd deal with that later. It was with a mixture of relief and anxiety that he saw the headlights of the ambulance coming towards him. It came to a halt and Harry walked out to greet the ambulance men, then escorted them into the house.

RICK STARED HARD at the ambulance that had just pulled up a few yards in front of him. He gaped open-mouthed as he watched the middle-aged bloke and the ambulance fellas go into the women's house. What the hell was going on in there? There were a lot of people in the house now. He thought for a minute and counted carefully: at least five. And how the bloody hell was he supposed to watch five people? There was only one of him. He chewed on his nails. What was he to do? He looked at his watch: five to nine. Well, he'd wait another few minutes until nine, then he'd call Alun. He felt uneasy about this because Alun had never mentioned ambulances, but he'd best wait, just to be sure; after all, it was only a couple of minutes.

EMILY SAT IN her armchair and watched the minute hand on the living room clock. Why did it move so slowly when you were watching it, and go like the clappers the second you turned your back? she wondered. She chewed on her lip and once again her eyes drifted towards the living room door. She'd heard the sound of a vehicle pulling up outside, followed by the murmuring of voices a few seconds ago. Would that be the ambulance men arriving? She felt her pulse quicken at the thought and looked down at her injured hand. Something was wrong with it, that bruising was definitely getting bigger, but was it another stroke? She thought back to the time when her first stroke had occurred, and looked again at her hand. Sure, her arm felt numb and clammy, but it didn't feel the same as that first stroke. She shuddered, thinking back; that stroke had felt very different— She heard footsteps approaching and Christine's voice speaking softly and her lips tightened; she knew she'd been a nuisance creating all this fuss and then this happened, just when she'd been trying to prove to Christine that she could cope, as if that girl hadn't got enough on her plate already. Well, there was one thing she could do: she could prove to them that she wasn't soft, no matter how bad the pain.

There came a brisk knock on the living room door and a paramedic walked towards her. He smiled and said breezily, 'Hello there, I'm Steve.' He crouched down beside her. 'And you're Mrs Brett, aren't you? Would you mind if I called you Emily? I hear you're the lady that's had an argument with the bathroom mat.'

'And the mat won,' said Emily. She held out her hand. 'Just look what happened to me.'

Steve grinned and gently took hold of her hand and examined it. After a while he looked at her eyebrow and said, 'I'll put a temporary dressing on that until we get you to the hospital.'

Emily looked at him in alarm. 'Do I have to go to the hospital? We've only just come from there this afternoon. Couldn't you give me a couple of painkillers and fix it?'

Steve shook his head. 'They'll need to have a look at you, love.' He winked at her. 'Just in case they spot something I've missed.'

He turned to his colleague. 'Get us the wheelchair, Mick.'

Emily looked at him. *I don't want all this fuss,* she thought. 'I can still walk,' she snapped.

Steve looked doubtful. 'Let's play safe, love, it's only 'til we get you into the hospital.'

Emily said irritably, 'Well, all right but I've still got two legs that function, you know, it's only my hand that's injured.'

'Get the wheelchair then, Mick,' the paramedic called. He looked at Christine. 'Your mum will need her coat and a warm scarf.'

'I'll get them,' Christine said. 'Don't worry, Mam, it's best that the hospital check it out.' She wrapped the coat around Emily's shoulders, buttoned it at the neck and gave her a reassuring hug. 'And I'll be with you all the while.' She took her mother's arm, helped her into the wheelchair, locked the door and watched as she was wheeled out to the ambulance.

IT WAS PRECISELY nine o'clock and Rick was keying in Alun's number when the two women—one of them now in a wheelchair—the two paramedics and the middle-aged bloke reappeared and made their way to the rear of the ambulance. Rick watched as the ambulance doors opened and the two women were assisted into it. The middle-aged one leaned down and said something to the bloke, then the doors were closed and the ambulance drove off.

Rick sat with his mobile crammed against his ear and gaped at the departing vehicle. Were they using the ambulance as a getaway car? And the wheelchair? Loads of stuff could be hidden in a wheelchair; any shoplifter would tell you that. And if the ambulance decided to use the blue lights and siren they couldn't half get some speed up! What was he to do? The ringtone from his mobile continued relentlessly. 'Come on, you stupid sod, pick up,' he yelled.

HARRY STOOD IN the middle of the road and watched the ambulance drive off into the night. He turned to glance at the Bretts' house; he knew Christine had locked the door but she'd forgotten to turn the lights off, but perhaps that was for the best. At least she'd have a welcoming light when she returned from the hospital. He'd given Christine his phone number and told her to phone him as soon as she had any news, then he'd drive up to the hospital and pick them up. Friday nights were usually hectic at the A&E so he knew they'd have to make their own way home.

He walked up the path to his own home and tried to dismiss the uneasy feeling that all was not well. As he reached his kitchen door he looked again at the house across the road. What if those prowlers were to return there again tonight? As he stood there the sound of an engine starting up made him jump. He looked along the street and saw an old black car drive off at speed. He sighed as he opened the door and went into his own house. Best tell Martin what's going on, he thought as he walked into the living room.

# TWENTY-THREE

'HELLO.'

'Alun?'

'Yeah.'

'Where the hell have you been?'

Alun recognized Rick's voice and sighed. 'It's only a few minutes past nine, Rick.'

'I've been calling you for ages.'

'So where's the fire?' Alun said.

'It weren't a fire; they've gone! The women! They went in an ambulance, I think it was an emergency one. Anyway they've just left. Oh, and another thing; the middle-aged woman found the box.'

'What!' screeched Alun. 'When was this?'

''Bout half six.'

'You bloody idiot! Why didn't you call?'

'Now look here, you said, "Call me at nine," and that's what I've done, see. You told me to keep watch. It's not my fault you don't tell me nothing.'

Alun's head throbbed. Questions whirled in his mind. He felt a desperate urge to strangle Rick, or knock the hell out of him, but common sense told him he must wait until later. Now he needed answers. How had the woman managed to find the box so early? She wasn't supposed to find it until Saturday; that was the plan, so what had happened?'

'What do I do now, Alun?' Rick's whining voice reached him.

'Who went in the ambulance?' Alun demanded.

'Just the two women. There was a bloke but he just stood there, then went home.'

Alun tried again. 'You say it was an emergency ambulance, so who was hurt?'

'I reckon it was the old woman in the wheelchair, but you told me to keep watch, remember, and that's what I did. And before you ask, I couldn't see if they took the box with them; they could have put anything into that wheelchair.'

Alun groaned. 'So they're going to the A&E and we don't know if they have the box or if it's now…in the house?'

'No. So now what?'

'Get the hell up to the hospital. Park as near as you can to the A&E unit and I'll join you there. But if they should come out before I reach you, call me, then follow them.'

'I'll get done if I use a mobile when I'm driving, and I've already got nine points on my licence,' protested Rick.

Alun thought again about what he was going to do to Rick once this job was over. He bit down on his lip and, with difficulty, remained silent.

'Alun?'

'Haven't you gone yet? Now what?'

'Where exactly is the A&E?'

'Leeds Infirmary, you moron! Now get off this bloody line, will you. I've got calls to make.'

Alun switched off his mobile and scrubbed at his forehead. He tossed the phone onto the table and went to get some paracetamol; his head was throbbing and he needed to think. He sprawled out on the sofa, stared at the mobile on the table and waited for the painkillers to kick in. He'd have to phone the boss; but when he did, where should he begin? He was still puzzled by the fact that the beige-haired woman had found the box so quickly. Again that feeling of something badly wrong gripped at his guts. He'd missed something. What was it? He must remember. He got to his feet, reluctantly picked up his mobile and stared at it. With a sigh he keyed in a number. As he waited for the boss to pick up the phone, his mind returned to the woman who'd witnessed their recent robbery.

Even then his gut feeling had been that they should call it quits and get out of the country fast. It would have been the safest thing to do; after all they'd got plenty of cash from their last raids. But the boss hadn't agreed; being a gambler, the boss always wanted more. So they'd executed plan 'A' and it was all going wrong. Again his mind went back to the woman. How had she found the box so quickly? What had aroused her suspicions? He thought again about how they'd delivered the box; there'd been no lights on in the woman's house, they'd put it in the shed without a sound and, credit where credit was due, Rick knew about padlocks all right. There hadn't been anyone lurking about; the night had been mild after the rain, it had been a bit slippy in the garden— He clicked his fingers. There. He had it. The mud! They must have left shoeprints.

'Yes?' said a voice.

Alun cleared his throat. 'Just calling in to report, boss.' He took a deep breath. 'Everything's going to be okay… although we might have to go to plan 'B'….'

'What's happened?'

'Rick's just phoned and told me the two women have gone off in an emergency ambulance.'

'There's been an accident?'

'Must have been but you know what an idiot Rick is, I couldn't get any sense out of him. I've tried to warn you about him before, he's trouble—'

'But an expert with locks.'

Yes, but there's something else.'

'I'm waiting.'

'She found the box…the woman, I mean. I know it was a day early—'

'She what? How did this happen?'

Alun gulped. 'Sorry, boss, but there's more. The women left in the ambulance and the old woman was in a wheel-chair, so we don't know if they've taken the box or if it's still in the house.'

There came a long silence.

Alun said quickly, 'I'm driving up to the hospital now to join Rick and keep an eye on things.' He held his breath and waited.

'I'll get back to you,' came the icy reply. The phone went dead.

'WHAT'S HAPPENING, DAD?' Martin asked as Harry came into the kitchen. 'Is that lady's mum ill? I saw them getting into the ambulance.'

'Mrs Brett, that's Christine's mum, has had an accident,' Harry said. He went to the fridge, got out a can of lager, thought about it, then put it back. 'I'd best have a coffee.' He filled the kettle. 'I've told Christine, that's the lady that phoned from here, that I'd drive up and collect them from the A&E once the medics had seen them.' He looked at his son. 'The ambulance won't bring them back, and it's a devil of a job getting a taxi on a Friday night.'

Martin looked at him closely. 'She's a nice-looking woman,' he said. 'It's good to know you're getting friendly with your neighbours; we always worry about you living up here on your own.'

Harry made his coffee. 'Now don't you go jumping to any conclusions.' He gestured at the fridge. 'Help yourself to a lager if you want, or there's tea or coffee.'

'No, thanks, I've got a drink in the living room already.'

'Well, come on, then, let's go and join Sheila; we don't

want to leave her sitting there all by herself.' Harry made as if to move into the living room.

Martin blocked him. 'In a minute,' he said, 'there's no rush. Come on, Dad, tell me more. It's not like you to go rushing off into a neighbour's house like that. I mean, you were always the "Good Morning, Good Evening," type of man, but as far as the neighbours were concerned, you and Mum more or less kept yourselves to yourselves.'

'Yes, well, this was an emergency,' Harry blustered, 'you could see that, couldn't you?'

'I could see the way that lady looked at you.' Martin smiled.

Harry felt his face grow hot. 'That's you and your overactive imagination. I was only helping a friend out.'

'So now she's a friend, is she? I thought you said neighbours.' Martin grinned.

Harry brushed past him into the hallway; he glanced up the stairs. 'Liam asleep already?' he asked in an attempt to change the subject.

'Yep—' smiled Martin '—it was way past his bedtime. So come on, Dad,' he persisted, 'what has suddenly turned you into the Sir Galahad of Leeds?'

Harry's gaze drifted down the hall. He saw the phone and remembered; what a lifesaver, he thought. 'You go and join Sheila,' he said. 'I have to report Christine's phone being out of order.' He watched Martin go back into the living room and then picked up the receiver and dialled 100.

'Operator assistance,' a voice answered.

'Can you give me the number for faults, please?' Harry said, then he dialled the number given.

'Faults department,' another voice announced.

Harry took a deep breath. 'I want to report a telephone line out of order, and the matter is urgent. The lady there has no other form of communication; her mother is disabled and we think she's suffering from a stroke. Yes, I do know it's late at night, but this can't wait until morning, it's imperative— All right, I'll speak to your manager then, thank you.' After a few more minutes' insistent conversation with the manager, Harry replaced the receiver. He'd been assured that they would send someone out straight away, that the matter had top priority.

For a while he stood in the hall and wondered; should he tell Martin and Sheila? After all, there was nothing wrong with his growing affection for Christine; it was all perfectly natural—that is, except for the prowlers, and the police. As if on cue his neck began to ache. He tried not to touch the sore bit, but the polo-necked sweater wasn't helping. Christine should never have whacked him like that. How on earth could he explain that incident to Martin without appearing to be a bloody idiot?

He'd try to distract his son and get him off the subject; then he had an idea. He walked into the living room and looked at his son and daughter-in-law watching TV. 'Er, I hope you two won't mind if I switch channels,' he said, 'but there's a rugby match on in five minutes. It's only on for an hour and a half....'

# TWENTY-FOUR

*A&E unit*

'HERE WE ARE, MAM,' Christine said as they entered the emergency unit. 'They'll soon have you sorted.' Christine placed her hand reassuringly on Emily's shoulder and looked down at her mother's anxious face. Not surprising she was upset, she thought, this place must be bringing back old memories. She looked around; the room was large and rectangular shaped, the nurses' desk was on her left near to the entrance, and on her right there was a long row of curtained cubicles. The air smelled of antiseptic and vomit, mingled with the stale smell of alcohol. Nurses and doctors bustled about the room, charts in hands, some entering the curtained-off cubicles, some emerging and hurrying towards the exit doors at the far end of the room, where, she supposed, the X-ray rooms and the scanners were situated.

A young nurse, chart in hand, came up to them. 'Mrs Emily Brett?' she inquired.

'That's me,' said Emily.

'Right then.' The nurse smiled down at her. 'Please come with me.' She led the way to a vacant cubicle. Christine, pushing Emily in the wheelchair, followed her. 'If you'd like to come in here and sit down whilst I just sort out the paperwork...shouldn't take a minute.'

Emily seated herself in a chair and looked nervously up at the nurse. She tried not to appear frightened. It was only her hand that hurt, not like the other time when.... She looked again at her injured hand. The thumb seemed to be turning blue. Maybe it was only a bruise, but then why couldn't she pick things up? That was the worrying bit.

'Now then, may I call you Emily?' asked the nurse.

Emily nodded.

'What the doctor will need to know, you see, is what medication you're on.'

Christine fished in her handbag and got out a piece of paper.

'I've brought a list of my mother's tablets with me,' she said as she handed them to the nurse, 'and as your records will show, she suffered a CVA just over eight months ago. Her left side is impaired, and I was worried in case this time—' She broke off and gestured towards Emily's injured hand.

The nurse nodded, took the list and made some notes, then said, 'I see.' She smiled down at Emily. 'Can you just take your coat off and roll up your sleeve so that I can do a quick blood pressure check before doctor arrives? And then we'll need a blood sample.'

Emily sighed and stood up. *Here we go again,* she thought, as she allowed Christine to help her off with her coat whilst the nurse set up the machine. *Dear God, please don't let it be anything like...that other time. I've been enough bother for Christine already.* She looked at her daughter's worried face and fought back her own fear. *I mustn't let her see I'm scared. I've got to be brave for her sake. I've got to fight back.* She tightened her jaw, sat herself back on the chair and allowed the nurse to take her blood pressure. She waited until she had finished, then said, 'All done?'

'Your blood pressure, yes.'

'Bet that's through the roof, isn't it?'

The nurse nodded. 'A bit.'

Emily smiled. In spite of her pain she looked around, then she sniffed and said loudly, 'By the heck, it doesn't half smell of pee round here.'

'Mother!' Christine reprimanded, whilst the nurse stifled a laugh.

Emily grinned. *I'm back on form again,* she thought.

Half an hour later the doctor arrived. 'Hello.' He smiled. 'I'm Dr Shan, sorry you had to wait so long but you picked a busy night.'

'We did that on purpose,' said Emily. 'We thought we'd keep you lot on your toes.'

'Mam,' Christine warned, but Dr Shan just grinned.

'Let's see your hand,' he said. He looked at it and examined the fingers gently, then peered closely at Emily and said, 'At what time did you fall, Mrs Brett?'

'Be about half past eight, I reckon, although I never looked at the clock.'

'And did you call out to your daughter?'

'Oh, I did that all right, gave me a heck of a shock, falling like that.'

Dr Shan nodded, then looked at Christine. 'Your mother's speech is not impaired, and that's always a good sign. Have they done the blood tests?'

'About ten minutes ago,' Emily replied before Christine could speak. 'I reckon you lot must have a gallon of my blood in stock by now. They took some this afternoon, you know. If they keep taking any more one of my arms is going to be empty.'

Dr Shan laughed. 'There's definitely nothing wrong with your speech or your comprehension, Mrs Brett, so now let's check out your bones.' He paused, then removed the dressing from Emily's eyebrow. 'That'll need a butterfly plaster; I'll have X-ray check that out as well as your hand, but first let's get you off to the scanner, then we can see what's what.' He wrote rapidly on the chart, smiled at them again then said, 'I'll send a porter along in a minute to take you there and I'll see you again when we've got the results.'

'Can I go with her?' Christine asked.

'As far as the scanner unit, yes,' said the doctor. 'I don't think it's a stroke, but let's be sure and check everything out first.' With that, he pulled the curtain aside and was gone.

Emily watched him go, then turned to Christine. 'He didn't believe in wasting words much, did he.'

Christine looked annoyed. 'We seem to have been here for ages and they're telling us nothing.'

Emily licked her lips. 'I could do with a cup of tea,' she remarked. She looked at Christine. 'And I never did get to drink that glass of wine you brought me. It's still there on me bedside table.' A thought occurred to her. 'Do you think it'll go off?'

'Mother,' said Christine, 'let's not worry about glasses of wine for now. We do have other things to think about, remember? Now, I'll go find nurse and see if I can get you a drink.' She strode off in the direction of the nurses' desk.

Emily sat quietly and examined her surroundings; a stretcher-type bed took up most of the cubicle. It was placed alongside the curtain which separated the cubicles and two chairs were placed close to the wall. Not exactly BUPA, but then who could afford private medicine these days? A voice crept into her mind: 'You could,' it whispered, 'with all that cash Christine has found.' Emily sat bolt upright. 'Thieves' gold,' she said out loud. And her mind returned to the events of this week. She sighed. One thing was certain; if the good Lord was going to take her off into the Great Blue Yonder, the cause of death sure wouldn't be boredom. Christine hadn't told her how much money there was. She hadn't even told her what she was going to do with it, although Emily felt sure she'd call in the cops— Emily frowned, but the thing that really worried her was that money was still there…in their house… all by itself.

CHRISTINE HURRIED THROUGH the big doors at the end of the room. 'It's the first turning on your left and then a few yards along you'll see a lift, which will take you down to the restaurant,' the nurse had said. Christine reached the lift, pressed the button to summon it, then checked her watch; close to ten, she thought nervously, and she still didn't know how bad Mam was. They'd just have to be patient. Maybe a warm drink would help them both.

As she bought the teas and some packs of biscuits her thoughts returned to Harry—and, of course, to the money. She felt relieved that she'd managed to hide the money before Mam had had her accident. What would have happened if she had fallen whilst she was still counting it at the kitchen table? Don't even go there, she told herself sternly as she strode back towards the A&E unit. But what about Harry? He'd been kindness itself, and she'd been such a nuisance, especially when his family was visiting. Once she knew what was wrong with Mam she'd phone him, although she felt sure that the doctors would want to keep her in for observation. She sighed; that was going to be another battle royal…. Her thoughts returned to Harry and the problems with the phone. She'd felt such a fool having to rush over to his house. Odd, though, that the house phone had gone dead like that; it had certainly been working when she'd phoned for a taxi earlier. Maybe there was a loose connection somewhere; she could have loosened it when she'd been vacuuming…but then, she hadn't been cleaning today. She thought again about the prowlers, and the shed, and the money; it would certainly be to their advantage if she couldn't phone the police. All it would need would be for someone with some knowledge of telephones to take out a circuit; they wouldn't need to enter the house to do it.

Strange, though, Christine thought, as she pushed the large doors open and walked back into the A&E unit. Why was it that Harry, nice as he was, was always around when something was going wrong? He was the only person who'd seen these prowlers and even then, he couldn't describe them. The thing was, was he being nice to her and Mam because he really liked them and wanted to help… or was there a darker reason for his friendliness? *Stop it!* she told herself sharply as she reached the curtained-off cubicle where Mam was resting. *Now you're getting paranoid.* She pulled back the curtain to see the porter already helping Mam into a wheelchair.

'I tried to tell him I can walk, Christine,' Emily said irritably, 'but he keeps on saying "Doctor's orders".'

The porter grinned at them. 'Got to do as I'm told, you know. So come on, you ladies, let's get you along to the scanner.'

'Give me that tea,' said Emily.

Christine handed the beaker to her. 'Careful, Mam, it's still hot.'

Emily took a grateful sip and looked up at the porter. 'Let's get a move on, then, now I've got tea to go.' With that he wheeled Emily briskly down the ward and through the doors with Christine following.

# TWENTY-FIVE

ALUN HURRIED DOWN the stairs and out onto the street. For a second he stood, keys in hand, and looked at his car that was parked there. Further along he could see the firm's grey van, which he shouldn't use unless it was on the firm's business. He gave a wry smile as he strode towards it; it was one of life's little perks, and it saved him a fortune in petrol. As he drove off, Alun's thoughts returned to the middle-aged woman, the money, and how it had all gone wrong. 'This woman must be silenced,' the boss had insisted, and he, fool that he was, had thought he'd cracked it.

Only this morning he'd sent off an anonymous letter to the police. The boss had mentioned that the local cops were fed up with this woman always reporting her neighbours; they'd pounce on an excuse to classify her as an 'unreliable witness'. When the police found the money in her shed they'd be convinced that she was involved with the thieves and the robbery. Alun sighed; putting the money in the shed had been a necessary sacrifice, but the boss had thought it would surely do the trick.

But now the stupid woman had gone and found it! Bloody bad luck on his part. How the hell was he supposed to know it would rain last night? He scowled. He knew the boss would blame him for everything and he must think of a way of, one, finding out where the money was now; two, getting it back and three, most importantly, silencing that blasted woman. Alun's hands tightened on the wheel as he drove into the car park of the A&E. The question was, how?

RICK SAT IN his car in the car park, elbows over the wheel, and glared at the sliding doors of the A&E unit. The waiting room was well lit and he could see lots of people. He couldn't see any sign of the old woman or the middle-aged one, though. He'd seen the ambulances parked down the side of the hospital—perhaps they'd come in another way. Maybe there was another entrance. He'd thought about getting out of the car and walking into the waiting area, and pretending he was looking for someone, but then he thought about Alun and he scowled. Alun had said to come here and watch out for the women, not to go find them, and if he were to get out of his car and Alun turned up there'd be another row, so he'd best stay put, with his eyes peeled.

As SOON AS he drove into the hospital A&E car park Alun spotted Rick's car. It was parked as near as Rick could get to the A&E waiting room. He saw that Rick was seated in the vehicle; at least he'd not gone walkabouts. He parked the van a few spaces away, went down to Rick's car and got in. 'Anything happening?' he asked as he slid into the seat beside him.

'Not much,' Rick said coldly, 'no sign of the two women, but the cops haven't half been busy; two lots of police cars have just pulled up and frogmarched some drunken yobbos into the waiting room in the last half hour. I'll bet the nursing staff aren't half thrilled.'

'Friday night's fisticuffs night,' Alun said. 'Trouble is, some of those little sods like having a punch-up, and if they're carrying knives they can't half cut up rough.'

'They'd better not try using knives on me,' Rick said.

He stared at Alun meaningfully, then said, 'I know all there is to know 'bout self-defence.'

Alun nodded and thought, *You mean you think you do, but I can handle you, mate, only not just yet.* Aloud he said, 'You stay here and keep watching whilst I have a scout round.' He got out of the car, strode across to the waiting room and up to the reception desk. With a charming smile he addressed the receptionist. 'I've come to collect two ladies; they came with the emergency ambulance just after nine o clock,' he looked around the waiting room, 'only I can't see them in here.'

The receptionist looked at him. 'Do you have their names?'

Alun said, 'It's a Mrs Brett, and I think the other lady is her daughter.'

The receptionist's fingers traced over the list in front of her, then she looked at the computer. 'Would that be a Mrs Emily Brett?'

'I wouldn't know about that…look, love,' he said, 'I've just come to pick them up. I'm only the taxi driver.'

The receptionist shook her head. 'Then you might have to wait a while. Mrs Brett is still receiving treatment.'

'Oh well, thanks, then. You don't know how long she'll be? Only, the meter's ticking.'

The receptionist shrugged and shook her head again. 'Impossible to say.'

'Right, I'll wait outside,' Alun said. It had been worth a try, but he already knew that tonight was going from bad to worse. He went out of the door, got back in his van and tried to think things through.

CHRISTINE SAT IN the waiting area outside the X-ray room, her eyes fixed on the flashing red light over the X-ray unit door opposite. On the door a notice read: Please do not enter when red light is on. As if anyone would, Christine thought; surely everyone knew about the risks of radiation by now. She glanced at her watch and gave a deep sigh. 10.15 p.m.; Mam had only been in that X-ray room for five minutes, but to Christine it seemed like five hours. What would they find? She'd been so sure it was the start of another stroke that she'd not given a lot of thought to the possibility that there might be fractures to Mam's hand, and she'd been surprised when Dr Shan had asked them to check out her mother's eyebrow. Still, it was good they were being so thorough but she felt sure that Dr Shan would recommend that Mam stay on in the observation ward overnight. She bit on her lip. *Stop worrying, just take one thing at a time,* she told herself firmly.

The X-ray room door opened and Emily, assisted by the radiographer, came out. The radiographer seated her carefully near the door then went back into the room.

Christine joined her mother. 'That wasn't all that bad, was it, Mam?'

'How would you know?' Emily growled. 'You've never been in there.'

'Still, it's all done with now,' Christine said reassuringly, 'we'll soon find out what's what.'

'They pulled me hand backwards and forwards and just about stood me on my head looking at me eyebrow,' Emily grumbled. She looked along the corridor. 'They told me to wait for the porter again, said the results will be along later.'

'Right,' said Christine. She smiled down at her mother. 'How do you feel now?'

Emily rubbed at her injured hand. 'The pain's gone off a bit. I feel a bit dazed, though.'

*That'll be the tablets the doctor had given her kicking*

*in,* Christine thought. She heard the sound of a wheelchair and saw the porter approaching. 'Looks like your carriage is arriving,' she said as he came up to them. She watched as the man assisted her mother into the wheelchair, then followed them back to the A&E unit.

DR SHAN PULLED back the curtain of their cubicle and beamed down at them. He looked at his clipboard, to which were attached two X-ray photos. 'How do you feel now, Mrs Brett?'

'Not bad,' Emily said, 'but I'll feel a lot better when you tell me what's wrong with me.'

'You want to know the damage, eh? Right then, the bad news is you've got a hairline fracture on the second pha-lange of your middle finger, and we think that's why you couldn't pick things up. So we're going to give it some sup-port, we're going to strap it to your ring finger.'

'Like a boy scout's salute?' Emily inquired.

The doctor grinned. 'Not quite, wrong fingers, but you were close. Now, your thumb is heavily bruised and it's probably causing more pain than the fracture. But the good news is your blood is fine, and there's no indication of a stroke. As for your eyebrow, it's just a cut, no damage to the bone—'

'I can go home then?' Emily asked eagerly. She stroked her hand and felt a sense of relief. *I can cope with this,* she thought. 'When they've strapped this up, I mean?'

Dr Shan hesitated and looked at Christine. 'We think it might be wiser if you were to stay with us overnight. You had quite a fall, Mrs Brett, and shock can do many things after an accident.'

Emily felt her mouth begin to quiver. She tightened her

lips and looked at the floor. 'I want to go home,' she whispered stubbornly.

'But Mam,' Christine bent over her and urged, 'it really might be best if you were to stay here; I'll stay with you if you like?'

Emily glowered up at her. 'But what about…y'know… the house?'

Dr Shan looked from Emily to Christine, then after a while he said, 'It's your decision, Mrs Brett, but I'd strongly recommend you stay in the observation ward overnight.'

'Mam? Please…you know it might be safer.'

'I want me own bed and I want you safe as well. I'm not stopping. So if they'll just fix me fingers…?' She held up her hand.

Dr Shan shrugged. 'Your choice, your decision.' He turned away and said, 'I'll get Sister to do the dressing and fill in the form.'

'I'm sorry about this, Doctor, but my mother is pretty stubborn. I'll do my best to look after her.'

Dr Shan smiled briefly and pulled back the curtain. 'Sister will be along shortly.' He turned and left.

Christine waited until she saw Sister approaching with the dressings trolley then turned to her mother. 'Sister's going to see to you now. I'll phone and let Harry know what's happening,'

'We are going home?' Emily insisted as she tried to control the anxiety in her voice.

'Yes, Mother, although…' Christine looked doubtful.

'Don't start that again,' Emily said. 'I'm going home if I've got to walk there myself.'

'I'm not going to argue with you when you're in this mood,' Christine said. 'I'll get back to you as soon as I've spoken to Harry.' She walked out of the cubicle and down the ward.

*10.30 p.m.*

HARRY PICKED UP the remote and switched off the television. The rugby match hadn't been too bad, but his mind had kept drifting to Christine and her mother over at the hospital. He got to his feet, went to the window and peered through the curtains. He could see that the lights were still on in the Bretts' house, but otherwise there was no sign of any cars or people lurking about. He glanced at the clock: 10.30 p.m. It was still early yet for the return of any prowlers; it had been closer to 1 a.m. the other night.

He wondered how Christine's mother was coping; she'd looked very frail when she climbed into the ambulance. Still, she was in the right place, the medics would take care of her but that could take a while, unless she was lucky and got to see a doctor straight away. His mobile buzzed, startling him. 'Hello?'

'Harry? It's me, Christine.'

'How are things over there?' Harry asked. 'Any news about your mum?'

'Yes, well I thought I'd phone and tell you that it's not a stroke—I'm really relieved about that.'

'So am I,' said Harry. 'She didn't look at all well when she left here.'

'What it is,' Christine continued, 'is damage to her middle finger. They're strapping it up right now. The doctor wanted her to stay in overnight in case of concussion, but you know what Mam's like.'

Harry couldn't help but grin. Only too well, he thought. 'At least she got seen to pretty quickly. When do you want me to pick you up?'

'That's just it, I know it's getting late and you've got your family visiting, and I don't like to bring you out all this way when I could get a taxi—'

'Nonsense,' Harry interrupted, 'of course you don't need a taxi. Martin and Sheila have already gone to bed, so no one's bothering them at all, I'll just get the car and—'

'Harry, hold on a while. Mam's still having treatment, then she's got to sign herself out and we'll also need to get painkillers for her from the ward sister. And I've no idea how long that's going to take. I think the best thing I can do is to call you again once we've got that sorted, then we can sit and wait for you in the A&E waiting room. Is that all right with you?'

'Whatever you say, Christine.'

'And Harry, Mam and I are really are grateful for all of your help. And I'm sorry about last night, really I am.'

'It's okay, but there definitely were two prowlers in your garden, I wish I could convince—'

'You've convinced me already. I know for sure we had trespassers—I can prove it—but I'll tell you more about that later, when we get home.'

Harry smiled to himself—at least she believed him now. 'All right then, Christine, but just to be sure I'll go have a quick check round outside your house whilst I'm waiting. The last thing you need is any more "visitors".'

'Thanks, Harry, I'll call as soon as we're ready. Bye.'

'Bye.' He hung up and thought for a while. Now at least Christine knew that he'd not been lying and that he was not some sort of peeping Tom. Those men had been there, all right, but what were they up to? And what was in the box they'd been carrying?

He walked into the hall, pulled on his jacket and went to get his torch. He was about to open the back door when he had an idea. He walked back into the hall, rummaged in the under-stairs cupboard and finally brought out an old cricket bat. He stood and wielded it experimentally, smiled in satisfaction, then marched outside and down his drive. If any more prowlers came his way tonight, he'd be ready for them.

As he strode down the drive he felt pleased he'd had the foresight to park Martin's car down on the road and leave his own car on the driveway once the ambulance had gone. Now he'd be able to drive straight to the hospital without any fuss or bother.

He crossed the road and went into the Bretts' front garden; no sign of any disturbances here. He wandered round to the back of the house, checked the back door, then shone his torch on the windows, making sure that none had been left open; all had been secured. Turning round he almost bumped into the conifer tree and memories of last night's incident returned. He poked at it angrily with the cricket bat and was rewarded for his efforts with a spray of raindrops. Brushing them from his face he returned to the front of the house and walked back up the drive.

It was then that he saw Kay crossing the road towards him, or rather coming towards the Bretts' house. She was clutching a small white box and her keys. 'Hello, Kay.' He smiled at her as she came up to him. 'And where are you off to at this time of night?'

Kay seemed startled to see him. 'Oh, it's you, Harry... I just wondered, has there been an accident? Only I saw an ambulance moving off a while ago. Of course, it might have been for someone who lives further down the road, but then I've been meaning to visit Christine with my peace offering, belated as it is. I thought I'd check if everything was all right.' She looked up at the Bretts' house. 'The lights are still on, I might just manage to catch her before she goes to bed.' She made as if to move past him.

'Just a minute, Kay,' Harry reached out and touched her arm. 'Yes, you did see an ambulance. Mrs Brett had a fall, but that was well over an hour ago. They're up at A&E now.'

Kay looked anxious. 'Oh, I'm so sorry. That poor old lady. Harry, I'm such a scatterbrain, I should have come out to see what was wrong when I saw the ambulance but I was waiting for an important phone call, and they don't have my mobile number so I couldn't leave the house.' She searched his face. 'Is there anything I can do? Anything at all?'

'I can't think of anything, but at least as far as I know, Mrs Brett is okay, it's not another stroke.'

Kay smiled. 'I'm relieved about that.' She looked down at the box she was carrying. 'Now, the question is, what can I do with these cream cakes? I wonder if Christine has remembered to lock the back door....' She took a step closer to Harry and gazed up at him. 'If not I could just slip in and pop these in her fridge with a note.' She licked her lips. 'It would be such a pleasant surprise for them when they got back, don't you think?'

Harry shook his head. 'Both doors are locked and the back door's bolted, Kay. I made sure of that before Christine left.' He looked down at the box. 'Perhaps you could leave the cakes until morning?'

Kay pouted. 'The cream might be sour by then,' she muttered sulkily, 'and I might have to go into work tomorrow—I've so much catching up to do.'

'If you'd give the cakes to me, I'll see that they get them, along with your apologies.' He reached out to take the box but Kay shrank back.

'No...thanks all the same,' she said stiffly. 'Don't be offended, Harry but I'd much rather do my apologies myself. I'll try to see Christine some time tomorrow.' She turned and started to walk back towards her own house. 'Goodnight,' she called.

Harry watched her hurry up her driveway. As she did so he saw her fumble in her jacket pocket and bring out some keys. It puzzled him. 'Wonder why she needs two sets of keys,' he muttered as she let herself into the house.

He looked along the road—not a soul about—and went back to his house. Christine might phone again within the hour. He walked into the kitchen and made himself a cup of strong coffee. Stifling a yawn he drank it slowly; it looked like it was going to be another long night.

'RIGHT THEN, MAM, let's get back to the waiting room,' Christine said, their footsteps hollow echoes as they walked along the corridors. She clutched her mother's arm tightly, steadying her as they moved along. 'It would have been better if we'd waited for the porter to bring us back up here, much easier on your legs.'

'That porter has more important things to do,' Emily said. 'There are a lot of sick people in that ward, they have to come first.' She scowled at her daughter. 'Besides, what makes you think I've lost the use of my legs all of a sudden? It's my finger that's gone on sick leave, nothing else.' She looked around as they walked along. 'Me mouth's ever so dry, though, I could do with another tea or coffee…is there a machine anywhere?'

Christine glanced at the bag of medicines she was carrying, and then looked at her mother. *It'll be the side effects of the painkillers that the doctor had given her that's making her feel thirsty,* she thought. 'I can remember seeing a drinks machine when I phoned from the waiting room earlier,' she said. 'Soon as we get there I'll get you a drink. We're almost there now, just through this door.' They walked back into the A&E waiting room and looked around. 'Now,' said Christine, 'let's get you settled and then I'll phone Harry to come and get us.'

Emily sat down near the door and Christine crossed the room to the drinks machine. It didn't do hot drinks so she put the money in and got a bottle of water—it would be a better choice than large amounts of Coca-Cola, she thought.

Having given Emily her water she fumbled in her purse for change, then went over to the phone booth. When she'd dialled Harry's number she listened to the ringtone and her thoughts returned to the money that she'd hidden. She felt her pulse quicken; what if someone had already got to it? What if the police had had a tip-off and gone and ram-raided the back door? She swallowed hard; she knew that sort of thing did happen, she'd seen it on TV. The police usually struck at about three in the morning, but—

'Hello?' said Harry.

Christine gulped. 'It's me,' she managed, at the same time wondering just how much she should tell him. 'We're ready to come home.'

'Right then, I'll be with you in half an hour. Try and stay near the door and I'll come and find you; if it's busy I might have to park some distance away. Is your mum okay?'

Christine looked over her shoulder at her mother quietly sipping her water. 'She's very tired, she could hardly walk straight, but otherwise she's all right.'

'I'll get there as soon as I can,' Harry said. 'See you in a while.'

'Thanks,' Christine whispered, but the line had gone dead. She put down the phone, went and sat beside her mother and looked around. The waiting room was nearly full. The patients, a lot of them looking like victims from some senseless brawl, were mostly young men. There were some girls who had had more than a few drinks too many sitting with their heads in their hands staring at the floor, and in the corner of the room a fat man sprawled in his chair was singing, 'You'll never walk alone,' in a slurred and tuneless voice.

Christine's gaze moved on. Over by reception a woman stood talking to the receptionist, holding a blood-stained cloth to the side of her face whilst beside her a little girl tugged at her coat insistently. The doors slid open and a young mother with a whimpering infant in her arms rushed across the room towards the duty nurse and addressed her worriedly.

'Makes you think, doesn't it, how much we take for granted,' Emily said quietly, nodding in the direction of the receptionist. 'You wonder how these people manage to cope with the rougher side of life.'

'I thought you'd gone to sleep, Mam.' Christine looked at her. 'Can I take it you don't feel up to telling our singer over there just who he can walk off with?'

'Not tonight.' Emily gave a tired smile. 'I just want me bed.' She tried to rub at her eyes, then scowled in irritation as she realized she was using her injured hand.

'Harry'll soon be here, Mam,' Christine said reassuringly. She leaned forward and pulled Emily's coat collar up around her neck, then looked hopefully at the door. 'Not much longer,' she said.

## TWENTY-SIX

HARRY DROVE INTO the A&E car park and, ever the optimist, drove towards the twenty-minute short-stay area near the reception waiting room in the hope of finding a space there. After five minutes he gave in. This place was always crammed full at weekends; he would have to park much further back.

Having found a space and fed the meter he walked towards the waiting room. As he approached the well-lit area he looked at the cars that were parked near there. Perhaps any minute now one of the vehicles would drive off, he thought hopefully. If so he'd have to run back to the car and grab the space—it would at least save Mrs Brett from having to walk so far. He looked along the rows of vehicles and his gaze sharpened; surely that was one of the garden centre's vans? He went towards it; it looked like the same grey van that delivered in his area. As he approached he could see that the driver's window was open and in the half light Harry saw the face of the driver, who was smoking a cigarette. Yes, it was the same lad, the one that— He stopped in his tracks as he saw a man cross the road, stride towards the grey van and angrily address the driver.

Harry stood stock-still. 'Hell's bells,' he said, 'I'm being haunted!' He recognized the man as Mr Longley, the garden centre manager, and it was plain from Longley's body stance that he was furious. Harry stood without moving for a while. He tried to eavesdrop on what Longley was saying but he was too far away to pick out the words—he could only hear the angry tones. After a minute or so he started to walk towards the waiting room again, but he felt uneasy. He knew there were such things as coincidences, but he'd seen this man three times in less than twenty-four hours—not counting his nightmare—and to his mind that was pushing coincidence a bit too far. He approached the glass doors, saw Christine and smiled and, dismissing all suspicious thoughts of Longley, strode towards her.

ALUN LIT ONE cigarette from the butt end of the other and tried hard not to cough. He knew he was smoking too much but what else could he do? The cigarettes were the only thing keeping him awake. He was trying not to doze off; he had to deal with enough dozy buggers as it was—he shot a vicious glance in the direction of Rick's car—without him falling asleep as well. He rested his elbows on the steering wheel and stared again at the waiting-room doors. Were these women ever going to come out of there? he wondered. A thought occurred to him: what if they were kept in there overnight? He shook his head. 'Don't even go there,' he muttered. In an attempt to clear the smoke from the van he wound down the window and tried to fan it away. As he did so he glanced in the wing mirror and stiffened. 'Oh shite!' he groaned. Today had been lousy enough but now it was going to get worse. He stared again in the mirror and at the familiar figure approaching him; no doubt about it, trouble was heading his way....

# TWENTY-SEVEN

'STAY IN THE WARM, Christine,' Harry said. 'I'll run back and bring the car up to the door.' He turned and hurried away.

'Are we going home or aren't we?' Emily muttered as she sank back down on a chair.

'Be patient, Mam,' Christine said. 'Harry won't be a minute, and you don't want to walk all that way to the car, do you?'

'All I want is me bed.' Emily sighed. She looked thoughtful, then said, 'Well that and a nice relaxing drink.' She gazed up at her daughter with an innocent expression.

Suspicion dawned in Christine's mind. *I'll bet she's gone and remembered that glass of wine,* she thought, and wine is the last thing she needs when she's on strong medication.

'If I remember rightly,' she said, 'we've still got some of that lovely hot chocolate that you like at home, and if I'm not mistaken there's a tub of double cream in the fridge, which I could put on top. That should be nice and comforting for you—'

'I was saving that cream for the apple pie on Sunday,' Emily snapped irritably.. 'Apple pie doesn't taste right with just…custard.'

'All right, Mam,' Christine said soothingly, 'we can always get some more for Sunday. It's not as if there's a world shortage of cream.' She looked through the glass door and saw with relief that Harry's car was pulling up outside. She helped her mother to her feet. 'Come on, then, Harry's here, let's get off home.'

ALUN SAT AND watched the women come out of A&E, get into the bloke's car and drive off. He keyed in Rick's number. 'They're out, Rick, get ahead of them. Looks like they're going home.'

'I saw 'em as well as you,' Rick yelled. 'And that bloke's back with them, did you notice?'

'I'm not blind and I'm not deaf, so watch it, will you,' Alun snapped.

'I've been sitting in this sodding car for hours now,' Rick protested. 'I'm tired and I'm hungry, and there weren't no sign of any bloody box, either. I reckon it's still in the house and I've had all this bother for nothing.'

Alun's patience snapped. 'Shut it, will you,' he shouted. 'Get off that sodding mobile and move it! I'll follow. The boss will deal with you later.' He watched as with an angry squeal of brakes Rick's car roared out of the car park. So much for discreet surveillance, he thought wryly. The boss should never have taken Rick on; he'd always said that. Except for his skills as a safe man, Rick was a walking disaster area.

Alun gave a deep sigh and drove out of the car park. He felt irritable and bone weary and he knew that tomorrow wouldn't get any better. He'd already taken an ear-bashing from old Longley tonight 'cause he'd spotted him using the firm's van and followed him here, and now they had to sort out this bloody woman. He pounded his fist on the steering wheel; who would have thought that one stupid witness could manage to ruin the whole bloody plan? It should be simple to silence her…but now there was this bloke. Who was he? Yes, he knew he was the man he delivered gardening stuff to, but what was the man's connection with the woman? He glanced hopefully down at his mobile on the seat beside him…and still no further instructions? He rubbed at his eyes as he drove along; they felt gritty and dry. Best do as he'd told Rick; drive back to the house and make sure they got there, and that all was well.

As HE DROVE along Harry looked in the rear-view mirror at Emily, who was seated in the back. She had her eyes closed and seemed to be dozing. He smiled at Christine, who was sitting beside him. 'How is she?' he asked quietly.

'She's coping well, but she's tired. She should have stayed in overnight like they said, but she wasn't having it.' Christine gave a weary smile. 'You know what Mam's like—'

'I heard that!' said a voice from the back seat of the car. 'Will you two stop talking 'bout me as if I was gaga?'

Christine turned in her seat to look at her. 'I'm just telling Harry what happened, about how the doctor said you should stay in.'

'Well I didn't, so there!' Emily said. 'Not when we've got all these goings on at our house.' She hesitated, then said quietly, 'Are you going to tell Harry what happened just before I fell?'

'I was about to…' Christine looked at her mother meaningfully '…but somebody keeps on interrupting me.'

There came an irritated snort from the back seat of the car, then, 'Go on then, get on with it.'

'I'm all ears,' Harry said, smiling encouragingly at Christine.

CHRISTINE TOOK A deep breath and instead of looking at Harry, stared at the road ahead. She wanted to tell him what had happened—he'd every right to know and he'd been so kind to them—but…. An uneasy thought stirred in her mind. She knew from bitter experience that men were not always what they seemed to be. She thought about Charles, her ex-husband, and repressed a shudder. How many times in the past had she trusted him and how many times had he betrayed her? She risked a swift glance at Harry's rugged face; but this man was not Charles and she must at least tell him something. He'd been right about seeing two men with a box and she should tell him that she'd found it, but, the question was, she thought, warily, should she tell him about the contents? Did she really trust him enough to tell him about the money? And where she'd hidden it?

'Come on, Christine.' Harry's voice reached her. 'I was right, wasn't I? Someone was prowling around in your garden last night, and I really wasn't trying to pinch your lawnmower as you thought.'

In spite of her cautiousness Christine smiled at him. 'Yes, I'm sorry I doubted you last night, I was wrong about that.' She looked at him anxiously and asked, 'How is your neck, by the way?'

Harry pulled a face and fingered his polo-necked sweater. 'It stills aches a bit, but enough about that. Tell me, did you find the box?'

Christine swallowed hard and glanced away. 'Yes, I did. And you were right about that as well.'

'Well that's a relief,' Harry said as they pulled up out-side her house, 'I was beginning to think I was halluci-nating.' He got out of the car, went to the rear door and helped Emily out, then turned back to Christine. 'Did you find out what was in it?' he asked.

Christine took a deep breath, avoiding his gaze, then said, 'No, I thought it looked suspicious and I decided that I'd better leave it as it was.' She looked down, fumbled with her house keys and opened the front door. 'I was going to phone the police, but then, as you know, Mam fell and then my phones didn't work....'

'And that's when you came to our rescue,' Emily said as she limped through the door. She stood on the threshold and looked over her shoulder at Harry. 'And usually I'd say come in, Harry, and have a hot drink, but I'm blooming freezing and I'm just about asleep standing up, so I'll say thanks again and I'll see you in the morning.' She went into the hall.

Christine watched her go then looked at Harry. 'I'm sorry, I'll have to go. I don't want her climbing those stairs by herself. I'd better make sure she's all right, in case she stumbles again.' She gazed up at Harry with troubled eyes, kissed him lightly on his cheek, then edged towards the door.

'Yes, of course,' Harry said. 'I've reported your phone, by the way, it should be okay. Oh, and Kay wanted to visit you; she was about to call on you earlier with a peace of-fering—' he glanced along the road at Kay's house '—but she'll come and see you tomorrow, she said.' He looked at her; he wanted to give her a reassuring hug but she seemed tense. He took a backward step. 'We can talk more to-morrow.'

Christine seemed not to hear; she looked anxiously at the door and edged towards it.

He got in the car and called, 'Meanwhile, if there's any-thing, anything at all, you know where I am.'

'Thanks, Harry, for all that you've done.' Christine smiled and then quietly closed the door.

Harry sat in the car and stared at the closed door. Some-thing was not quite right, he thought. He didn't know what it was, but there was something in Christine's attitude that didn't fit. He drove the car up his drive, got out and went into the kitchen, his mind awash with the events of the night. He stood for a while listening, hoping that he'd not disturbed his family but all was still. He'd felt tired earlier, but now he was wide awake, and didn't feel a bit like going to bed. *Perhaps the coffee I drank earlier was too strong,* he thought. He wandered into the living room and picked up the evening paper; that might take his mind off things.

It was no use; as soon as he opened the paper there it was, a bloody great half-page advert of the garden centre proclaiming its special offers. Harry sighed in exasperation and his thoughts began to ricochet from garden centre to van to Longley to driver to box and to Christine. That was it! Christine and the box. That was the question. Why hadn't Christine opened the box?

It was so unlike a woman, Harry thought. The newspaper dropped unnoticed to the floor as his mind went back to the days when his late wife received parcels and packages and he smiled in reminiscence. Susie was always so excited when she received a parcel or a present; she would dash into the kitchen to get the scissors and attack it with gusto, eager to see what was inside. She would never have waited calmly until the next day.

Was Christine so calm and so controlled that she would behave that way? Harry grinned and shook his head. From what he knew of her she'd never struck him as being the calm unflappable type; not only that, she was downright nosy. So why wasn't she telling him the truth? A scary question crept into his mind: what the devil was in that box?

AFTER A FEW minutes Alun turned into Poole Road and parked the van some distance away from the women's house. He glanced at his watch: close to midnight. He looked along the road: no lights on anywhere except for the women's house. He saw the man drive his car up the driveway and go into his house and felt a slight sense of relief. So far so good; everyone was now back where they should be, at least for the time being. He looked further along the road and saw Rick's car parked without lights. With a weary sigh Alun flashed his headlights at him and his mobile rang instantly in response. Alun picked it up. 'Hello?'

'They're all in,' Rick said peevishly, 'now can I go home?'

'You may as well.'

'What about tomorrow, then?'

'I dunno…I'm waiting for instructions from the boss.'

'Will I be needed?'

'I keep telling you, I don't know. I'll call you first thing if you are.' Alun's phone went dead. He watched as Rick's car shot past him and then he slumped deeper into his seat. He scowled down at the mobile that he'd flung onto the seat beside him as if willing it to ring. It remained silent. He brought out a pack of cigarettes and lit one. For the time being there was little else he could do, except to follow his instructions and wait for the boss to call.

EMILY WALKED INTO the house, cast a quick look over her shoulder and headed for the stairs.

'Where you going, Mam?' Christine called up after her.

'Gotta use the loo,' Emily said.

'Hang on a second, I'll come with you.'

Emily stopped on mid-stair and glared at her daughter. 'I do know where the loo is, and just because I fell doesn't mean I need potty training.'

'Better safe than sorry,' Christine said as she climbed the stairs to join her. 'These steps are pretty steep, Mam, and the painkillers they gave you were strong ones. I know you'll be all right in the bathroom, but I don't want you slipping on the way there.'

Emily reached the landing and turned to stare at her daughter. 'I hope you're not going to start following me around like this.' She eyed her bedroom door, then turned towards the bathroom with reluctance. 'This is my home, I know my way around it and just because I hurt my hand, it doesn't mean I'm going doolally.' She limped into the bathroom, locking the door behind her.

CHRISTINE LOOKED AT the bathroom door. She was about to reason with her mother when she remembered the glass of wine on her mother's bedside table. The penny dropped. So that was what she was up to. She smiled and hurried into her mother's bedroom. It was not that she begrudged her a drink, but she'd taken strong painkillers and there was the risk of concussion.

Feeling like a mean spoilsport she picked up the glass and looked at it. She heard the sound of the bathroom door being unlocked and knew she was short of time. She'd never get past Mam with the wine now. There was only one thing to do: she gulped down the wine and hid the glass in her coat pocket. She was only just in time.

Emily stood in the doorway looking at her. 'Now what are you up to?' she said as her gaze strayed towards the bedside table.

'Just looking for your hot water bottle, I thought it might ease the pain on your hand.'

Emily clicked her tongue. 'It's where it always is, hanging up in the bathroom, as you well know.'

'You're right, I forgot,' Christine said. 'Are you going to stay up here and get undressed whilst I make you that hot chocolate? I'll bring the hot water bottle up with it in a minute.'

Emily sank down on the bed. 'Yes, that would be nice,' she said. 'I think I could manage a few biscuits as well.' She looked at the bedside table. 'Do you know, I'm sure I left a glass of wine on there.' She looked at her daughter inquiringly.

'You did?' Christine looked around. 'That's funny, I must have cleared it away earlier,' she lied, 'but never mind.' She smiled at her mother reassuringly. 'You can have a glass with your lunch tomorrow. You know as well as I do, alcohol and painkillers don't work well together.'

Emily stifled a yawn. 'Well, I would have liked...but I suppose I'd better play safe.' She shot a quick look at he daughter, then said quietly, 'And I suppose you were playing safe when you didn't tell Harry 'bout the cash.'

Christine edged towards the door. 'What Harry doesn't know can't worry him; he's done enough for us, besides I'm not yet ready to tell him—'

'Fair enough, if you feel you can't trust him....'

Christine bit on her lip. 'Mam,' she said, 'after the way Charles betrayed me, I've found that trust, when it's broken, takes a long time to heal.' She turned and walked out of the room.

# TWENTY-EIGHT

EMILY LISTENED TO the sound of her daughter's footsteps going down the stairs and sighed; she undressed and eased herself into bed. Leaning back against the pillows she nursed her injured hand and scowled at it in irritation. 'I bet I'll have to sleep on me back now I've done this,' she muttered, 'then I'll start snoring again.' She stifled another yawn; she needed to sleep.

*Think of something else,* she told herself, *then you won't feel the pain so much.* She thought about Christine and about the money that was downstairs, and remembered that her daughter hadn't told her how much it was. What cunning and cruel people those crooks were, attempting to corrupt Christine like that. She searched for the right word; entrapment, yes that's what folk called it, making it look as if her Christine was involved in their crimes…how evil was that?

From what she'd seen of the money it looked like it could be a lot, and in their circumstances with only her pension and disability allowance, and with Christine being out of work it was very tempting— A question sprang into her mind. Startled, Emily eased herself upright into a sitting position. How did the crooks know about their finances? It wasn't the sort of thing that she or Christine would talk about to strangers. She pondered; it had to be someone who knew them.

CHRISTINE WENT INTO the kitchen, got the milk for the hot chocolate from the fridge and noted with relief that the box was still in there. Closing the fridge door she straightened up and scanned the room anxiously; no sign of any break-in from the back door and the lock on the kitchen window was still intact.

She made the drink and placed it on the tray, put some biscuits on a plate and tried to stop herself from hiccuping. She should never have gulped Mam's wine down like that, especially since she'd not eaten much, but she'd had to stop Mam from drinking it. Picking up the tray she paused, and for a split second her gaze drifted towards the pantry door; that, too, was still bolted. She nodded with satisfaction and went upstairs knowing that, for the moment, everything was as before.

*1.30 a.m.*

'SOD IT ALL to hell!' Alun woke to the smell of burning and slapped furiously at the hole in his jeans where his cigarette had fallen. On the seat beside him his mobile rang insistently. Angrily he picked it up. 'What? Oh, it's you,' he said irritably. 'I was beginning to think you'd never call me back.'

'You know me better than that.'

'Well, you could have called earlier, I've been sitting here half the sodding night, babysitting these bloody women, and I'm just about dead on me feet.'

'Be quiet. You can sleep later. I have some jobs for you. Get a pen and some paper.'

'What the hell—? Can't you just tell me what you want, boss? I'm not a bleeding secretary, you know.'

'That's enough. There are several things I want you to do. Everything has gone wrong on this job. Write this down so that there can be no more mistakes. Do you get that? Now, get paper and a pen.'

'All right! I'm just as pig sick of this as you are,' Alun said. He rummaged in the glove compartment, found an old delivery note and a stub of pencil and pressed the paper against the dashboard in readiness. So? What now?

'This is what I want you to do....'

CHRISTINE CAME BACK downstairs into the kitchen, pulled out a chair and sank down on it. She felt strangely numb. Emily had just told her of her suspicions and she was surprised that she'd not thought of them before. She had been convinced it was the van driver, but to discover there might be someone else involved, someone who knew all about them? What was she to do?

Her gaze drifted towards the hall phone and she hoped that it was working. She should phone the police right now and tell them about the money, but.... She looked at her watch: 2 a.m. Would they come out at this hour of the morning, especially as she'd called them out the night before?

She folded her arms on the kitchen table and rested her head on them for a second. She should phone the cops, or at least check if the hall phone was okay, but the wine had made her drowsy. She'd do it in a minute, she told herself. Her stomach rumbled and she frowned, trying to remember the last time she'd eaten something. She didn't feel all that hungry so she eyed the biscuit tin, then shook her head; she couldn't fancy anything sweet; better to make a sandwich. A fried egg one would do. She got up, got out the eggs, switched on the cooker and stared sleepily at the halogen hob as it turned red.

Having made the sandwich she bit into it with relish and felt much better. Walking into the hall she picked up the phone and checked the ringtone. Yes, all was well. Her thoughts returned to Harry; if it hadn't been for him helping them out with the phone and giving them a lift, what would she have done? She smiled shyly as she thought about him, such a kind and thoughtful man, but…was he all he seemed to be? Was he all that she wanted him to be? Her thoughts drifted again to what her mother had told her earlier. Or would she be betrayed once more?

*Pull yourself together, woman,* she told herself sharply, *you have other things to think about; the money, for instance, the police, and most importantly*—she walked to the stairs and stood listening to the faint sound of her mother snoring gently—*Mam.*

Christine returned to the hall phone and stared down at it again. At the moment it was her only lifeline; she would have to get to the shops and get a new mobile as soon as she could. Her hand hovered indecisively over the receiver…she should phone the police. If she didn't, and the line went down again, and the thieves came and tried to get their money back, then what would she do?

'You'd run outside and scream like hell, like any sane woman would,' she muttered. She looked again at her watch. In a few more hours it would be daylight and yet she felt too scared to go to bed.

Her lips tightened and she wandered into the living room, crossed to the window and peered out into the night. Darkness all around, not a soul about. She went to the sofa, punched a few cushions and flopped down. There was little she could do except wait until daybreak.

# TWENTY-NINE

THE ALARM CLOCK rang loudly, forcing Alun to leap from his bed and knock the clock, still ringing, to the floor. He picked it up, switched off the alarm, then stared at the time in disbelief: 7 a.m., it couldn't be that time already, could it? He'd hardly closed his eyes. He pulled on a sweater and his jeans, staggered into the kitchen and peered at the wall clock: five minutes past seven. It was no use, he'd have to get a move on and get the van back up to the garden centre, then persuade one of the early shift workers to drop him back here.

He thought again about the boss's instructions and shook his head—no way could he risk using the firm's van after Longley had told him off last night. Walking over to the fridge he got out a can of Coke and took a large gulp from it; he needed the caffeine. Then he went into the bathroom and washed his face, rinsing his gritty eyes again and again with the ice-cold water. He had to be awake, he had to be alert, and most of all he needed time to think. Fishing in his jeans pocket he pulled out the crumpled bit of paper and re-read what the boss had dictated to him. Then he picked up his keys, went down the stairs, got in the van and drove to the garden centre.

'ARE YOU READY, Grandpa?' Liam jiggled up and down beside the kitchen table. 'Dad's got the car out.'

'All right, Liam.' Regretfully Harry abandoned his toast and got up from the table.

'Don't rush yourself, Dad,' said Martin. 'It won't hurt him much to wait.'

'No, it's all right; we've got a good hour's drive ahead of us,' Harry said. *I'm not going to spoil Liam's day out just because I've been up half the night,* he thought. He walked towards the door and said, 'I wonder what Thomas the Tank Engine has for breakfast, Liam. Do you reckon it might be cornflakes?'

Liam looked astonished. 'Don't be silly, Grandpa, don't you know steam engines only eat coal?' He trotted off down the driveway.

Liam's mum, Sheila, was already down at their car waiting when Harry joined them. She and Liam got in the back whilst Harry went to sit next to Martin, who was driving. As Harry climbed into the car he looked across the road at the Bretts' house, but the curtains were still drawn. He'd meant to tell Christine he'd be away for today but with all the drama of last night he'd forgotten to mention it. It was still early, just past eight o'clock. Perhaps he could phone her later? Then he remembered he'd given her his mobile number; he felt sure that if there was anything urgent she'd call him.

'Ladies across the road still asleep, then?' Martin smiled as they drove off down the street.

'I suppose so,' Harry replied. 'They had a busy night, but the old lady, that's Mrs Brett, is okay. She gave us a bit of a scare, though. We thought she might be having another stroke.'

'And who is "we"?' Martin teased. 'Now, Dad, what have you been up to?'

'Just helping out ladies in distress,' Harry said, 'not that it's any of your business.'

'I like to be in the loop,' Martin said. 'We don't want any surprise elopements, you know.'

Harry felt his face flush and he touched the sore patch on his neck instinctively. 'You keep your eyes on the road and don't you worry about me.' He looked over his shoulder at Liam. 'We don't want your dad getting lost on the way to see Thomas, do we, Liam? That would never do.' He glanced at his son. 'So, if you take the M1 and head due north, we might be lucky and manage to get ahead of the traffic.'

Martin nodded. 'Already heading that way, Dad. No worries.'

Harry leaned back in his seat and stared blankly out of the window; he felt a bit tired after rushing around last night. Of course, nodding off in the armchair, waking at 3 a.m. and having to creep up the stairs to his bed in fear of waking his family hadn't helped much, either. He watched the flow of traffic coming relentlessly towards them, all heading for the city of Leeds. Business was business, and on a Saturday the city centre would be hectic. It was a good job that they were heading in the opposite direction. *In what direction are you heading, Harry?* The question came without warning into his head. What exactly were his feelings about Christine? Christine was a good-looking woman; more than that, she was a caring woman, he'd seen that in the way she looked after her mother, but a sense of wariness overcame him. She was over-imaginative—too bloody over-imaginative at times—and why hadn't she told him the truth about the box? Knowing Christine he was sure that she'd opened it. As for the contents—

'Are you taking a quick forty winks then, Dad?' Martin's voice reached him.

'No,' Harry blustered, 'just watching the world go by. Whereabouts are we?' he asked, leaning forward and peering through the windscreen.

'Just about to turn onto the M1,' Martin said. 'At least

the traffic's getting a bit thinner.' He looked at Harry. 'I was thinking, on the way back, if there's time, that is, I wondered if we could drive over to Halifax and have a look at the Eureka Museum? Some friends of ours have told us it's a great place for kids.' He glanced at his son. 'And fun for budding engineers.'

'Fine with me.' Harry smiled. He looked back at his grandson.

'Let's see how much time we've got when we've seen Thomas. What do you reckon about that, then, Liam?'

Liam leaned forward excitedly. 'Will there be lots of toys there, Grandpa?'

Harry pursed his lips. 'Oh, I should think we might find one or two.'

# THIRTY

*Saturday 11 a.m.*

EMILY GROANED AND opened her eyes. Trying not to move too much she tentatively took hold of her throbbing hand and held it to her chest. Her fingers touched the dressing and she remembered. She peered at the injured hand and gave a deep sigh. 'Thank God it wasn't another stroke,' she whispered. 'This, I can put up with.' Slowly she eased herself out of bed and got washed with difficulty, and then with a struggle, managed to dress herself. She put on her glasses and looked in the mirror. What she saw made her start with shock. What stared back at her was an old woman with a nasty-looking black eye. Emily removed her spectacles, gave them a thorough rub and, putting them on again, refocused…the result was the same. She touched the injured area gingerly, her hand hovering over the butterfly strips on her eyebrow. 'I look like Dracula's daughter.' She went out onto the landing and eased herself down the stairs. *What I need now is fortification,* she thought, as she clutched the handrail. A good strong cup of tea and a couple of painkillers will do for a start.

Christine was on the phone and had just finished talking to the police when she looked up and saw her mother coming down the stairs. Horrified, she slammed down the receiver and clasped her hands to her mouth. 'Mam!' she cried, and rushed towards her.

'Don't fuss, girl,' Emily said, 'it looks far worse than it

is, but by the heck, I couldn't half do with some of those pills from the hospital.'

Christine took Emily gently by the arm and guided her into the kitchen. 'Sit yourself down for a minute.' She stared down at her mother and chewed on her lip.

'Now what?' Emily said.

'It's just…when I think…I brought all this on you, and you have to suffer like this.'

'You only forgot to take up the bathmat. That could happen to anyone.'

'Mam, you know what I'm talking about. I meant the robbers, and the money.'

'I heard you talking to the police,' Emily said, 'are they coming round?'

'Someone's coming, yes, so don't worry. I couldn't get hold of the sergeant in charge of the case, but the officer who took the call earlier wrote down my message and said he'll get it to him as soon as he can.'

Emily looked up at her daughter. 'And then what?'

'Well, I would hope he'll come round here; or phone me.'

Emily thought about this for while. 'Did you tell them how much money we've got here?' she asked slyly.

Christine looked flustered and avoided her mother's gaze. 'No, I didn't, I mean it's not something you would say over the phone. I'll tell them when they get here.' She went to the cupboard, got out the bottle of tablets and read the label. 'Now it says you've got to have some food before you take these,' she said briskly, changing the subject. She smiled down at her. 'So tell me, what would you like to eat?'

A slow smile spread over Emily's lips as her gaze drifted towards the fridge. Opportunity, she thought, never knocks twice. 'A couple of sausages would do for a start, and if I remember rightly there's some bacon in the fridge, and I wouldn't mind a couple of eggs as well—I could really fancy a good fry-up.'

'Mother!' Christine protested.

Emily sat bolt upright and stared at her daughter. 'After all,' she said defiantly, 'I am an invalid, and after what I've been through, what with me arm, me eyebrow and these bloody robbers, I reckon I've more than earned it.'

'All right then,' Christine said with reluctance. She went to the fridge and got out the food. 'But you know as well as I do that a fry-up like this is poison for you.'

'I've got past caring,' Emily said blithely as she watched her daughter putting the sausages in the frying pan. 'I'm getting quite gung-ho about it all.' She leaned forward, sniffed at the aroma of the frying sausages and licked her lips. 'And you might chuck in some mushrooms and fried bread as well,' she added. 'After the week I've had I might as well go the whole hog.'

Christine stood silently in the kitchen doorway watching her mother enjoy her breakfast, then she picked up the bottle of pills again, placed two tablets on the kitchen table and remembered with a start that the hospital had only given her a twenty-four hour supply. Today was Saturday! The local chemist's would certainly be closed tomorrow. She wondered if she could ask the chemist to deliver the tablets, perhaps she could phone— She paused, remembering that her mobile was now useless, and, after the problems she'd had with the hall phone, she needed to get another one. The question was, when?

Emily finished her breakfast, swallowed the tablets and turned round to look at her daughter. 'Now what's the matter? You've got that panicky look again.' She eyed her critically. 'Have you eaten anything this morning? I've not seen you touch a thing.'

'I had an egg sandwich last night,' Christine said, 'and I've had a glass of water this morning. I feel too queasy to eat anything yet.'

Emily got up, picked up her plate and put it in the washing-up bowl. She turned on the tap. 'Perhaps you'll feel better when the cops have been.' She grinned at Christine. 'I just hope it's not the Pinky and Perky that visited us the other night.' She was about to wash up the breakfast things when Christine intervened.

'Leave it, Mam, I'll do that. You go sit down.' She went over to the sink, washed up and cleared the breakfast things and as she did so, she wondered how long it would be before the police came to see her, or even returned her call. Surely it would be sometime this morning, but if it wasn't? What then?

She turned and walked through the hall into the living room. Crossing to the window she looked out across the road at Harry's house. Not a soul out there, she thought, and no cars parked outside either. Perhaps they'd all gone into Leeds shopping. If so, they should be back sometime in the early afternoon.

She looked further along the road at Kay's house; no sign of life there either. Harry had said something last night about Kay coming to the house to apologize while they were at the hospital. He'd said she'd even brought some cream cakes for them. Christine frowned at the thought, but then Harry had added that Kay had said she would call on her this morning, Christine sighed; so far there was no sign of her.

Christine thought again about Harry; maybe she should phone him and ask him to get a mobile phone for her. He'd told her she should call him if she needed anything, and if he was already in the city then— She stopped short, her hopes dashed. It was no good, he couldn't get Mam's tablets; the chemist wouldn't issue them without a prescription and she had that here.

'I thought I heard a car drive off early this morning.' Emily yawned as she joined her daughter at the window. 'But then again it might have been the milkman.'

Christine turned round, letting the net curtain fall back into place. 'Harry's got visitors, Mam. His son and his wife and grandson are here for the weekend, I guess they've all gone out for the day.'

'Wish we could,' Emily said ruefully, stifling another yawn. 'Instead we're stuck here waiting for the rozzers or the robbers, or whoever decides to visit us first.'

'Mam! You can't really think that the thieves would have the nerve to return here in broad daylight?'

Emily frowned. 'Don't you ever read the papers? Most burglaries happen in the daytime…you should know; you witnessed one yourself.'

'But that was different.'

'Well I'm not going to argue with you.' Emily sat down and struggled clumsily to pick up the remote and switch on the TV. 'We'll just have to wait for the cops to arrive.'

Christine watched her with concern. 'Mam?' she said cautiously, 'I've been thinking, if I were to phone for a taxi, you could go and visit Uncle Jimmy for the weekend. I'll phone him, I'm sure he won't mind, just until this blows over.'

Emily switched off the TV and turned to stare at Christine in alarm. 'You want me to go see our Jimmy?'

'Just for today and maybe tomorrow. You've been through enough and I thought—'

'You'd really wish my brother Jimmy on me? In my state of health? You know very well it's not Easter, and we're two months away from Christmas—it's bad enough that we have to visit him then.'

'He's your big brother, Mam, and you'd be safe there.'

'You know what it's like in our Jimmy's house; he lives in a permanent fog, him and his ruddy pipe, he's always puffing away. It makes me eyes water every time I go see him.'

'But it might be better than here. You're not very well, and what with all this stress….I could just phone him— shall I?'

Emily struggled to her feet and glared at her daughter. 'You'll do no such thing! I'm not leaving you here by yourself. I tell you this, I am not going there, not without a respirator, and even worse, if you phone him now and tell him what's happened, *he* might come *here!*' She pushed past Christine, went into the kitchen and switched the kettle on. 'These tablets are making me thirsty,' she said crossly, by way of explanation, 'so I'm making myself another brew.'

Christine followed her and noticed again how shaky her mother's hand was as she poured the boiling water into the mug. *No,* she thought, *that won't work, she's too agitated, and if I pressure her it will make it worse.* 'It was just a thought, I'll leave it, so don't worry.'

Emily stirred her tea furiously and managed a brief nod.

Best get out of the way for a while, Christine thought. 'I'm just going to tidy the bathroom, then,' she said, 'I noticed a few blood spots on the tiles.' She went upstairs.

Emily didn't deign to reply. She picked up her mug, sat down at the kitchen table and drank her tea. Where did Christine manage to get such daft ideas from? Fancy expecting her to go and stay with Jimmy, just when all this was going on here. As if she would ever leave her here all by herself to deal with the cops, or the crooks.

She gulped down the last of her tea, got up, rinsed the cup at the sink and placed it on the draining board. When she'd done that her gaze flicked down towards the oven;

she'd already earmarked it for cleaning this week. It was a job she always hated but now....She looked at her injured hand and smiled; at least she'd got a good excuse for postponing it.

She looked around the kitchen; there must be something she could do, even with an injured hand. She didn't want to wander round the house doing nothing, or sit watching the telly all day; she'd be bored out of her skull by teatime. She glanced at the ceiling and listened; she could hear Christine moving about in the bathroom, cleaning. She'd wanted to ask her about so many things, such as where the money was, and how much was there, for she knew she'd hidden it. What would Christine tell the police sergeant, when he finally got here? Another question crept into her mind: what would her daughter tell the thieves if they contacted her?

Emily shivered at the thought, went into the living room and stared out of the window. The road was empty, not a soul about. She walked back to the hall and looked up the stairs. Hearing the sound of the vacuum cleaner being switched on she pulled a face. The bathroom had been thoroughly cleaned on Thursday; there was no need for that. She knew that Christine was avoiding her because she had so many questions, but she needed answers.

Wandering back into the kitchen she stood in the doorway looking at the wall cabinets. Her gaze came to rest on the small cabinet over the draining board next to the back door. Christine called it the spices cabinet, but that was the posh name for it; she knew it as the 'odds and sods' cupboard, wherein just about everything was stashed. She nodded happily and limped towards it; it was bound to need tidying.

Upstairs Christine switched off the vacuum cleaner and listened yet again for the ringing of the phone but there was nothing. She sighed, put away the vacuum cleaner and went into her bedroom. She looked in the mirror; if the police were coming to see her she'd better freshen up and make herself look presentable. Having done this she looked at her watch: close to two. Surely the police hadn't forgotten?

SERGEANT FARRELL STARED at his mobile and thought about the call he'd just received from Leeds HQ. 'We've received an anonymous letter regarding the Brett case,' the officer had said. 'It claims that a Miss Christine Brett is involved with the recent hypermarket robbery and that there is evidence at her house to prove it. Can you please investigate further.'

He sighed and fought back a sense of frustration. Here he was, stuck in York, trying to close a case and meeting with constant delays. He'd already received an urgent message from Leeds about the Brett case first thing this morning; and now this. There was nothing else for it—he'd best phone her. He keyed in the number.

The hall phone rang and Christine raced down the stairs and picked up the receiver. 'Hello?' she said anxiously.

'Miss Brett?'

'Yes.'

'It's Sergeant Farrell here.'

'Oh, thank heavens for that, I called the police—'

'Yes, I know and since then we've received some further information,' Sergeant Farrell replied, though he didn't mention what that information was. 'I got your message and I'm doing my best to get to your house as soon as I can, only, the thing is I'm stuck here on a case in York. I'd hoped we'd have finished with it by noon, but it's dragging on. Anyhow, I'll get to you at some time today, probably by early evening.'

'Can't you give me an exact time?' Christine pleaded.

'I wanted to get a prescription made up from the chemist. They close at five, and I don't like leaving my mother alone.'

'Isn't there a friendly neighbour that could stay with her?' the sergeant said. 'Surely you can find someone?' He gave a weary sigh then said, 'Miss Brett, I promise you, I'll be with you as soon as I possibly can.' There came a click and the sound of an empty line.

Christine stared at the receiver, then slammed it down on its rest. That was just the problem, she thought: apart from Harry, she didn't have any friendly neighbours; *you brought this on yourself because of your nosiness,* a small voice in her head reminded her.

'Was that the police?' Emily called out from the kitchen.

'Yes.' Christine joined her mother. 'It was a Sergeant Farrell, seems he might not get here until early evening.'

'At least you know he's not forgotten us.'

'But I have to get your medication, Mam. You've only enough pills for today.'

'I'll be all right by myself; get yourself off to the chemist.'

'I'll have to get a taxi—it'll be quicker than getting the bus. I need to go into town to get a new mobile as well—' She stopped in mid-sentence as she saw Emily's guilty look. 'Oh don't look so upset, Mam, what you did could have happened to anyone.'

'But I keep making more and more work for you; it isn't as if you've not got enough to deal with already.'

'Things happen, Mam,' Christine said as she went to the freezer, got out a lasagne and placed it on the draining board. 'I thought we'd have that for dinner.' She looked at her mother. 'Now what would you like for lunch?'

'Don't worry about me, I've just had a big breakfast and if I get a bit peckish there's some leftover soup from yesterday, I can soon warm that up,' Emily replied. She watched as Christine hurried into the hall, picked up the phone and began to dial, then she sighed and limped into the kitchen. *Once she's gone,* she thought, *I'll make a start on the cupboard.*

# THIRTY-ONE

'THANKS, MATE,' ALUN called as he jumped out of the van, 'have a good day.' He watched as the driver pulled away. He looked at his watch and tried to suppress a sense of panic: just after two. There was a job to be done; two problems to deal with. He was running out of time.

All would have been well if he hadn't been press-ganged into doing an extra delivery and helping the other bloke with some loading, all because some silly sod driver had decided to call in sick. He'd wanted to argue, but he didn't want to draw any more attention to himself. He cursed silently; it was going to be one of those days.

'Focus,' he told himself, as he ran up the steps and entered his flat. He looked down at his ready-packed hold-all; all he needed was in there. He went into the bedroom and did a final check: drawers and wardrobe all empty; no letters or papers lying around. All he needed to do now was to take the bed linen down to the Salvation Army used clothing bin at the end of the road—shove it in there and it would be as if he'd never existed. He picked up the linen and the holdall, took one last look around the living room and walked out of the door.

A few minutes later he got out his mobile and keyed in a number.

'Hello?'

'Pack your gear, get hold of Pete, don't forget your passports and get yourselves round to my place by half three.'

'This is it, then?' Rick said. Alun could hear the excitement in his voice. 'I know for a fact that's Pete's all ready; he's been raring to go for days now. We're at "go" then?'

'Yep. Just two problems to deal with, and this last job, then it's over.'

'I'm on my way.'

'Don't forget to clear up—' Alun yelled then stopped in midsentence: he was already speaking to an empty line. He switched off angrily. 'Bloody moron, he never listens.' He keyed in another number. The boss answered immediately. 'Everything okay?'

'The lads are on their way.'

'Remember what I said about the vehicle and keep your phone switched on. I'll call if there's a change of plan. Now, you know what I want?'

Alun sighed wearily. 'You've said it often enough.'

'Until later, then.' There came a click and the line went dead.

Alun went to his car, slung the holdall onto the backseat and drove off. Where would he find a vehicle at such short notice? He tried not to look at his watch and his thoughts returned to his boss as he cruised along the back streets of Armley and Kirkstal, where lots of used vehicle depots were situated. 'Look for something conspicuous, yet inconspicuous,' the boss had said. He gave a weary sigh; the boss often talked in riddles, so the first problem was to find a suitable vehicle. Then came the other 'problem' and after that the intended raid tomorrow—the last big haul.... And then? At last: freedom. Straight to the coast, onto the ferry, then onwards to Brazil...and a new life. Would he ever get there? His lips tightened; he sure as hell would try, but there must be no more mistakes.

Alun scowled at the thought; he was tired, and tired people made mistakes, especially when they had to work with idiots. And then there was Pete. Pete wasn't the brightest spark in the universe, but he was big, anyone would think twice before picking a fight with him, and he did what he was told. The trouble was he always took Rick's side when there was an argument because he and Rick were mates. Thank God, he thought, he wouldn't have to work with them much longer.

He cruised slowly on; glancing from left to right at the used cars and vehicles depots, there looked to be plenty of choice. Then he saw it. He smiled in relief and parked the car. As he got out he looked at the vehicle. It was a bit old, but the tyres were still good. It would be perfect as long as the engine wasn't knackered....

# THIRTY-TWO

*Around 3 p.m.*

EMILY STOOD IN the doorway and watched Christine climb into the taxi. She gave a brief wave then closing the door repeated Christine's instructions: 'Lock both doors and don't open up for anybody,' she chanted. 'Makes me feel like a little kid,' she grumbled, 'giving me orders. Does she think I can't look after myself?' Having bolted the door she limped through to the kitchen and did the same with the kitchen door. 'That'll show her,' she muttered. Then she returned to the spice cabinet.

For a while she stood staring at the vast assortment of packages, cartons and tubs, most of which were grubby and crumpled and half empty, then with a sigh she held up one packet. 'Bouquet garni?' She peered at the date. '1997! Where the heck have you been hiding?' She tossed it into a bin liner and continued to root through the packets and tubs, ruthlessly throwing away the ones that were past their sell-by dates until she came to the salt mill. She shook it, gave it an experimental twist and some grains of salt sprinkled out in response. 'You don't need refilling,' she said and placed it to one side. Next came the pepper mill, but this time when she shook it, it gave a forlorn rattle. Unscrewing the top and peering inside she saw that only two peppercorns remained. 'Better sort you out, though,' she said, but when she searched through the cupboard no black peppercorn refill packets could be found. All she could find was a container of ready-ground white pepper. She shook her head. 'We'll have to make do with that for now.' She picked up the two condiments, limped through to the living room and placed them on the dining table. She returned to the kitchen, picked up the bin liner and, unbolting the back door, took it outside to the dustbin. She was coming back into the kitchen when the hall phone rang.

'That'll be Christine,' she said as she went towards it as fast as she could. 'Maybe she's testing out a new mobile.' Breathlessly she picked up the receiver: 'Hello?' but there was just the sound of a dead line. 'Blooming cold callers,' she grumbled. She slammed down the receiver and started to limp back to the kitchen. 'Shouldn't be allowed.'

She'd just reached the kitchen doorway when the phone rang again. Emily turned sharply at the sound and without warning she felt light-headed. She clutched the door frame in alarm and realized too late she'd used her injured hand. A sharp pain swept through her and she bit tightly on her lip. After a moment she took a deep breath, steadied herself, then limped towards the ringing phone. 'Christine, is that you?' she said weakly as she felt the waves of nausea sweep over her. Silence, then a sharp click, and once more the line went dead.

'Christine? Are you there?' Emily said anxiously, but there was nothing.

Emily keyed in the caller ID number and waited. 'You were called at 3.12 p.m. The caller withheld their number,' came the automated reply. Emily replaced the receiver, then grabbed at the hall table with her good hand as she felt the dizziness return. Her heart began to thud loudly as she tried to take a deep breath and control her fear. 'Dear God,' she muttered, 'please, not another stroke…at least, not right now.' After a couple of minutes she eased her way into the living room and looked at the clock: 3.15.

'Best thing is to sit down,' she said. 'I don't right fancy collapsing in a heap on the floor.' She smiled at the thought. 'Even then,' she added, 'knowing me I'd break something.'

She sat down carefully in the armchair, glanced at the living room clock again and thought back. Christine had given her those pills just before two o'clock, she remembered, and most medication took at least one hour to kick in. At this thought she felt the relief flood through her. It wasn't a stroke coming on; it was just the pills doing their job. She did feel drowsy, though, so it couldn't do any harm to rest for a while. Emily leaned back in the chair and switched on the TV. 'Let's have a look at the news,' she muttered, 'that'll take my mind off the pain.' She sat watching the news, then she began to doze....

*3.30 p.m.*

ALUN EASED THE van to a halt and parked it outside his flat. He got out, lit up a cigarette and looked along the road. He had not long to wait for after a couple of minutes he saw Rick coming towards him. Rick looked eager and excited and ready to go, although he was struggling slightly under the weight of a large backpack.

'Got everything?' Alun asked.

'Yep,' said Rick. He patted the backpack. 'It's in here, paperwork and all.'

Alun raised an eyebrow. 'Got your gloves and balaclava?'

Rick slapped his trouser pockets. 'In here.'

'Where's Pete, then...? You did tell him?'

''Course I did, he's just dumping his old banger. He'll be here in two ticks.'

'Get your gear in here, then,' Alun said as he slid open the door of the van.

Rick unstrapped his pack and peered inside. 'This looks big enough—tons of room here. He grinned up at Alun. "Course, we're going to need it,' he said. He turned and kicked the front tyre experimentally. 'As long as the engine don't pack in.'

'That's not your problem,' Alun snapped. 'I know what I'm doing. I'm not like you.' He saw Pete approaching and beckoned to him.

Pete came up struggling with his case and waved his car keys. 'What'll I do with these?'

'Chuck 'em,' said Alun and indicated a nearby drain. He watched as Pete dropped the keys down it, then said, 'Let's get going.' The two men climbed into the van and Alun went round to the driver's side and got in. He sat for a moment and looked at them. 'Sure you've both remembered everything? Not left anything behind?' They nodded, eager to be off.

'You've both had your instructions from the boss?' Alun queried.

They nodded again.

Alun sighed. 'This time there can be no mistakes.'

'Not like the last job when you blew it,' Rick blurted.

Alun's knuckles gleamed white as they gripped the steering wheel. 'Just shut it, you. You know we've got a problem, and we've got to sort that first.' He looked at Rick and Pete and saw their frustrated expressions. 'You've had your orders,' he insisted, 'you've been told to do exactly as I say.'

Rick snorted, then quickly covered his mouth.

'One more wrong word from you,' Alun snarled, 'and I'll boot you right out of here—you'll be finished.'

'Oh for God's sake you two, let's get going!' Pete intervened. 'Let's get this bloody thing over with and do the job, then I'm buggering off to Ireland.'

## THIRTY-THREE

HARRY SAT AT the café table outside the station and watched his grandson tuck into the peach and ice cream sundae. He looked at his own sundae and feeling only a slight twinge of guilt, dug into it with gusto. He tried to remember when he had last eaten an ice cream sundae; it must have been donkey's years ago when Susie was.... He looked again at Liam; how Susie would have loved to see him now, sitting here in the October sunshine enjoying his food.

Across the road Harry could see the distant figures of Martin and Sheila. They were browsing at the souvenirs stalls, looking for mementoes to take back to their friends. He thought again about the conversation Martin had had with him earlier when he'd invited him to come south to stay with them through the winter and Christmas. Harry was tempted. He looked again at his grandson and knew he would love to be there on Christmas morning and watch Liam as he opened his gifts from Santa; these were the precious years.

But then, Christmas was still two months away, and there was nothing to stop him visiting once he'd helped Christine. He smiled as he thought about her; such a kind girl once you got to know her, and so caring, even though she was incredibly nosy. He'd tried to phone her earlier on his mobile to see how she and her mother were, but couldn't get a signal. He'd phone again when they got home, or better still he could nip cross the road once they got back. After all, he had a good excuse; he had found out the van driver's name—Alun Rhodes. He grimaced; that was about the only useful information he'd managed to glean from Mr Longley. He'd tried to look for an Alun Rhodes in the phone book, he'd even checked the internet, but there was nothing.

Harry frowned as he thought again about Longley; why had he been so reluctant to give out any details about the driver? Was that the firm's business policy, or was there a more sinister reason? Was there a connection between Longley and the van driver? And had his being 'accidentally' trapped inside the garden centre really been an accident?

'Gotta start making tracks for home, Dad.'

Harry looked up to see Martin and Sheila, clutching carrier bags, standing at the table. He looked at his watch. 'It's not even four o'clock yet.'

'Traffic's likely to be heavy on a Saturday,' Martin said. He looked meaningfully at Liam. 'Besides we've got another little visit to make—that's if a certain someone has been good?'

'Oh Daddy, Daddy...I have been good! Can I have a present, *please?*' Liam bounced on his chair excitedly. 'I know where the station gift shop is, 'cause I saw it when we came in, and Grandpa said....' Liam leapt off his chair and tugged at Harry's jacket.

'I did say you could have a new train.' Harry smiled, getting to his feet. 'The question is which one is it to be?'

'Can I have Hiro, please? Or maybe Belle?' Liam grabbed Harry's hand. 'I'll show you, the shop's just along here.'

# THIRTY-FOUR

*3.45 p.m.*

CHRISTINE STOOD IN the queue at the prescription counter and tried not to get irritated; she hadn't thought there'd be such a crowd waiting to hand their prescriptions in. It might have been better if she'd decided to get the mobile later and gone to the local chemist instead of coming into town, but she'd needed both of these things urgently. She looked around impatiently. She knew that in this store they sold their phones on the first floor; if she were to run upstairs and get the mobile first instead of hanging around here waiting, it might be quicker, but then again there might be customers waiting at the mobile phone counter as well. It was, after all, Saturday afternoon.

For the twentieth time she checked her watch; coming up towards four o'clock. Well over an hour since she'd left home and still she'd got nowhere. Her thoughts returned to her mother and her anxiety increased. What if Emily should decide to snoop around and try to find where she'd hidden the money? She'd avoided talking about it all morning because she didn't want to worry her, but in truth Mam had every right to know where it was; it was her house, after all. Christine sighed. It was all her fault; if only she hadn't been so nosy about reporting everyone she'd never have got herself and Mam into this terrifying situation. Another thought occurred to her: she'd instructed her mother to lock both front and back doors and not open them for anyone, but what if Sergeant Farrell should arrive on their doorstep having got back from York earlier than he'd estimated? Surely in that case he'd phone first? She tried to reassure herself but her sense of unease grew.

'Next, please!' called an impatient voice.

Christine turned to look at a harassed young assistant. He gave a tight smile. 'Can I help you, madam?'

'Oh, yes,' Christine handed him the prescription, 'this is for my mother.'

He glanced at it, then looked at her. 'She's over sixty?' Christine nodded.

'Then you've to sign on her behalf,' he indicated a section on the paper, 'down here.'

With a flushed face Christine scribbled her name; she should have thought of that while she was waiting. She handed him the completed form.

The young man took it. 'Be about twenty minutes,' and he walked away.

Christine stared after him in exasperation. 'Twenty minutes!' she said under her breath. 'Just for a few pills.' Then she thought about buying the mobile phone—she might just manage it in time. She hurried off towards the escalator.

Thirty minutes later Christine, clutching a carrier bag containing Emily's pills and the new mobile, came out of the store and into the Briggate shopping area. Turning right she hurried down the street. I'll make for the taxi stand at City Square Station, she thought. She turned right again onto Boar Lane, racing past the tempting shop window displays and shouldering her way through the crowds of shoppers. She looked about her in distraction; was it her imagination or was Leeds extra busy today, even more than usual for a Saturday afternoon? There seemed to be hundreds of families on the streets. She hurried on and crossed the road towards City Station. I hope Mam's okay, I've left her for far too long.

As she reached the taxi rank, she stopped short in dismay: there was not a taxi to be seen. Not only that, there were long queues of families, all with suitcases, standing waiting at the rank. Where have they all—? Then she had it. It was the end of October; half-term school holidays. That must be why there were so many children about. She looked around in desperation—what should she do? She looked across City Square to where she usually got her bus home, not that there'd be a chance in hell— But wait, there it was! Her bus. She knew it stopped at the end of Poole Road. Run! Risking life and limb she raced through the traffic and leapt on the bus just before the doors closed.

'That was a near thing, missus,' muttered the driver as he took her fare.

Too breathless to answer, Christine managed a nod then sank down onto a nearby seat.

# THIRTY-FIVE

*Around 4.15 p.m.*

KAY WAS UPSTAIRS in her bedroom sorting out suitable light-weight clothes for her trip abroad when she heard the sound of a vehicle pulling up outside. She walked to the open window and looked out. She could see a large gas board van parked in front of Christine's house. As she watched she saw three men hurrying through the Bretts' gate and down the path. Kay stood at the window and thought about this; she'd seen Christine leave after lunch and get into a taxi. She'd heard her calling out instructions to her mum, so the old lady must be in the house.

Kay shrugged and returned to her task of sorting out what clothes she would take with her. She looked in her suitcase and checked that her good pieces of jewellery were safely packed away, then began to pack the light-weight shoes and sandals she would need. As she did so her thoughts returned to the Bretts; she wondered what was going on. As far as she knew Christine had not returned home. Kay checked the time: just coming up to 4.30; surely Christine wouldn't leave her mother alone longer than was necessary?

*4.30 p.m.*

THE KITCHEN DOOR of the Bretts' house inched open and Alun slid through it. For a second he stood silently, listening, his body pressed up against the wall. He heard voices coming from what he thought was the living room; he held his breath but then realized it was the TV. He stood motionless and listened for any other sounds in the house, but there was nothing. Satisfied, he returned to the back door and beckoned the two men inside.

EMILY WOKE WITH a start. What was that? She'd heard something. Had that blasted phone been ringing again? Or had it been something on the TV? She shivered and rubbed her arm. There was a draught —had she left the living room window open? She switched off the TV, then stood up and listened. Silence. Well, if it had been their phone whoever it was would just have to call back later. She stretched, limped over and checked the window, pulled back the net curtain and looked out. She'd hoped to see a familiar figure approaching, but instead to her surprise she saw that a large van was parked outside. Emblazoned on its side was the logo of the gas board. Must be an emergency call-out or a delivery, she thought. You don't usually see them out on a Saturday. She peered further along the road. Funny, though, Mrs Gibbs next door has gas central heating, but I'm sure Christine said that they were away on a cruise for the next two weeks.

Emily straightened the curtains, turned away from the window and stood frozen in shock, her hands clasped to her chest.

Three men stood framed in the living room doorway. One of them moved towards her. 'Don't scream, love,' he said. 'We just want to talk to your daughter.'

# THIRTY-SIX

*Around 4.30 p.m.*

CHRISTINE GOT OFF the bus and hurried along Poole Road. She'd been fortunate to catch it. Could it be that for once her luck had turned and was on her side? She certainly hoped so. If she'd waited for a taxi it would have taken her much longer to get home. Her thoughts turned towards Sergeant Farrell and whether he'd arrived at the house yet. She smiled and wondered if Mam would let him in or force him to stay outside until she returned. As she looked further along the road her attention was drawn to the large van that was parked outside the house. It seemed to be from the gas board. Perhaps their neighbours, the Gibbs, had a problem with their gas central heating. She looked closer, but if so why would the driver park outside their house when there was plenty of room on the street? Maybe he was trying to leave a parcel for them with Mam.... She increased her pace; she'd better go see.

'GET OUT OF my house!' Emily yelled at the top of her voice.

Instantly the man rushed towards her and clamped a hand over her mouth. He scowled at her. 'Now, missus, didn't I tell you to be quiet?' He looked down at the trembling old lady, eased his grip on her mouth and his face shifted into a sly smile. 'Look, love, I don't want to hurt you. All we want to know is where is your daughter?'

An odd sort of mumbling came from Emily.

'What was that? Listen, darling, if I take my hand away, will you answer my questions…and no more yelling? Nod once for "Yes".'

Emily's head bobbed up and down rapidly.

'All righty.' Slowly the man removed his hand from her mouth.

She spat straight in his face.

'You wicked old bitch!' He grabbed her by the shoulders and shook her.

'Ease up, Alun,' one of the other men called out, 'can't you see she's got a broken wing?'

The man called Alun released her. Emily tried to stop herself trembling; her heart was pounding and she leaned back against the dining table for support. As she did so her good hand touched the plastic pepperpot. She grasped it and eased it into her cardigan pocket.

'Shut it, Rick,' snarled Alun.

'You watch your bleeding temper. We don't want to get done for topping her,' Rick said.

'Shouldn't hit old ladies,' said the third man. 'It's not right; she looks a bit like my gran.'

The man holding Emily turned to glare at them furiously. 'What did I tell you two?'

'Who bloody well cares?' said Rick. 'Just find out where the other woman is.'

'She's not here,' Emily whispered defiantly. 'She's gone, she's never coming back.'

'Check it out, Rick,' Alun said.

Rick ran up the stairs and returned again a couple of minutes later. 'Clothes is all there, and suitcases, and there's two toothbrushes in the bathroom. There's no one else here.'

Alun stared hard at Emily. 'Who's telling porky pies, then?' He looked at Rick. 'You'd best get back in the van and keep watch. You know what she looks like; if you see her coming, bang on the horn.'

'Right,' said Rick and he went out of the door.

'JUST WAIT ANOTHER five minutes, Liam,' Harry said. 'That's if we don't get stuck in another traffic jam,' he muttered. He turned to look at the small boy seated behind him who was clutching a large paper parcel. 'We'll soon be home and you can get your train out.' He smiled at his grandson; it had been such a long day for the little lad and he'd behaved so well.

Harry felt a sense of pride as he looked at his small family. It had been a day well spent and he'd enjoyed every second of it.

'Know where we are now, son?' Martin asked as they turned into Poole Road.

Liam peered out of the window. 'Think this is the street where Grandpa lives.'

'Right first go,' Harry laughed. His gaze travelled along the familiar street and his thoughts returned to Christine. He'd tried to phone her again without success, so now that they were back home he was eager to see her. He needed to tell her about— He stopped in mid-thought. In the distance he could see a large van, which appeared to be parked right outside the Bretts' house, and looking along the pavement he saw the figure of Christine walking home. He saw her hesitate and stare at the van, then hurry towards her house.

KAY WALKED TO the window again and looked out. She saw one of the men come out of the Bretts' house and climb into the van. A few minutes later she saw the distant figure of Christine returning and a blue car driving along the road. Kay noticed that as Christine approached her home the blue car drew level with her. She heard the sound of a horn as the car turned into Harry's drive. She raised an eyebrow: Harry has visitors, she thought.

She went back to her suitcase and closed the lid and wondered whether it would be a good time to take her little 'peace offering' over to the Bretts. I'd like to see Christine before I leave, she thought. Smiling, she went down the stairs and out through the back door to where her car was parked ready for loading. Again she checked the oil and petrol and as she did so she felt the excitement grow within her. Soon it would be time to go.

As CHRISTINE APPROACHED her house she looked at the van and saw there was a driver seated inside it. It's probably a delivery, she thought as she opened the gate and walked down the path. As she did so she heard a car close behind her, followed by the sound of a horn. She looked over her shoulder and saw that the car was turning into Harry's drive. That would be Harry's son. She gave a casual wave, then put her key into the lock on her front door. It turned but wouldn't open. She rapped on the door. 'It's me, Mam,' she called. 'Let me in.'

# THIRTY-SEVEN

CHRISTINE POUNDED AGAIN on the front door. 'Mam,' she called, 'let me in.' She stood and listened for the sound of her mother's approaching footsteps but there was nothing. 'Mam,' she called again, 'will you open the door? My key won't work.'

'Go on round to the back,' she heard Emily call; 'the bolt on the front door's stuck.'

Christine thought her mother's voice sounded shaky. 'You all right, Mam?' she asked, but there was no answer. She hurried down the path. Why had Mam suddenly decided to bolt the door? She distinctly remembered telling her to lock the doors; she'd not said anything about the bolts. They were new and bound to be stiff. Hurriedly, she pushed at the back door. It swung open and she strode inside; and where was the man from the gas—? She froze as the door closed swiftly behind her and a strong hand gripped her arm. She looked up at the large man who was holding her and opened her mouth to speak, but the words wouldn't come. Then her mother, escorted by a tall, pale man whom Christine instantly recognized as the getaway driver, came into the kitchen.

'We've been waiting for you, love,' the man said. 'She,' he nodded at Emily, 'swore you'd gone and left home forever, and I thought to myself, there's no chance of that, you'd not leave your mum, would you now?'

'What do you want?' Christine finally managed to gasp. 'Get your hands off my mother.'

'Let the old girl sit down, Alun,' said the large man who was holding Christine, 'she looks like death.'

'I'm in charge here,' the man replied, but he pulled out a chair and moved Emily towards it. 'You do as I say, Pete. Not the other way round.'

Christine looked at her mother; she looked pale, but her lips were set in a determined line. She wanted to go to her, to reassure her. She tried to move forward but the large man, called Pete, held her back. 'Stay put,' he said firmly.

'Now to business,' said Alun. He glanced again at Emily. 'Don't you want to sit, too?'

'I'll stand,' she replied.

'Suit yourself.' He walked towards Christine and smiled down at her. 'You do know why we're here, don't you?'

'I know you're going to jail for illegal entry and for assaulting my mother, that's for sure,' Christine blurted out.

Alun sneered. 'Come on, now, let's have less of your joking.' His expression changed to that of a scowl. 'So... where's the money?'

HARRY GOT OUT of the car and followed Liam and Martin through to the living room. Liam was already seated on the floor and busily trying to pull away the wrappings from his present. Martin squatted down beside him to help. Harry stood and watched them for a while and smiled with satisfaction.

His thoughts returned to Christine and he went outside to see if the van was still there. It was. Perhaps there was some problem with the Bretts' gas installation? If so that could be dangerous; gas explosions were nasty. But wait... did the Bretts' house have gas? He frowned; but they must have, otherwise the gas board van would not b— *As for me, I wouldn't have gas in the house.* Emily's words echoed clearly in his mind. When had the old lady said that? It must have been on the night he'd had dinner with them. So what was the man from the gas board doing in Christine's house? Was he dealing with some other matter? He couldn't be sure but…. He drew a deep breath; he would go over and find out. Besides, he needed to tell Christine the name of the van driver. He called through the kitchen doorway, 'Back in a minute,' and dashed across the road.

RICK SAT IN the driver's seat of the van and looked out at the houses on either side of him. They all seem different in daylight, he thought. He shifted uneasily in his seat; he had the distinct feeling he was being watched. He felt edgy; he wanted to get this over with and be on his way. He looked around again. All he needed now was for that old geezer with his dog from the night before to…. He peered in his rear-view mirror and, as if on cue, the slight figure of the old man and his dog emerged from his gate and walked along the pavement towards him. 'Hell's bells,' Rick growled, 'talk of the devil and he bloody well appears. What to do?' He watched as the old man came ever closer. Would he recognize him? Maybe not. He was in a gas board van now, not in his old battered Ford. But what to do if he did? At best the old boy would be sure to reckon that he was some kind of stalker.

He fished in his jacket pocket, searched for his ciggies, and having found them realized he'd got no lighter. He cursed loudly. He knew exactly where the lighter was; he'd lent it to Alun half an hour ago.

Irritably he swung round in his seat and glared at the woman's house. She'd gone inside a few minutes ago so what the hell was keeping Alun and Pete? He gave a nervous snigger; perhaps they were having afternoon tea?

The sound of someone calling out made Rick look in the rearview mirror again. He watched as the bloke opposite hurried down his drive, crossed the road and went straight towards the woman's house. Rick straightened up. 'This looks like trouble,' he muttered. He got out his mobile and wondered whether he should warn Alun. And if he did? As usual Alun would yell his head off. Well, he was not having that; but he would have to do something. He reached for his backpack. Delving deep down into it he pulled out a gun. He hesitated, eyeing it nervously, then checked it was loaded. He thought again about all the money at stake. His jaw set determinedly; he put the gun in his pocket and got out of the van.

# THIRTY-EIGHT

HARRY HURRIED DOWN the Bretts' path past the front door and round to the back of the house. As he approached the kitchen window he slowed his pace. He could hear Christine's voice; she sounded frightened. He tried to peer in through the window but the Venetian blinds blocked his view. He listened. A man spoke harshly: 'Come on, tell us. Don't make us hurt you.'

Harry froze; then he heard the 'click' of the garden gate and his heart pounded. Quickly he moved closer to the back door and pressed up against the wall. Someone was coming down the path. Desperately, he looked around for a weapon, anything at all…then he saw it. A garden spade propped against the wall, near the dustbins. He grabbed it; he didn't want to use it. He listened again. Whoever was coming was almost on him.

As the man came round the corner Harry saw he was holding a gun. The words of Harry's TA instructor sprang into his mind: 'Never hesitate when dealing with an armed man; it can cost you your life.' Harry lunged forward and whacked the man over the head with the spade with all his strength. The man slumped to the ground. Harry picked up the gun, put it in his pocket, then leaned back against the wall, listening. He waited for the back door to open, but no one came. He bent down, touched the man's neck and felt a pulse; at least he wasn't dead. He crept up close to the door and listened again.

'How many more times do I have to tell you? It's not your money!' Christine shouted. 'You're a thief! You stole it.'

'And you nearly broke your neck trying to give it back,' Alun sneered.

Christine glared at him. It was on the tip of her tongue to blurt out that she'd already informed the police, but caution ruled and she remained silent.

'That's shut you up, hasn't it?' He looked at her meaningfully. 'Listen, love, it's not as if I want to be…unreasonable. *You* weren't meant to find that money,' he grinned slyly, 'that was for the coppers to discover, and now *you've* gone and blown it, y'see, 'cause now the cops are going to come here convinced you're one of us. They're not going to believe a word you say; they'll think you're barmy.'

'Of course they'll believe me; I've got the money.'

'That's why we're here. But there is a way out of this. If you can forget all that you saw, all that you found, and tell the police you've had one of your turns, brought on by stress and that accident last night with your old mum…I'd make it worth your while to keep schtum.'

Christine's lips tightened as the significance of his words sank in. 'You know what? You disgust me. Do you really think I'd take stolen money from you?'

'Could come in very useful.' He looked around at the furnishings. 'From what I see here of this scruffy old stuff, you look like you could use it. Otherwise,' he stared at Emily, 'I might have to take more drastic measures.'

'Don't you look at my Mam like that, she knows nothing.'

Alun grinned. 'Don't get excited,' he moved up close to Emily, 'I've hardly touched her…yet.'

Emily stared up at him stubbornly and fumbled in her cardigan pocket.

'Keep away from her,' Christine blurted, 'just leave her alone.'

'Leave it out, Alun,' Pete said quietly, 'we only want the money.'

Alun grinned at him. 'But we'll need some insurance.' He glanced again at Emily.

'If I give you the money,' Christine blurted,' you'll leave us in peace…and you'll go?'

'Just tell us where it is, my love.'

Instinctively Christine's eyes flicked towards the pantry door. Quickly she tried to look elsewhere, but too late. Alun had seen it.

He strode over to the pantry and rattled the doorknob, then slid back the bolt. Looking over his shoulder he leered at Christine. 'It's in here, isn't it?'

'No.' In her heart Christine knew they would not just take the money and go. Hardly daring to breathe she watched as Alun pulled the door wide and peered inside.

'Blimey, what have we got here, then, all this stuff,' Alun scowled, 'but we will find it, so you may as well tell us now.'

'Not on your life!' Christine shouted.

'No?' Alun grinned. He grabbed Emily and pulled her to him.

'Well then, maybe on hers.'

Christine was filled with rage; how dare he touch her mother. She broke free from Pete, and flew at Alun, clawing at his face. 'Get your filthy hands off her!' she screamed.

HARRY HEARD CHRISTINE scream. It was enough. He burst into the kitchen and took in the scene, saw that she was struggling with a tall man. 'What the hell's happening?' he shouted as he rushed in to help her.

'Get them off me!' Alun yelled as Emily joined them in the attack.

'You old bitch,' Alun shouted as he tried to push her away.

'Do something, Pete, she's kicking me,' he cried, as he leaned forward and grabbed at his leg.

Pete rushed to help him just as Emily whipped out the pepperpot and yelled, 'Christine and Harry, stand back,' as she tossed the contents into the thieves' faces. They screamed and rubbed frantically at their eyes.

Staggering back, Harry and Christine picked up the kitchen chairs and jabbed at the men with them, forcing them to retreat into the pantry. 'Help us, Mam,' Christine shouted as Harry forced the door shut and leaned against it whilst she tried to bolt it.

Leaning against the pantry door, Harry said to Christine, 'This door won't hold for long—call the police.'

'They should be on their way,' she said, 'but I'll ring them again.' She ran along the hall towards the phone.

Harry called after her, 'Come on, now, love, you've got to tell me. What's this all about?'

'The money, what else?' said Emily.

The doorbell buzzed, startling them all.

'Who's that?' asked Harry.

'It's probably the police,' Christine called as she ran to answer it. 'Sergeant Farrell did say….' She opened the door.

SERGEANT FARRELL DROVE slowly into Poole Road and looked at the houses, searching for the right house. Number 47, the office had told him, that was the Bretts' house. Ah, there it was up ahead on his right. As he parked the car he watched as a young blonde lady crossed the road and rang the doorbell. He watched her closely. She was smartly dressed and very attractive and she was carrying a white confectioner's box. The front door was opened and the woman went inside. Must be a visitor invited over for tea, he thought, and his stomach rumbled in agreement.

Focus, he told himself, that's not what you're here for. His thoughts returned to Miss Brett's file; her phone call of this morning and the anonymous letter that Leeds HQ had received today and informed him about. A later call from Leeds HQ had told him that no identifying fingerprints had been found on the letter. So where did he go from here? Surely Christine Brett wouldn't write anonymous letters to the police about herself? The alternative was that she was involved in the robberies, perhaps even a member of the gang. Or could it be that someone really had it in for her? He got out of the car and keyed in the Bretts' number as he walked towards the house....

# THIRTY-NINE

'HI THERE,' SAID Kay. She was standing on the doorstep and holding a white confectioner's box. She smiled at Christine, then pushed her aside and moved briskly into the hall, closing the door behind her. 'Good afternoon, Christine, I've caught you at home at last. I tried to come and visit you last night.'

'Oh, I'm sorry,' Christine stammered breathlessly, 'Mam had an accident, and we—'

Kay looked down at the box. 'I thought I'd bring you a peace offering.'

'Thank you, but this isn't a good time,' stammered Christine, 'perhaps later?'

Kay smiled; she had no intention of leaving until she knew what was going on. 'I'm pushed for time; I'm going away tonight and we ought to made amends.' She brushed past Christine, marched towards the living room and glanced in. 'Is your mother in the kitchen?'

'Yes,' Christine said as she hurried after Kay down the hall, 'but the thing is—'

'Ah, Harry!' Kay called out as she came into the kitchen. 'You're here as well? We could almost have a party.'

'Not now, Kay, I think you'd best go back.' Harry moved towards Kay whilst Christine went to reassure her mother.

'What's all this noise? What on earth's happening here?' Kay frowned at the shouts coming from the pantry.

'Something bad, I can tell you that,' said Harry. 'Now,

you get off home—the police will be here any minute to arrest these thugs.'

'Oh no.' Kay pouted. 'I can't go now, I'd miss all the excitement.' She slid the box onto the table and fished inside it. 'And I don't think anyone's going to get arrested… at least, not if I have anything to do with it.' She straightened up; she was holding a gun.

Harry stared at the weapon. 'What are you doing, Kay? Don't be silly, those things are—'

'I know how dangerous they are, Harry, but needs must. Now,' she said sharply, 'get over there beside the women.'

Harry moved to stand in front of Christine and Emily. 'And then what?'

'I want you to get my men out of there and if any of you argues, I'll shoot. You!' She waved the gun at Christine. 'Get that door open.'

Harry kept his eyes on her. This is incredible; Kay's a criminal. 'Stay put, Christine,' he said with as much authority as he could manage. Then he eased the gun he'd picked up out of his pocket and pointed it at Kay. 'Looks like we have a stand-off.'

Kay gaped at the gun but said coldly, 'I'm not joking, I want that door open. I want my men released and I want our money. Do as I say or I will shoot.'

'*Who* will you shoot?' Harry said. He walked slowly towards her. 'Even if you shoot me, there's still Christine and her mother.' He paused. 'There's only one of you.'

The phone rang. Kay flinched and glanced down the hall.

It was enough. Harry grabbed her arm and twisted it. The gun clattered to the floor. He pinned her against the wall. 'Answer that,' he yelled at Christine, 'then call 999.'

Christine raced into the hall and picked up the phone.

'It's Sergeant Farrell. He's here now—he's outside,' she called. She ran to open the door.

'Tell him to call for backup,' Harry shouted. He looked at Emily. 'Got anything to tie this one up with?'

She hurried over to a cupboard and got out an old clothes line.

Harry took it and tied Kay's hands. 'Now, you keep your eye on her,' he picked up Kay's gun, 'whilst I make sure these crooks don't get out of the pantry until backup arrives.'

Emily glared at Kay, then limped to the sink and picked up the skillet from the draining board. 'Don't worry, I'll watch her,' she said grimly. She waved the pan warningly in front of Kay. 'One wrong move from you, lady...I've been waiting for this chance for years.'

# EPILOGUE

*Eight months later*

EMILY CAME DOWNSTAIRS and stood unnoticed near the kitchen doorway. She heard the chatter of voices, the deeper tones of Harry and Sergeant Farrell and a sudden burst of laughter from Christine. Emily smiled. It did her heart good to hear her daughter laugh again; there'd been times when she'd thought Christine had forgotten how. She limped into the kitchen, got out some juice and poured it into a glass. She was on her way to the living room when Christine said, 'Aren't you going to join us, Mam? Sergeant Farrell here has just told me I'm going to get an award for being a good citizen. Apparently those crooks almost got away with millions; they'd made dozens of raids and got away with it. The police have been after them for years, so at least I think I deserve it. I'm to get a small reward from the hypermarket as well—that'll be great, won't it?'

'Wonderful,' agreed Emily as she edged ever nearer towards the hall.

Harry, who was sitting with his arm round Christine, patted the chair beside him and said, 'Come and join us, Mrs Brett, we don't want you sitting in the living room all by yourself.'

'Ah,' Emily hedged, 'well, you see, there's the wrestling on soon, and I don't want—'

'Oh,' Christine laughed, 'let her go, Harry. She'll not miss the wrestling, come what may.'

'See you in a bit, then,' Emily said. She limped quickly into the living room, sat down and placed her glass carefully beside her. Having picked up the remote and switched on the TV, she looked over her shoulder at the open living room door. She could still hear their chattering voices. Good had come out of the robbery; although who would have thought that Kay was the mastermind behind it all? It just goes to show, you never really know who your neighbours are. Still, it had brought Christine and Harry together. Emily smiled; they were well suited, those two. Of course, she'd have to get a new hat for the wedding and their Jimmy would have to be invited; he'd just have to smoke his smelly old pipe outside, that's all. Emily scowled as she thought about it. There was only one real downside to that marriage, though; she'd be doomed to listen to 'The Robbery' episode forever.

She still shivered when she recalled the day the thieves had invaded her home and held her hostage. And by golly they'd been on the very brink of finding the money, too. Later, when Sergeant Farrell had arrested them, she'd asked Christine where the money was. 'I know it was in the pantry, but just where did you hide it?'

Christine had grinned and replied, 'That's when I remembered my lessons from you, Mam. You were always telling me, "Never put all your eggs in one basket, girl." So that's what I did. The money wasn't in one place you see, but in several.' Emily eyed her glass of orange juice and chuckled. At least the lass did take her advice sometimes.

She got up, wandered over to the window, pulled back the net curtains and stood for a while looking along Poole Road. There, at the end of the street, she could see Brian Sharpe exercising his dog. She smiled; he seemed to have taken over Christine's role of resident nosy parker these days, but for all that, it suited him. Brian and his dog had never looked happier.

Letting the curtain fall back into place she walked to her chair, sat down and, picking up the remote, switched over to the wrestling channel. With any luck the Undertaker might be on. She snuggled into the chair and relaxed; it was time for a bit of celebrating. Fishing in her cardigan pocket, she brought out a miniature vodka bottle, tipped the contents into her juice, then slipped the bottle back in her pocket. 'Cheers.' She grinned as she took a sip from it. 'Now with any luck I'll be able to get on with the rest of my life.'

\* \* \* \* \*

# REQUEST YOUR FREE BOOKS!

## 2 FREE NOVELS
## PLUS 2 FREE GIFTS!

**MYSTERY**

# W⊙RLDWIDE LIBRARY®
TM
### Your Partner in Crime

**YES!** Please send me 2 FREE novels from the Worldwide Library® series and my 2 FREE gifts (gifts are worth about $10). After receiving them, if I don't wish to receive any more books, I can return the shipping statement marked "cancel." If I don't cancel, I will receive 4 brand-new novels every month and be billed just $5.49 per book in the U.S. or $6.24 per book in Canada. That's a savings of at least 31% off the cover price. It's quite a bargain! Shipping and handling is just 50¢ per book in the U.S. and 75¢ per book in Canada.* I understand that accepting the 2 free books and gifts places me under no obligation to buy anything. I can always return a shipment and cancel at any time. Even if I never buy another book, the two free books and gifts are mine to keep forever.

414/424 WDN F4WY

Name _____ (PLEASE PRINT)

Address _____ Apt. #

City _____ State/Prov. _____ Zip/Postal Code

Signature (if under 18, a parent or guardian must sign)

### Mail to the **Harlequin® Reader Service:**
**IN U.S.A.:** P.O. Box 1867, Buffalo, NY 14240-1867
**IN CANADA:** P.O. Box 609, Fort Erie, Ontario L2A 5X3

**Want to try two free books from another line?**
**Call 1-800-873-8635 or visit www.ReaderService.com.**

* Terms and prices subject to change without notice. Prices do not include applicable taxes. Sales tax applicable in N.Y. Canadian residents will be charged applicable taxes. Offer not valid in Quebec. This offer is limited to one order per household. Not valid for current subscribers to the Worldwide Library series. All orders subject to credit approval. Credit or debit balances in a customer's account(s) may be offset by any other outstanding balance owed by or to the customer. Please allow 4 to 6 weeks for delivery. Offer available while quantities last.

**Your Privacy**—The Harlequin® Reader Service is committed to protecting your privacy. Our Privacy Policy is available online at www.ReaderService.com or upon request from the Harlequin Reader Service.

We make a portion of our mailing list available to reputable third parties that offer products we believe may interest you. If you prefer that we not exchange your name with third parties, or if you wish to clarify or modify your communication preferences, please visit us at www.ReaderService.com/consumerchoice or write to us at Harlequin Reader Service Preference Service, P.O. Box 9062, Buffalo, NY 14269. Include your complete name and address.

WWL13R

# *ReaderService*.com

## Manage your account online!

- Review your order history
- Manage your payments
- Update your address

---

*We've designed
the Harlequin® Reader Service
website just for you.*

---

## Enjoy all the features!

- Reader excerpts from any series
- Respond to mailings and
  special monthly offers
- Discover new series available to you
- Browse the Bonus Bucks catalog
- Share your feedback

*Visit us at:*

**ReaderService.com**